*to chocolate*

# The Adultery Diet

# The Adultery Diet

Eva Cassady

POCKET BOOKS

New York  London  Toronto  Sydney

Pocket Books
A Division of Simon & Schuster, Inc.
1230 Avenue of the Americas
New York, NY 10020

First Pocket Books trade paperback edition August 2007

POCKET and colophon are registered trademarks of Simon & Schuster, Inc.

For information about special discounts for bulk purchases, please contact Simon & Schuster Special Sales at 1-800-456-6798 or business@simonandschuster.com.

Designed by Carla Jayne Little

Manufactured in the United States of America

10  9  8  7  6  5  4  3  2  1

Library of Congress Cataloging-in-Publication Data

Cassady, Eva.
    The adultery diet / Eva Cassady.—1st Pocket Books trade pbk. ed.
        p.   cm.
    ISBN-13: 978-1-4165-3272-9
    ISBN-10:     1-4165-3272-2
    1. Chick lit. I. Title.
PS3603.A868A38 2007
813'.6—dc22                                              2007005491

# Acknowledgments

*My thanks to all those who have hungered,
only to prove that living well is the best revenge.*

# The Adultery Diet

# 119

Everybody asks how I did it. Women gather around me at parties, stop me in the halls at work, their eyes measuring my new body, their smiles tight with the long history of their failures.

*Tell me,* their eyes plead. Every one of them has a shelf full of diet books at home: low-carb, no-carb, Weight Watchers and Zone, South Beach, Dial-a-Meal, and hamster diets of lettuce and seeds. They've done Marnie and Jane and Beto, yoga and hip-hop, Tae Bo, Buns of Steel, and the Ab Lounge. They've hired personal trainers, had their stomachs stapled or their lipo sucked. Now they're angry and ashamed. They feel like failures. But even more, they feel betrayed—all the books and commercials have lied to them. And let's face it, they have lied to themselves. They come to me for the truth.

"There's no secret," I tell them. "Just diet and exercise."

But that's a lie, too. Every diet has a secret: vanity, wounded pride, rage. Or desire. "You have to want it," I say, and they nod.

But the world is full of *its*. You need something stronger than crème brûlée, more seductive than chocolate, more powerful than hunger itself. And in the end, you learn that the *it* doesn't matter. It's the *wanting* that gets you to the gym in the morning, propels you past the bakery on your way to work, carries you back to the gym in the evening for the unforgiving cardio with the Lycra-clad gazelles from Ford and Elite. You have to hunger, not starve. You have to be driven to walk those twenty-four blocks to work, then turn left toward the stairs instead of joining the crowd at the elevators. Something has to be eating at you.

"Eva looks great," the men say to my husband, and I see him smile. What man doesn't want to be envied? What man doesn't want to get his wife back at forty-four, finding—to his surprise—a younger woman emerging from under the weight of the years like a flower growing from a snowbank? They don't say it aloud, but their eyes say, *How did she do it? Can she teach my wife?*

Sure, boys. But be careful what you wish for.

Fall 2005

# 176

When did the bathroom scale become the tyrant that rules my life? I used to laugh at women who weighed themselves every morning, back when I was a hot young thing: leather miniskirt, cup of coffee and a cigarette for breakfast, out the door. But the times, they are a changin'. Even Dylan probably owns a scale now and growls at it every morning when it breaks his heart.

"What time does Chloe's plane leave?" David comes into the bathroom and reaches for his toothbrush. I step off the scale and quickly slide it under the shoe rack in the closet.

"Two thirty." I slip my bathrobe on and step into my slippers. "And she's not even close to packed yet."

"She's a junior in college. She'll figure it out." He glances at me in the mirror. "Might be time to get you a new robe."

I look down at my no-allure velour, threads pulling

at the seams, hem unraveling. "Chloe gave me this for Mother's Day. When she was eight."

"You'll still be her mother, even if you get a new robe."

I imagine silk, poured over lean curves. But I'd need a new body first. "Maybe she can get me one in Paris. Do they have Mother's Day over there?"

David smiles. "I think the French have a different idea of motherhood."

Slim and chic, probably. Audrey Hepburn wheeling a carriage along the banks of the Seine. Did Parisian women own bathroom scales?

"Do you have a busy day today?"

David shakes his head. "A meeting in the afternoon with Maribel Steinberg and her agent. I'll have to get the contracts ready this morning."

Maribel Steinberg. I'd spotted her new book in the stack of manuscripts on David's bedside table: *The Be-True-to-Yourself Diet*. I'd picked it up and flipped through it while David got ready for bed. The agent's letter described it as "a diet book for women who don't believe in dieting."

"Isn't that like selling guns to Quakers?"

David glanced over at me. "What do you mean?"

"Well, you may not like guns, but if you buy one, you want it to work."

He shrugged. "Our marketing people like it. They've got a whole publicity campaign ready to go. Straight talk about weight loss. Manage your weight without self-hate."

"Catchy."

But the numbers don't lie. Three weeks of positive self-concept, moderate exercise, and goal-oriented self-reward, and I've lost a grand total of two pounds. True, my daughter is flying off to Paris for a year, and the magazine I write for is going through a major redesign to revive its sagging circulation, both substantial "stress factors," according to Maribel Steinberg, that can lead to "destructive self-modeling." But *two pounds*?

"Mom, I can't find my passport!"

David looks up at me, his mouth full of toothpaste. It's a look that says, *She called for you.* The same look he used to give me when she was three, crying out in the middle of the night. His hair (what remains of it) and beard are silvered now, and he's heavier around the middle, but there are still moments when I catch a glimpse of the twenty-six-year-old grad student, with his passion for poetry and social justice, hidden beneath the middle-aged editor.

Does he think the same when he looks at me?

Chloe sits on the floor of her room, piles of clothing and open suitcases scattered around her. She's got her purse on her lap, her wallet in one hand. "I can't find my passport," she says again, plaintively. "I had it in my purse when we went to the bank yesterday, but it's not there now."

"You want me to look?"

She gives me an impatient look. For a moment, she's fourteen again, wearied by her mother's inability to comprehend the complexities of a teenager's life.

"Where'd you put your traveler's checks?"

She opens her purse, takes out an envelope. When

she opens the envelope, she finds her passport tucked inside among the packets of checks. "Oh, for God's sake." She slips it into the inside pocket of her purse, where she keeps her cell phone, then stuffs the envelope of checks back into her purse. I notice a condom packet lying next to the hairbrush in her purse and look away quickly. At least she's being safe.

"And you've got your ticket?"

She rolls her eyes in exasperation. "Yes, I've got my ticket." She shoves her wallet back into her purse, zips it closed. "I'm not a child."

I leave her there among her luggage. It's her story now. David and I are just the parents she comes home to for a few weeks in the summer, the unchanging background against which the changes in her own life can be accurately measured. For her, the future's all possibility: college, Paris, career, and yes, sex. We're what she has to leave behind. We've made our choices, and now she wants us to get out of the way so she can make hers.

David's in the shower now, steaming up the mirrors. I sit on the bed listening to the traffic on Riverside Drive. Is the story really over at forty-four? If you're basically happy and successful—good jobs, nice apartment, a child in college—what else would you really wish for? It's hard to think that the story now might be simply more of the same or, even worse, a slow decline, like dust settling in an empty house. When did life stop being about hope?

But even in the midst of that thought, I can't help reaching for a scrap of paper, scribbling down *Old houses as easy metaphor for our lives. Is that why we love them?* One of the pleasures of my job as an editor at *House & Home* magazine, among the endless photo tours of overdecorated celebrity homes and stories on refinishing hardwood floors, is my monthly column. At times, it's hard not to laugh at the idea of someone who's spent the last twenty years living in apartments on the Upper West Side of Manhattan writing a monthly meditation on what architecture means to our lives, for a readership of wealthy professionals blessed with the luxury of restoring Victorian homes. My publisher had his doubts when I first proposed the column, but it proved surprisingly popular with readers, and I've even received invitations to appear at home shows and on a public television program devoted to restoring old houses. Invitations I've politely declined, not wanting to reveal my fraudulence. Writing a sex-advice column for single women in their twenties, or tips for surgeons performing open heart surgery, would be almost as unlikely as what I'm doing now.

David's out of the shower now, humming to himself as he towels off. It's my turn now, but it's a small bathroom, and I find myself feeling strangely self-conscious (the numbers don't lie), so I go into the kitchen and eat a cup of nonfat yogurt standing at the sink.

Sex advice for single women. *Enjoy it while you can, honey. You won't have that body forever.* I'd carried condoms in my own purse once, merrily fucked my way through college and then half the pubs on the Upper West Side in my first year in the city. Shouting, "I'm looking for a job in publishing!" over the Eurythmics while the guy waved frantically at the waitress for more margaritas, like a soldier terrified of running out of bullets in the middle of the battle. The results were predictable enough: I'd studied my share of ceilings, taken my share of early morning taxi rides, and in the end, I'd met David—just a few weeks too late to fuck my way into an editorial assistant's position at a big publishing house, since I'd just taken a job at *House & Home* that might actually pay my rent. (An old joke there, which one of David's male colleagues had once told at a Christmas party: "She took an editorial assistant's position." Bent over the copy machine, apparently, with her panties around her ankles.)

But now it's all joists and tuck pointing. Home, after all, being where the heart is.

David comes into the kitchen as I'm throwing away my empty yogurt cup. "So, you can run Chloe out to the airport?"

It's the third time he's asked me this question since yesterday, when we agreed that I'd take her because of his meeting. As always at these moments, I'm faced with three choices: (1) scream; (2) murder; or (3) reassure him that he shouldn't feel guilty for not seeing her off.

"Liz is picking us up at ten," I tell him.

"You think that's early enough?"

I look at him. "To get to LaGuardia? Yeah, I think we'll make it."

"Provided Liz doesn't get you lost on the way out there."

"I'll navigate."

Liz is my oldest friend in New York, and as long as I've

known her, she's always gotten lost. She could be driving around the block looking for a parking space, and she'd make a wrong turn and find herself in the Jersey Pine Barrens. David's theory is that it's a single woman's cry for help. But the truth is much simpler: she gets to talking and loses track of where she's going. When she wants to make an important point, she likes to emphasize it with a change of direction. And since she can talk passionately on almost any subject—especially the untrustworthiness of men—any trip in her car includes abrupt lane changes and sudden turns.

Still, she's offered to drive Chloe to the airport, excited to see her off on her Parisian adventure. "With French men, at least you know where you stand," she assures my daughter as we head out of Manhattan. She jerks the wheel hard, cutting off a transit bus. "When you aren't lying down, that is. It's impossible to believe anything a man says in bed."

Chloe nods. She's got one hand on the dashboard, the other clutching her seat belt, looking terrified. Is it Liz's driving, or her romantic advice? What twenty-year-old wants to listen to a jaded single woman in her forties on the topic of love? It's like getting medical advice from an undertaker.

To make it worse, the car's full of cat hair, which is playing hell with my allergies. Liz got two Siamese when she turned forty, saying, "If I'm not going to have kids, I need something else to torture." She named them Touchy and Surly, and likes to hand-feed them bits of raw liver from the butcher at the Food Emporium on Broadway. "I'm training them," she tells me. "The next guy who lies to me, I'm going to cut out his liver and feed it to my cats."

My streaming eyes and the hairball forming in my throat are the only reasons I can ride with Liz without terror. Five minutes in her car, and I don't even notice the trail of rage and destruction we leave in our wake: the cab driver screaming at us from the shoulder, where we've forced him off the road, the pimped-out Caddie that pursues us for ten blocks with the driver waving a gun from his window. By the time we arrive at the airport, any terror Chloe had about her flight or the prospect of life in another country is gone. She happily yanks her suitcases out of the car's trunk and leads us through the terminal at a trot, saying, "Really, Mom, you don't have to wait."

But it's my job to sit there, the worry building inside me until I say something so exasperating that my daughter rolls her eyes then leaps up to join the line for security like she's trying to force her way onto the last chopper out of Saigon. One last hug, and then Liz and I stand beyond the Plexiglas, watching as Chloe moves slowly through the line, slips off her shoes to put them through the scanner, then waits to be waved through the metal detector. On the other side she gathers up her things, pauses to give us a last jaunty wave, and she's gone.

"Well, that's done," Liz says, as we walk back to the car. "I think you handled it very well."

I'm sobbing. My baby's gone forever, and I forgot to remind her to write. She'll return like Sabrina, full of elegance and soufflés, a confident woman with a string of French lovers to her credit and strong ideas about accessories. I'll look like a frump next to her when we walk down Broadway, just another Upper West Side hausfrau out with her lovely daughter.

"Let's go get you drunk," Liz suggests.

The ride back to the city is a blur of screeching brakes and sickening thuds, through which we pass on a steady current of Liz's chatter, like a comet through fiery skies. We arrive at her building's garage without a scratch, although insurance companies from here to Boston stagger and fail under the carnage. She takes me upstairs, makes martinis in her kitchen, and we sit beside an open window, where I can breathe the sooty Manhattan air as her cats prowl the entryway, lying in wait for unsuspecting men.

"I should call the office," I sigh after the first martini. I've taken the day off, but you never know what can come up in your absence. Someone might have invented a new spackling compound. Track lighting might have made an unexpected comeback. After the second martini, I say, "Where did the years go?" By the time we finish the third, the subject is blowjobs. Why so many? And to so little effect?

By six I have to be poured into a taxi for the bleary ride back home to hearth and husband. I'm a middle-aged mother who's just sent her only child off to be ravished by God knows how many odiferous Frenchmen, but for some reason, I can't stop giggling. Earlier, Liz had gone to the kitchen for more drinks, and after a moment I heard her bellowing, "No! Stop that! No!"

Her cats came tearing out of the kitchen, tails high, but they slowed to a languid walk as soon as they'd left her behind. One of them walked a cautious circle around the other one, sniffed at the base of his raised tail, and then casually mounted him.

Liz came back into the living room at that moment carrying our drinks, and she stamped her foot and shouted, "No! Stop it!"

As the cats vanished down the hall, Liz stood staring after them in despair. "As if it wasn't bad enough that there are no straight men left in this town, I end up with gay cats." She handed me my drink. "I caught them fucking on my bed last week." She glared at me. "Stop laughing. It's my bed, not some furry little Fire Island. You think I want to sleep in that? Anyway, *I* should be the one fucking in it."

*Only Liz,* I hear David saying. And, *Who can blame them? She's probably had that effect on lots of men.*

I giggled. "Maybe you shouldn't have gotten two males," I told her.

"They're *brothers*. That's what makes it so gross. How was I supposed to know they'd spend all their time humping each other?"

The cab's two blocks from my building, and now I'm giggling again. David will be appalled when he sees me, and that thought alone makes it impossible to stop. I force myself to take a deep breath, tighten my jaw, and gaze out the window at the blur of Broadway. It all looks so . . . *lurid.* Is this really where I live? How did that happen?

But it turns out David isn't even home. There's a message from him on the machine. He's taking Maribel Steinberg and her agent to Michael's for dinner to celebrate the contract. Walking the author, he calls it, showing her off to all the other editors. What will she order? Will she be true to herself, or just pick at a salad?

I peer at the leftovers in the refrigerator. There's a box of two-day-old mu shu calling to me with all the seductive power of three martinis. I sit at the kitchen table and eat it cold, straight from the box. It's oddly pleasant to sit here in an empty apartment, no one to feed. Chloe's winging her way across the Atlantic at this moment. She likes the shades down on the window during a night flight, preferring the faint womblike light of the enclosed cabin to that expanse of darkness beyond the glass. She'll read, then sleep. And when she wakes up, she'll see the red roofs of Paris. What could be more pleasant?

I leave the empty takeout box in the sink, stagger into the bedroom, and crawl beneath the covers. The light's on above me, but I lie there dreamily, eyes closed, imagining my daughter's excitement. It's oddly arousing. Hope. Change. French food. French men. It's the opposite of marriage, motherhood, and middle-age. It's the hollow feeling in your belly that tells you anything is possible at this moment. You're open to the world, just waiting for it to sweep you off your feet. Terrifying, but also breathless and thrilling.

The light's still on, but I can't make myself get up

to turn it out. I'm too tired, and the room's spinning slightly—just a pleasant whirl, like waltzing with a count in a Russian novel. Snowdrifts and candlelight. Pale girls in furs.

David will turn the light out when he gets home.

# 178

How can any girl be true to herself in this world? They bring in pastries at my office when we're on deadline. If you're not careful, you can get mauled by a bearclaw before you know it. My column's late, and I'm hung over from Liz's martinis, and this morning David asked me, "Don't you think those pants are a little tight?"

Seriously. Like he was trying to help me. I was standing in front of the mirror putting on my makeup—trying to create a convincing illusion that my eyes were really open—and he comes up behind me, stands there for a moment with this expression like he's giving the problem serious thought, then he says it.

"Don't you think . . ." (a pause here, thoughtful, then a slight nod of the head toward my barely contained hips) "those pants are a *little* . . ." (his voice going up slightly here, like the word is almost too tiny to say) "tight?"

Spear thrust, right in the heart.

I blame Maribel Steinberg, the bitch. She ordered a salad, then spent the evening telling him that it's a myth that women naturally gain weight in their forties. If you're *true to yourself,* to your *inner woman,* then your husband will *never* have to ask you if your pants are just a *little* . . .

The thing is, he's right, damn it. I can barely move in these pants. At the time, I was too hungover to get into a fight and too humiliated to change. *"No,"* I told him, "I *don't* think these pants are too *tight."* I gave him what passes for a withering look when you can't get your eyes more than half open, snapped my makeup case closed, and stalked off to the kitchen. Breakfast was out of the question now, and I couldn't picture myself sitting over a cup of coffee while he told me about his lovely evening with the charming and svelte Maribel Steinberg (the skinny bitch).

I stood at the sink just long enough to drink a glass of water, which promptly set the room spinning again. I knew this once, in college. Liquor dehydrates. Water re-hydrates. If you drink a glass of water the morning after, it wakes up the alcohol lurking in your system. Better to stick to coffee and cigarettes. Only, I gave up smoking years ago, which is why my ass is now so big that my pants don't fit. That, and Chloe. Maribel Steinberg is probably childless. And a smoker. That's why Liz is still thin. Of course, she's also bitter, single, and running a home for gay cats.

Some women have all the fun.

I left my glass in the sink, next to the empty takeout box, which David hadn't bothered to throw out when he got home. Chloe was gone for one night, and things were going to hell. It would have taken me a second to put the glass in the dishwasher and throw the box in the garbage can under the sink, but the message for David seemed clearer this way. He was still getting dressed when I left.

I got in line at the Starbucks at the corner, then had to juggle the cup on the subway all the way to Fifty-ninth Street. By the time I got to the office, my knuckles had burns on them and there was a coffee stain on my left shoe, but I'd made my point. When was the last time I'd left the apartment without breakfast? David would know I was angry.

Meanwhile, I was starving. And there were pastries on the conference table for our ten o'clock staff meeting. My fate was sealed.

*House & Home,* my publisher likes to remind us, has two kinds of subscribers: the gay couple who've bought in a changing neighborhood, and dentists. The average gay couple subscribes on a blow-in card after their first trip to Home Depot, where our magazine is strategically placed on a rack near the cash registers. ("They're urban homesteaders," Ron likes to say, "so they buy us instead of *House & Garden.* We don't do gardens.") Dentists keep us in their waiting rooms.

Actually, Ron's exaggerating on both counts. We're a prestige publication for suburban coffee tables, and a form of pornography for urban bathrooms. We market a fantasy of wood, tile, and beveled glass. "Reality has nothing to do with it," Ron likes to point out at our monthly staff meetings. "We're selling dreams, just like

Hollywood. Only the dreams we sell come with hardwood floors."

Ron Nunberg was born in the Bronx and grew up in
a three-room apartment on the Grand Concourse. His
father worked in a hardware store, so when Ron was
in high school, he spent his summers stocking shelves
with decorative hinges, window locks, and copper pipe.
"That's where I learned my business," he reminds us.
"Our readers are the people who like to wander through
hardware stores because they're fascinated by all the *stuff*.
What we offer them is a dream of order. Perfect objects
for a perfectible world."

Now he owns a Victorian farmhouse in Katonah,
which he visits one weekend a month to supervise its
restoration. The rest of the time, he lives in a cluttered
apartment on Park and Sixty-sixth, with stacks of old
magazines piled up on every surface. Architecture magazines, fashion rags, celebrity tabloids. One look at those
stacks and you realize that the house is just an excuse for
the magazine, and in this respect, he's not so different
from our readers. Everybody needs an ideal to live up
to, an aspirational image. It's what gets us out of bed in
the morning.

That's the theory, anyway. This morning, getting out
of bed seems to lead only to pastry and a confrontation
with my personal failings. My pants are too tight, my
deadline's approaching, and my column's just a vague
scrawl on a scrap of paper that I've left on my bedside
table. Something about old houses as a metaphor for our
lives. Except that houses rarely get bigger as they age.

Or do they? Chloe goes to college in a tiny New England village where it's all the rage to buy up lovely old houses and then double their size with modern great rooms and in-law apartments. The result, the owners seem to believe, will give them all the charm of an old farmhouse and all the space of a suburban McMansion.

*Frankenhouse,* I scrawl on my pad. *Preservation or abomination?*

We're seated around a glass conference table strewn with page proofs, photographs, and the wreckage of our diets. Ron's collecting the latest disaster reports: the photo shoot that ended badly, an architect stalking off his own project when the photographer refused to work with only natural lighting, the manufacturer of roofing shingles who threatened a lawsuit if we went ahead with a consumer report on his products. I'd slipped into the room early, as always, to grab the seat on Ron's right. He always goes around the table from left to right, which gives me forty-five extra minutes to come up with a subject for my column.

*Do our houses expand,* I scribble, *along with our waistlines?*

It's not much, but beggars can't be choosers. Anyway, everybody's looking down at their own pads, consumed in their own disasters. Would anyone notice if I grabbed another bearclaw?

Morris, our designer, is ending his report, and before Ron can say something scathing, Morris looks up brightly and asks, "Oh, and did anyone see that Michael Foresman won the Pritzker Prize? They announced it this morning."

It's a brilliant strategy. Everyone looks up from their

pads, interested, and Ron sits back, raises his eyebrows. "You're kidding. The Madman of Santa Monica won the biggest prize in architecture?" With no warning, his gaze lands on me. "You know him, don't you, Eva?"

"We've met," I say tightly, and look down at my pad in a way that I hope will signal that the topic is closed.

But Ron is enthroned at the head of his conference table, with his subjects gathered before him. He's here to dispense wisdom and, when necessary, justice. And let's face it, all is not well in The Kingdom of Ron this morning. The upcoming issue of *House & Home,* according to its editors' glum reports, will have no photo spread of the latest pop diva's Malibu love nest, no scathing exposé of the roofing tile industry, and (although he doesn't know it yet) no witty column on the latest fashion in home design. I should have known he wouldn't let it drop.

"You've met." He considers this. "Met how? Met like 'Hi, my name is . . .' or met like 'Please pass the condoms?' "

My face reddens. I force myself to look up at him reproachfully. "There were no condoms involved." (It was twenty-three years ago, and I was stupid then.)

He shrugs, raises both hands as if in surrender. "Okay, sorry. Just wondered if we had a connection there that was worth pursuing."

We move on, and when my turn comes, I describe my Frankenhouse idea. He nods, but I can see he's got his doubts.

"You don't think that'll offend our readers?" our circulation director asks. "It's not like they're all restoring houses to original condition. Lots of them put on additions." He glances over at the advertising director. "You might catch some flak from advertisers, also. Those additions sell a lot of building supplies."

The marketing director has been gazing longingly at the pastries, but she perks up at this. "I'd have some concerns about that. They're already angry about your column on replacement windows."

Ron winces visibly at the memory. "Maybe you should think of something else," he says to me. So much for freedom of the press.

Later, Ron appears at my office door. "Sorry if I put you on the spot this morning." He closes the door discreetly, making everybody on the floor look over to see what's going on. Ron takes a seat opposite me, then sighs deeply as if the weight of the world has been heaved onto his weary shoulders.

My impulse, as always, is to apologize for causing him such anguish. But I bite my tongue. I know this trick; he uses it every year during salary negotiations. I fold my hands in my lap and look at him with earnest attention.

"I'm just a little thrown by this Michael Foresman thing," he says, gazing thoughtfully out my window at the brick wall across the alley. "You remember he wrote that article in *Architecture* a few years ago called 'Against Beauty?' Now with this prize thing, he's going to be in all the newspapers. He's the flavor of the week. For our readers, it's going to feel like the devil's been elected pope."

"Ron, since when do we care who wins the architecture prizes? You can't even get on the short list for those things unless your latest project looks like a pile of cardboard boxes your kid kicked over. It's like fashion shows: everybody gets excited by the stuff nobody would actually wear. And that article he wrote was just a way of getting attention. Nobody thinks you're important in that profession unless you make somebody mad, like in the art world."

He nods. "Yeah, I know. I'm just thinking about our readers. They're going to be expecting us to say *something* about this guy. I mean, this is the guy who said he doesn't believe in houses. He thinks everybody should live in apartment buildings."

I can't conceal my surprise. "He said that?"

"In an interview last year." Ron takes a piece of paper from his pocket and slides it across my desk to me. "He also said that renovating old buildings is like eating somebody else's leftovers. Architecture should be the art of the new."

I take the photocopy of a magazine article, look down at a photograph of Michael gazing at the camera with a serious expression. He's older now, with some gray in his swept-back hair, but it's still the same face that once brought a hollow feeling into my stomach, as if just meeting that intense gaze might feel like a kiss, a caress, a wave that could sweep you away.

"He likes to be provocative," I say, passing the paper back to Ron. "I guess he likes buildings that do the same thing."

"You know him well enough to get an interview?"

His words send a rush of blood to my face. "He's probably doing interviews with *Newsweek* and CNN. Why would he bother with us?"

He gives me a cagey look. "We've got a personal connection."

❧

That's one way to put it. Michael Foresman and I spent most of a week in a *personal connection* the summer after my sophomore year in college. A girl whose parents had a place in Palm Beach had invited Liz (who promptly invited me) to come down right after exams to lie on the beach, drink margaritas, and take long, casual walks past the Kennedy compound. The bars were full every night, and Liz proved to be an expert at getting men we'd just met to buy us drinks. Among those men was a group of architecture students down from Harvard.

"You're *all* studying to be architects?" Liz looked like she'd just struck oil. They nodded. "And you're all at Harvard?" More nods. She sat back, sighed with pleasure. "Okay, so which one of you wants to marry me?"

She looked them over carefully, settling on one with dark, restless eyes and an impatient way of gazing off across the room when one of the others came out with something he thought was stupid. The other four men had crowded around us, one of them leaning across the bar to catch the bartender as he passed, anxious to get more drinks into us. But the dark-eyed guy remained silent, watchful.

"And what's *your* name?" Liz asked him, leaning past the others to rest her hand on his forearm.

"Michael."

"And you're the challenge in this group?"

He gave a smile. "That's me."

"I like a challenge."

It never would have occurred to me to talk to a man that way, and I couldn't help envying her. She came across as wicked and free. She called it, "celebrating her inner slut." Meanwhile, I sat in silence, watching.

He must have felt my gaze, because he looked over at me. Our eyes met, and I quickly looked away. One of the other guys was talking to me, and I smiled as if he'd said something smart and funny, but inside I was feeling slightly nauseated.

Eye contact. It's the rolled *R* of sex. ("Flirrrr-tation," Liz says, with Sadean delight.) Either you can do it, or you can't. In love, I flew blind, sending out faint shrieks like a bat, trying not to crash into trees.

Later, when the margaritas had wrought their usual havoc, we staggered out onto the beach to look at the moonlight or the ocean or some other part of the tourist brochure, and one of the architects—the one who'd been working so hard to make me smile—leaned over and threw up onto the sand.

"Who's for a swim?" Liz demanded. Then she reached down, unbuttoned her skirt, and let it fall to the ground. We stood there, watching her strip off her clothes and then run down into the surf. Several of the architects started pulling off their clothes. Liz's friend Andrea looked at me. "Are you going?"

I shook my head. She hesitated, then gave a laugh. "Then watch our clothes, okay?" She started unbuttoning her shirt.

I sat on the sand beside the pile of clothes. The guy who'd thrown up lay a short distance away, sleeping. I looked around and saw that Michael had turned, standing with his back to the ocean, looking at the row of hotels that faced the beach. I could hear Liz laughing over the sound of the waves. After a moment, Michael came over and sat beside me.

"I hate Florida," he said. "It's mindless."

I rested my chin on my knees. "What would you build here?"

"Nothing. Anything you built here would be overwhelmed by the site. It would be too dependent on its context to mean anything. I'd rather build in a city, where you've got all the other buildings to interact with yours." He was silent for a moment, looking out at the water. "Beaches limit your imagination. Think about what you see on beachfronts: houses or hotels with lots of glass facing the water. I'd put a solid wall facing the ocean and make all the windows face the land."

"What's the point in that?"

"To make people question their expectations."

I looked over at him. "What if they want to look at the ocean?"

"Then they should go stand in a different building." He looked back at the row of hotels behind us. "They've got lots of choices."

We were both silent for a while. I looked at the pile of clothes beside us. Liz had borrowed a silk shirt from me when we were getting ready to go out. (We wore the same size then.) Now it lay in a heap in the sand. I resisted an impulse to shake it out.

"So why'd you come here if you don't like Florida?" I asked.

"I'm interning with a firm in New York. They're building a performing arts center down here."

"Which way do the windows face?"

He smiled. "It's a couple miles from the water." Then he looked out at the bodies splashing in the surf. "So how long do you think they expect us to watch their clothes?"

"Tell me you didn't fuck him," Liz demanded the next morning.

"I didn't fuck him," I lied.

We were in the kitchen of Andrea's parents' house, Liz slumped at the table while I searched through the cabinets looking for Tylenol. I was wearing the fluffy bathrobe Andrea had loaned me, having snuck in twenty minutes earlier only to find the house empty. I'd just had time to make a pot of coffee and settle at the table with a bowl of Wheat Chex when Liz turned up, wearing her tiny skirt and my now-ruined silk shirt. Andrea still hadn't come home.

"Well, that's a relief," she said. "When we came out of the water and found you gone, I thought, 'The clever little bitch! She plays the quiet type while I'm off frolicking in the surf, and she makes off with the man I'm going to marry.' I thought I'd have to shoot myself in despair."

Instead, she'd gone home with one of the other architects and spent the rest of the night having athletic sex with him in the swimming pool of the apartment complex where he was staying. "We're going sailing later." She raised her head to look at me with concern. "You don't mind if I slip away, do you? I'd invite you, but apparently it's a small boat."

"That's fine," I told her. "I'm kind of tired today, anyway. I'm just going to hang out by the pool."

And that's how it went for four days. Every morning, Liz would apologize, but one of the architects simply *had* to teach her how to Jet Ski after he got off work. And I'd smile, assure her that I was perfectly capable of entertaining myself, then slip off to spend the evening in bed with Michael. It was never really clear why we kept it secret. Liz stopped sighing about him after a few days, once she'd fucked all his friends and it became apparent that they all thought he was arrogant. But the idea of hiding it from my friends somehow made it all the more exciting.

When the week came to an end, Michael wanted to take the morning off so he could come with me to the airport, but I shook my head. "I don't want to upset Liz. I'll call you when I get home. Maybe I can come up to Boston when you get back."

We talked on the phone a few more times that summer, and in the fall we spent a weekend on the Cape, never leaving our motel room. "What's there to see?" he said. "Just more sand and water. I'd rather look at you."

But even as he said it, I could tell his mind was elsewhere. It was his final year in grad school, and he had a job offer out in California. "It's an exciting firm. Lots of energy, and they're not afraid to take risks. I think it's a good match for me."

*What about me?* I wanted to ask. *Am I a good match for you?* But the weekend quickly ended, and that was it. There were a few more phone calls during the fall, but he was busy with his final projects, and he was flying out to Los Angeles over the holidays to look for a place to live. That spring, I took a class on the history of modern architecture and wrote my final paper on the tyranny of the view in American beachfront design. *Very provocative,* the professor wrote on the final page, A−. I called to tell Michael, but he wasn't home, so I left a message on his machine. That was the last time I ever spoke to him.

"I think you're overestimating my relationship with him," I tell Ron now. "He probably won't even remember who I am."

Ron heaves himself out of the chair. "Can't hurt to try, right?"

*D*ear Michael . . .

I'm stuck. All morning, the email has been on my computer screen, unwritten. From time to time, I pull it up, stare at it for a while, then get disgusted with myself and click the button to send it scurrying back to the bottom of my screen, like a rat vanishing into its hole. *This is stupid,* I think angrily. *I've got more important things to do.*

I let two days go by, hoping it might slip Ron's mind, but this morning he stopped me in the hall and asked, "Any luck on the Foresman interview?"

"Working on it," I assured him. "I'll let you know as soon as I hear something."

So unless I was happy to be a total liar, I actually had to try. I went back to my office, pulled up the website for Michael's firm, and found an email address. With iron determination, I hit the Compose key, typed in the address and a subject line that read *Congratulations!* Before I could have second thoughts, I typed *Dear Michael,* hit the Return key, and paused.

And that's where things stand.

I read somewhere that the late-night email to an old boyfriend is so common now that it's the flip side of the Dear John letter in the modern woman's gallery of self-inflicted wounds.

> *Dear John. How's everything? My life sucks. And by the way, what went wrong?*

Like drinking and dialing, it never leads to good. They should pass a law that all email servers shut down after 2:00 a.m. If you can't send it in the cold morning light, you've got no business sending it at all.

But how do you write something like this sitting in your office at eleven o'clock on a Thursday morning? I need Liz, with her gay cats and her martini shaker, to inspire this act of self-abasement; she's always been my muse in that department. Who else would take me shopping for clothes on my fortieth birthday, helping me to the realization that not only was I old and overweight, but helplessly uncool as well. We started out in the nose-ring and anorexia boutiques south of Houston and, when that didn't work, tried our luck at Prada, which lasted until I got a look at the price tags. By the end of the day, we were in Saks.

"Look at this stuff," she said, her voice dripping with fashionista disdain. "They ought to call it Sacks with a *ck*."

I tried to hush her, but the sales clerk gave us a dirty look. And I'd just found something I wanted to try on.

But how could I explain to Liz that I was writing to a

man I'd stolen from under her nose, then hadn't had the brains to hang onto until he became a celebrity? It was hard to know which she'd find more offensive.

So I'm on my own. Where are the pastries when you need them?

> *Dear Michael,*
> *I don't know if you'll remember me, but I wanted*
> *to send you my congratulations on the Pritzker Prize.*
> *I've followed your success with pleasure over recent*
> *years, and . . .*

Oh God, am I really going to tell him how much he deserved the award? It seems like the obvious thing to say, but does he really need to hear it from some girl he slept with more than twenty years ago?

Not that any of this really matters. I'll write the email and send it, and that'll be the end of it. He probably has an assistant to screen his email, some pretty young thing with a degree from Yale to decorate his outer office with her brisk, effortless beauty. She'll look at it for thirty seconds, just to make sure it isn't from somebody important, then delete it along with the rest of the day's flood of congratulations.

*. . . I was delighted to see your work recognized in such a public manner.*

Time for something personal, to remind him who you are.

*No beachfront properties, I notice. I'm glad to see you've stuck to your guns.* (Too casual? Too vague, maybe. He could have made that speech to lots of people. Young girls he wanted to impress. Still, there's your hook.) *Forgive the cliché* . . . (Brief reprieve, while I go searching for the accent mark), *but it really does seem like only yesterday that we were sitting on the beach in Florida* . . . (Pause. Too vague. Block, delete.) . . . *in Palm Beach* . . . (Pause. Too many *beaches* now, too close together. Block, delete.) . . . *in Florida, and you were designing buildings that turn their backs on the sea.*

Okay, that's not bad. A hint of humor, and the buildings are personified, which makes it easier for him to picture us sitting there on the sand. Should I hint at what followed?

*I'm glad you didn't turn your back on me* . . .

Ugh! (Block, delete.) Anyway, he had. Never returned my call, the heartless bastard.

*I was impressed by the clarity of your vision that night* . . . (among other things) . . . *and I'm glad to see you've stayed true to that vision throughout your career.*

Flattery, but with a judicious tone. Like you share his high standards, or even that you've been watching to see if he can meet your expectations. You're not begging for his attention, like other journalists. After all, you've seen him naked.

Anyone passing my office would see me smiling—Mona Lisa, alone with her filthy thoughts.

My phone rings. It's David, naturally. Are we free on the twenty-fourth? He's trying to schedule a book party. I check my calendar. Yes, we're free. Great. Your day going okay? Sure, fine. Yours? Busy.

We hang up and I sit staring at my computer screen, feeling oddly guilty. Ridiculous, really. It's just memory.

Like David doesn't think about girls he slept with when he was single?

The cursor blinks its reproach: get to the point.

*As it happens, I work for an architectural magazine . . .* (No, much too direct. Block, delete. Just renew the acquaintance for now, then you can ask about the interview when the moment's right.)

*I'm sure you must be terribly busy right now, but if you ever get a minute, I'd love to hear how you're doing.* (Swilling champagne and being toasted by the world press. Thanks for asking.)

Something personal to end it?

*I've thought about you often over the years.*

Not true, really. I've thought about him occasionally, as one does with old boyfriends, but who wants to hear that? This implies sighs and longing. And a hint of enticement? Just a hint that he could have seconds, if he's still hungry.

It makes me feel slightly naughty, which is rather pleasant. I probably won't get a response, but let him think about that girl in Palm Beach for a day or two. Wasn't she worth the whistle?

I sign my name, add *(from 1982, Palm Beach)* just to make it clear, and then in a sudden burst of daring, I hit Send.

I regret it immediately. Why would he want to hear from that girl in Palm Beach after so many years? And even if he did, what's left of that girl after twenty-three years of marriage, motherhood, and middle-aged spread? I wince. Would he even recognize me now?

I've seen *him,* in the newspapers, on his firm's website,

being interviewed on PBS after one of his more radical designs won a competition for a new museum in Berlin. By this evening he'll be on cable news. He still looks good. Sexy, in that windblown California way, like a man who's worked hard but also lived well. I could picture him on a sailboat, if he didn't hate the ocean. I can picture him walking his construction sites in a hardhat and a leather jacket, checking to make sure that every nail is driven according to his vision.

He looked like he hadn't gained a pound in twenty-three years—just wisdom, success, and public acclaim. That pretty young thing in his office, with her great legs and cool glasses and her degree from Yale, surely has a crush on her boss. He's just the kind of man she imagines herself marrying.

*So maybe your email will make her jealous.*

Fat chance. She'll glance at it, hit Delete, and that'll be the end of it. At least I can tell Ron I tried.

I spend the afternoon copyediting an article entitled "Kitchens to Fry For!" By the time I'm finished, I've got an irresistible craving for fried clams from some waterfront shack on City Island. I'm such a fraud. My idea of a perfect kitchen is one that comes with a waitress and a cocktail bar. I know my convection ovens and I can name the stovetop with the highest consumer satisfaction rating, but I'm the reigning queen of Chinese takeout: I know the phone numbers by heart, and which place to call for Hunan beef, the best kung pao shrimp, or a mu shu pork that will make your heart race.

When Chloe first left for college, David and I stopped eating at home altogether, unless you count pizza lifted straight from the box. We'd work until six, then spend ten minutes on the phone deciding where to meet for dinner. If the weather was lousy we'd sit on our couch with our feet up, eating takeout pot stickers while watching old movies on television with a feeling of sinful decadence. It was like being newly married again, and when we'd eaten all we could hold, we'd put the leftovers in the refrigerator, toss the empty boxes in the garbage, and stagger off to bed to make love like two whales in heat. For a few months it was glorious.

Then David read a manuscript entitled *The Myth of Middle Age,* which argued that men who exercise regularly and eat a low-fat diet after forty have higher levels of testosterone than men who allow their sluttish wives to tempt them with takeout. After that he began stopping at the health club in the evenings, while I miserably shopped for chicken breasts and prepackaged salads to serve for dinner.

What's he need all that testosterone for? I couldn't help wondering. Certainly not for me. With all that working out, he'd crawl off to bed shortly after dinner, leaving me to wash up the dishes and entertain myself for the rest of the evening. Old movies aren't nearly as much fun when you watch them alone. For a while, I exchanged emails with Chloe at school almost every night, until she started staying late at the library to study for midterms. (That's what she said, anyway.) After that, I surfed the Web, where it's always the soul's deep midnight, and the lonely discover how much they have in common. I searched for old boyfriends (including, I confess, Michael Foresman), then college classmates.

Nobody had won the Nobel Prize, thank God, but there was enough success—books published, doctorates completed, even a federal judgeship—to leave me feeling depressed for days.

"It's not that I mind David going to bed early," I told Liz one night when we went out for drinks. "I mean, he looks great, and he says he has lots more energy during the day. I just wish we could spend more time together."

Liz looked at me over her martini. "You mean you're not getting laid."

I shook my head. "I'm not talking about sex. We've always gone through phases when we had lots of sex and other times when one of us seemed to lose interest for a while. It's part of the cycle of a marriage."

"Bullshit." She lifted the olives out of her glass and popped one into her mouth. "You're upset because you thought you married a fun guy, and now you've ended up with a fungi. It's the classic situation, only before you always blamed it on Chloe."

"I never blamed it on Chloe!"

"I'm not saying that you *blamed* her, just that you always figured this was part of being parents. So now she's gone and you thought you'd get your husband back, but he's too busy hanging out at the gym." She shrugged. "So go fuck the doorman. That's what I do."

I stared at her in horror. "You didn't. *Harold?*" Harold the Doorman was her building's version of a gargoyle, except that he was too fat to be hoisted to the roof, so they kept him at street level where he could scowl at deliverymen and single women.

"Please," she said, shuddering. "Not Harold. The kid who replaced him during his vacation last summer. The surfer."

"With all the teeth?"

"Mmmm." She smiled, as if savoring the memory. "He wants to be an actor. I can certainly vouch for his performance." And she proceeded to do so, in great detail, and in a voice just a bit too loud for privacy. By the time she finished, the stockbrokers sitting at the table next to us looked pale.

I drained my drink. "Well," I said, "I guess that solves the problem of tipping at Christmas."

She raised her glass. "Service with a smile."

But my building doesn't have a doorman, so Liz's advice was of no immediate use. David continued to go to the gym every evening, and diet books began to show up in the stack of manuscripts on his night table. A food scale appeared on our kitchen counter, and he began to measure out his portions with scientific care.

"Have you considered that he might be having an affair?" Liz raised an eyebrow. "He's got midlife crisis written all over him."

I sighed. "Last night he mentioned that he's always dreamed of buying a Harley and riding it out to California."

"There you are: he's feeling his age." She gave a wicked smile. "Maybe *he* needs to fuck the doorman."

So there I am up to my ample ass in kitchen design, and all I can think about is fucking the doorman. Is this a common practice among New Yorkers? It must make it awkward when you bring home a date, or even when you go out for a newspaper. One of the delights of marriage was *not* running into people who've seen you howling in passion when you're buying groceries or picking up your dry cleaning.

Your husband doesn't count, of course, because you see him every day, and you've made an unspoken agreement not to smirk about it, unless seduction is in the air. Marriage is an institution based on a shared delusion of privacy: you won't notice that I hide cookies under the dish towels if I don't notice that you pick your nose. And neither will share the other's secrets with outsiders, *ever*.

Men seem particularly sensitive on this subject, perhaps because they fear that women are comparing notes behind their backs. And they're right, of course. Most women, I've found, marry only for the pleasure of complaining to their girlfriends about their husbands' failings. It's like bragging in reverse, a competition to determine who's pledged her life and eternal fidelity to the most loathsome jerk. (But just let the other women hint that your husband is loathsome, and you've got a fight on your hands.) It seems to be an expectation, one of the structural beams of female friendship. Liz is always complaining that I don't find more to loathe in David. As a married friend, I'm a disappointment. Where's the blood? Where are the steaming entrails for her to feast upon?

But I prefer privacy. It's like the takeout food of romance: easy, convenient, and you don't have to worry about cleaning up the mess.

If my mind keeps wandering, I'll never finish this article: vent hoods, power burners, splatter guards, all important for fried food. (And marriage?) David's low-fat obsession faded after a few months, and by the time Chloe came home from her first year at college, we were back to pizza and Chinese takeout. He still went to the gym several times a week after work, but he'd come home hungry, so it wasn't like living with a Spartan warrior. Chloe had put on some weight on the college's meal plan, so he got a family membership at the health club and the two of them would meet there in the evenings and work out together.

"At least you know he's not having an affair with some gym rat," Liz observed with her usual discretion.

I went with them a few times, but I found the whole thing embarrassing. What's the pleasure in sweating among strangers? Being in a room with people so focused on their bodies made me self-conscious, and don't even get me started on the clothing! My gym bag, with its hazardous cargo of Lycra and unwashed towels, lies under my desk at work, a daily indictment. But David and Chloe seemed to enjoy the time they spent working out together. They often came home laughing, practically snapping towels at each other like kids after gym class. My job was to make sure there was food ready when they came through the door, and as long as it didn't involve chicken breasts and prepackaged salad, I was happy to comply. My kitchen may not have had power burners and splatter guards, but it had a telephone and a drawerful of takeout menus. And who needs a vent hood when the food arrives trailing such delicious smells?

I finish the copyediting at last, drop the article in Ron's box, then go back to my office and call David to ask when was the last time we went out for fried clams. But he's away from his desk, and I get voice mail. "Hi, it's me. Just thinking of you." (A lie, but it doesn't seem fair to tell him that he's playing second fiddle to a plate of fried clams.) "Give me a call when you get a chance."

I check my email, but there's nothing from Michael Foresman, or anyone else for that matter. I try calling Liz, but her assistant tells me she's out with a client. Liz runs a very successful interior design business. She's developed a highly profitable niche market helping newly divorced women spend their ex-husbands' money decorating their new Park Avenue apartments—the designer of choice for angry women with a taste for the fabulous.

I try Chloe's cell, but she doesn't pick up. It's the café hour in Paris. She's probably out with some pale existentialist, letting her phone ring in her purse while she gazes deeply into his soulful eyes.

I've left messages everywhere, but the afternoon passes and nobody calls me back. I'm the forgotten woman. I spend the long, lonely hours in copyediting hell. Two freelance articles with not a decent verb between them. Where do we find these people? Ron's girlfriends, no doubt. He's always turning up some recent liberal arts graduate with lovely tits and a degree in English who's looking to get some freelance writing. The better the tits, the worse the writing. And it's up to me to sort out the mess, making sure the magazine's current issue has enough active verbs in it to qualify, under current legal statutes, as English.

But Ron's outdone himself this time. I can only hope

that he's getting what he paid for, because by four o'clock my head is throbbing, the pages are dripping with red ink, and it's still not clear to me that we've got an issue worth publishing. Outside it's raining, but I decide to dash down the block to Cupola before I start hacking at my wrists with a letter opener. Late afternoon is a bad time to hit the coffee bar. Everybody in there has a haunted look, like the day has finally turned on them, snarling with dripping fangs. We're all ready for alcohol, but there's still work to be done, so we stand blankly before the counter, gazing up at the list of mochas and lattes like refugees driven before the storm.

"Nonfat latte," I tell the girl, "with a shot of sugar-free almond syrup." There's a pastry case, but I force myself not to look. I'm a repeat offender: one more almond dream bar, and they'll send me up for life.

When I get back to my desk, the light on my phone is flashing. Chloe got my message, and everything's fine. David's going to be on the phone with an author, but he'll try me when he gets done. Liz is back from lunch with her client and ready to dish. It seems I'm not a pariah, after all. Or maybe they were all waiting until I'd been fully caffeinated and my wits restored.

To my surprise, there's email too. *FORESMANM,* says the first entry in my in-box.

My cursor hovers over his name for a moment, gathering its courage, and then clicks.

*Dear Eva. Thanks for your kind note. Of course I remember you! I've avoided beachfront projects all these years for fear of disappointing you.*

I pause, read that last sentence a second time. My heart gives a flutter.

> *This whole business with the prize is a little embar-*
> *rassing. In fact, it's proved impossible to get any work*
> *done since Monday. But one real pleasure has been*
> *hearing from old friends.*

Now my heart sinks. I'm just one of many. Probably lots of old girlfriends have written to him. He's acknowledging the gesture, politely.

> *I was in such a hurry as a young man, so anxious*
> *to prove something to myself and to the world, that I*
> *didn't always give my friends their due.*

Interesting. You wouldn't expect such a reflective tone from a man who's just won his profession's highest honor. But maybe success allows for a chance to measure the cost.

> *In most cases, I was simply selfish. I didn't see the*
> *real value in my friends, and now I find myself want-*
> *ing to apologize.*

Uh oh, getting a little maudlin. Too much champagne?

> *But there are other cases where I know it was*
> *my loss. I've thought about you often over the*
> *years . . .*

I've stopped breathing. My eyes can't seem to move beyond this phrase. Can he really be saying this?

> *. . . and I've often wondered what might have happened if we'd stayed in touch.*

In a flash, twenty-three years are gone. I'm young, thin, living in California with my architect boyfriend. The thought is both exciting and strangely sad. What would my life have been?

> *I hope you've had a good life . . .*

I have. David, Chloe, a job I mostly enjoy.

> *. . . and I'd love to hear about it when you get the chance. Until then, thanks again for your kind note, and for still thinking of me after all these years.*

> *Best wishes,*
> *Michael.*

I'm still staring at the screen in amazement when the phone rings. My hand lifts it automatically, brings it to my ear. "Hello?" I say absently.

A pause, and then David says, "Eva?"

Guilt floods through me. I've been in California with another man, walking on sunlit beaches, where all the movie stars' houses turn their backs on the sea.

"David! Sorry, my mind was on other things." I usually answer my office phone, "Eva Cassady," with a slight lift in tone on the final syllable, not quite a question but an openness to be engaged. Only at home do I answer the phone with a dull "Hello," and then only when I've been sleeping.

"Busy day, huh?"

"Yeah, lots of copyediting. More of Ron's writer girls." I click the button to diminish Michael's email, as if David might catch a glimpse of it over the phone.

"I got your message, but I've been on the phone for the last three hours. Everything okay?"

"Yeah—just needed to talk to somebody who knows what an active verb is. I tried Chloe and Liz, but I guess their verbs are too active."

"So what does that say about me?"

"That you're in publishing." I can hear his keyboard tapping in the background. Multitasking his wife.

"I'm not sure I like thinking of Chloe and Liz in the same category."

"Single girls. Get used to it." I click the button to bring up Michael's email again. Two can play at this game. *I've thought about you often over the years . . .*

"That's it? Nothing else on your mind?"

"Fried clams," I tell him. "When was the last time we went out to City Island?"

"Two summers ago?"

"I think we're due."

He's silent for a moment.

"Still there?"

"Yeah, I got distracted. We can go out there if you want fried clams. But not tonight, okay? You know Edie, in my office? She's trying to grab some manuscripts away from me again, so I've got to catch up on my reading. How about this weekend?"

"It's a deal." We hang up, and I read Michael's email again. Suddenly I have no interest in fried clams. Just the thought of all that grease makes me feel slightly nauseated.

    *. . . I'd love to hear about it when you get the chance.*

Is it too soon to answer? If I fire off a reply, it might seem like I have nothing better to do. But, really, what's wrong with an honest expression of pleasure at his sweet words? And anyway, Ron wants an interview for the next issue.

I hit Reply.

> *Dear Michael,*
>     *What a lovely message! You always knew how to warm a girl's heart.*

Too flirtatious? Probably, but I want to say it.

>     *And you certainly can't blame yourself for not giving me my due.*

Okay, that's definitely going too far. But I can't bring myself to delete it. Let's face it, he did me, and why pretend it's not a pleasant memory? It was more than twenty years ago. There's nothing wrong with a playful wink after so long, right?

>     *My life is good, if not quite as exciting as yours. I'm living in Manhattan, and I've got a daughter in*

*college who's off in Paris this year, boning up on . . .*
(block, delete) . . . *studying French, or at least
French men. Her name's Chloe, so I'm picturing an
Eric Rohmer film.*

Interesting that I didn't mention David. That seems
dishonest. After some hesitation, I reluctantly go back
and change the sentence to *I'm living in Manhattan, married, with a daughter in college . . .* Honesty's always the best
policy.

*How about you? Any kids to inherit all that talent?*

I can't ask about a wife, although I'm dying to know.
There's nothing in the newspaper stories or on his firm's
website to suggest one, but that doesn't mean one doesn't
exist. Tall, blond, and lean, probably. An elegant woman,
with a drawerful of French underwear to keep the sexy
young assistant at bay. If she's smart she's already be-
friended the girl, taken her to lunch and shopping in
Beverly Hills, showing her she doesn't stand a chance
against all that elegance. Maybe pause in a store to let her
try your perfume, so she'll show up at the office smelling
like his wife.

But wait. If there's an elegant wife, why all the regret
in his email? He sounds more like a man who's recently
divorced. Probably a workaholic who put his career before his family. Now he's achieved success, and there's
nobody with whom he can share it. His ex-wife's dating
her divorce attorney, and he sees his kids only on weekends. Even the sexy young assistant has a boyfriend, a

surgical resident at Cedars-Sinai. What's left but flirting with old girlfriends by email?

I consider deleting my reply, but what kind of heartless bitch would I be to abandon the poor guy now? I'm all he has! My eyes fill with tears, and I'm just reaching for a tissue when my phone rings. "Hello?"

Liz says, "You sound like you've been crying."

"I think I'm allergic to something."

"That explains the swelling."

Ouch. What law is it that single women over a certain age get a free pass for bitchiness? I blame Eve Arden.

"Did you call only to insult me, or was there something else on your mind?"

Liz sighs. "You called me, honey. Remember? You were bored with your life and you needed me to brighten your day. So you left a message with my assistant, and I called you back like a good girl, but now you've got something interesting going on, so you don't need me anymore. I'll die alone and unwanted, and my gay cats will feed on my rotting corpse."

"And that justifies calling me fat?"

"You're right—I'm a bitch. It's my hormones. I'd be much better if somebody made me moan like a whore."

Liz could do standup, but she's rarely on her feet that long. "Do you ever hear from old boyfriends?" I ask.

"Are we counting restraining orders?"

"Seriously."

"Well, one guy invited me to his wedding. I sent back the response card saying, 'No thanks. I'm holding out for the funeral.'" Her voice takes on a conspiratorial tone. "This is an interesting topic. What's up?"

"Actually nothing," I say, too quickly. "I was looking at a magazine at lunch, and there was an article that said the latest trend in relationships was old boyfriends coming back for seconds. You know, the late-night email—'How's everything? I miss you. Want to get together for coffee?' I just wondered if I was the only one who doesn't get those."

"You're a lousy liar, Eva," she says. "And I'm bitterly disappointed that you'd think you can put me off that easily."

"Seriously, I was just feeling insecure. I get that way when I read magazines. Everybody else seems to have a more interesting life."

"That's how you sell magazines, honey. Can you hang on a second?" She puts me on hold then comes back a moment later, saying, "Anyway, would you really want to hear from one of those guys? Personally, if they're not feeding me, fucking me, or paying my rent, I lose interest."

"What about James?"

"That's different. James is gay. We can go shopping and talk about what shits men are. He's much better as a gay friend than he ever was as a boyfriend."

"That's what you get for dating a guy you met in the dunes at Fire Island."

"He was having sexuality panic. I wanted to help." She sighs. "Apparently I was a big help with the whole 'women aren't my thing' question."

"You could start a service. Put up signs in the Ramble."

"Don't think I haven't considered it. Lots of cute guys,

a couple of dates each, and no expectations. That would have to be an improvement on my current love life."

After twenty-five years, I've learned that nobody can sniff out a lie like Liz. But I've also learned that it's easy to put her off the scent. Just get her talking about her romantic disappointments, and you're home free. We spent the rest of the call discussing why women can't simply date gay men, with whom they have so much more in common.

I checked my email, but there was no reply from Michael. I'd probably put him off by flirting too openly. Or with the reference to my marriage—that combination *could* be confusing. That's the problem with email: what seems playful when you write it arrives with no irony attached. Once, in an exchange with an editor at another magazine, I joked that the quality of the freelance work we were getting was so bad I was ready to open my office window and crawl out on the ledge. Ten minutes later, I got a call from building security. She'd phoned them in a panic, saying that a woman in their building might be suicidal.

Maybe I'm just not funny, but I prefer to blame the medium. What other form of writing comes equipped with little pictures to show you when to smile? I've always hated those little ;) winking at me like the village idiot, and don't get me started on *LOL*! People depend on hearing your voice to know when you're joking.

I spend the rest of the afternoon on the phone with our printer, arguing about photo reproduction. There are young people, I remind myself, who would *kill* for my job.

At five-thirty I'm still on the phone with the printer, or rather, I'm on hold while he talks to somebody on his production staff. As I wait, I casually check my email. Okay, I confess that my heart leapt slightly when I saw his reply. Three emails in one day! Didn't he have more important things to do than write to me? Interviews with the international media, congratulatory phone calls from wealthy clients, design groupies throwing themselves at his feet . . .

For a moment, I'm tempted to call David and crow. Don't go taking your old wife for granted, Jacko! She's got an old boyfriend writing to her *three times in one day*. On further consideration, I decide against it. Better to say nothing; just smile with quiet satisfaction like the intriguing and mysterious woman I am.

I click on his email. *Wife*, it says. *Child. House. Dog. The usual collection. I'm happy in all the ways that matter.*

My heart sinks. Of course he's happy. Not that I'd want him to be anything else, but . . .

I start to read the rest, and of course the printer picks that moment to get back on the phone, talking about pixel counts and digital resolution. We argue for twenty more minutes. By that time I'm thoroughly depressed with my life, and I turn back to Michael's email with something approaching dread. What blissful scenes will he choose to share with me? Some sunbaked California joy, no doubt. And I'll bet his wife doesn't spend her day arguing with printers. But she won't be the expensive bauble I'd imagined, either. She'll be a cancer researcher or a civil rights attorney. They're vegetarians, active in politics. She grows organic produce and somehow fits yoga into her busy day.

I take a deep breath and turn back to the computer screen. *Wife Mari, daughter Emma.* Mari? Not what I'd expected. She could still be elegant and wear French underwear, but there's also a hint of affectation. *Mary* with its nose in the air. I'll bet she spends her life telling people how to pronounce it.

*The dog's name, I regret to say, is Walter Gropius.*

I can't help feeling relieved. His idea or hers? It was supposed to be cute, but the poor dog!

> *Sorry if I sounded a little melancholy in my last message. This prize thing has proved a little unsettling. You know how something nice can happen and you should be celebrating, but all you can think about is what it cost you?*

Actually, no. I haven't won any major prizes lately. But I'll take your word for it.

> *I did three television interviews this morning, and I'm afraid I came off like a pompous jerk. But maybe I am a pompous jerk. I'm sitting there in the TV studio, all made up like some kind of eighteenth-century courtier, and the morning show hosts are chatting away about the latest celebrity divorce, then they sud-*

*denly turn to me and start talking about my work in this incredulous tone, as if I'd built all these ridiculous buildings just to get attention. It's nothing personal; I can see the woman reading off the cue cards. But suddenly I have to defend my life's work to America, as if I'm desperate for public approval. I felt like a whore. And they flash up pictures of my projects, and my work suddenly looks so self-important, like it's taking itself way too seriously. I came back from the studio feeling deeply depressed. So I open up my email, and there among all the fake congratulations from people who feel they need to suck up to me now, and the requests for interviews from reporters who don't have a clue what I'm trying to do in my work but think they can amuse their readers by making fun of it, I find you!*

Okay, so I'm feeling a little guilty, not having mentioned that I'm one of those people looking for an interview. But when was the last time somebody thought I was worth an exclamation point? I read on, quickly.

*You may not realize it, but you had a powerful effect on me. I wanted to impress you, and all those things I said to you were the things I wanted to be true, both about me and about my work. I've thought about you a lot over the years, and in a way, you've come to embody those aspirations in my mind. Whenever I wasn't sure about a design, I always imagined that I was showing it to you, and I could always tell if it wasn't working by how hard I was trying to explain it. It's a little embarrassing to confess this, but in a sense, you've been my muse, Eva. You're the beautiful girl on the beach who asked me why my buildings all turned their backs on the sea.*

I'm crying now, because his words are so sweet and because they seem so undeserved. What would he think if he could see me now, a forty-four-year-old woman sitting in her tiny office at *House & Home* magazine, struggling to get through the day without resorting to pastries or electroshock? It's not *me* he's been thinking about all these years, any more than it was me he made love to during our week in Palm Beach. It was some girl from his dreams, wise and clear-eyed, who would bring out the best in him.

*I can't tell you how many times I started to call you during my first years out here in California. I wrote several letters, but never worked up the courage to mail them. I wanted to wait until I had something I could be proud to show you, and by the time that happened, it all seemed so long ago that I figured you'd forgotten all about me.*

One of the secretaries walks past my office, stops, and comes to the door. "Eva? Are you okay?"

I nod, sniffling. "I'm sorry," I say, embarrassed. "It's nothing, really. Just a note from an old friend."

She looks at me with something close to pity. "Can I get you something?"

"Thanks, I'm fine." Just a little humiliated. After she's gone, I get up and close my office door.

*Anyway, no more interviews. They're bad for the
soul. I'm just going to get back to work and do my best
to ignore this circus that's erupted around me. I envy
you living in New York. At moments like this, I'd love
to be able to go out and walk up Broadway or Fifth,
letting the crowds carry me along. L.A. can be too
much like a television that stays on all day and night,
even though there's nothing on.*

*What do you do, besides musing?*
*Michael*

Panic! How do I tell him now? The disappointment
will be shattering. I stare at the screen for a few minutes, trying to think of a way to get out of answering the
question, but I can't stop my eyes from straying back to
his words. *You've been my muse, Eva.* My pulse starts to
race every time I read them, and I have to get up and
walk around my office, rubbing my hands together to
keep them from trembling. It's late. I should just shut
the computer down and go home; anything I write in
this state of mind will be stupid and ruin everything.

But I can't go home to David like this, either. I'm a
bundle of raw nerves.

I circle my tiny office twice before I notice the gym
bag under my desk. If there was ever a moment to strap
myself to a treadmill, it's now.

I call home and leave a message for David on the machine. "Hi, there. What a day I've had! I'm going to stop
at the gym and see if I can sweat off some of this printer's
ink before I get home. Won't be long. Bye!"

I shut down the computer and grab the gym bag, trying to picture the look on David's face when he gets my message. I must have sounded like a cheerleader in the last stages of dementia, just before she grabs the axe.

Ron's waiting at the elevator. He eyes my gym bag. "You look virtuous."

I smile. I spent the whole day flirting with an old boyfriend on company time, and all I have to do is pick up a gym bag to get a reputation for virtue.

"It's a competitive business," I say. "We've got to keep our edge." Then an inspiration takes me, and I glance down the hall. "As a matter of fact, I think I'll take the stairs."

He stares after me in surprise as I walk away. What can I say? It's a big responsibility, being somebody's muse.

# 176
## (and in serious pain)

'm an idiot. I don't know if it was the elliptical machine, the stair climber, the weight machines, or the sex, but I can barely crawl out of bed this morning. Every muscle hurts. David's in the bathroom whistling like it's the first day of spring, and here I am creeping down the hall for Advil like somebody beat me with a stick.

How do people do it? At the gym, they tear along on their machines like it's the most natural thing in the world. "I'm on my hamster wheel," Liz always says when I call her cell and catch her at the gym. It doesn't stop her from chatting; I just hear her breathing hard as she pounds along on her treadmill.

I left my phone in the gym bag, which I shoved into a locker. There's a row of treadmills in front of the window that looks down on Broadway, and I had to wait in line for a few minutes until one became available. The young woman who was getting off glanced over at me as she wiped the machine down. She looked like a marathon runner, and there was no mercy in her eyes.

*Keep sweating, honey,* I thought to myself. *Maybe someday, if you're real lucky, some guy will tell you you're his muse.*

For once I felt immune to the scales in their eyes. *Let 'em look,* I thought as I stepped onto the machine. *All they've got is their bodies. I've got a past.*

I've always wanted to be the kind of woman Marlene Dietrich would play, with smoky eyes that have seen their share of broken hearts, but still ready to kick off her shoes and walk out into the desert after the man she loves. For a while I followed that distant column of men into the sunset, walking steadily over the burning sands, but I kept getting distracted by the woman next to me who was striding along at an astonishing rate. If the treadmill were suddenly to have stopped, she looked like she might shoot out through the window, landing in the middle of Broadway. Her legs and arms were going furiously, and I found myself gradually picking up my pace to match hers, until I started gasping for breath and had to slow way down, clinging to the sidebars to keep from shooting off the back. I glanced at the digital clock on the control panel: I'd been on the machine for eight minutes. The woman beside me strode on, her eyes fiercely fixed in front of her, as if she were in pursuit of some prey that could not escape her, no matter how far or fast it ran.

That's the secret, I realized. You have to keep your eyes fixed on the road, never allowing the person working out beside you to enter your consciousness. Tortoise or hare, it's not a race you can win. The young women may stride

along as fierce as Spartans, but they'll always end up in
the same place as you, trudging along through the desert
of middle age. Better to follow Marlene's example and
chase that man vanishing on the horizon. Just keep your
eyes on him, and you'll get where you're going.

*It's a little embarrassing to confess this, but in a sense, you've
been my muse, Eva . . .*

I spent twenty minutes on the treadmill, then twenty
more on the stair climber, gasping like an asthmatic Sherpa
hauling his load up the long final ascent. *You're the beautiful
girl on the beach who asked me why my buildings all turned their
backs on the sea . . .*

I should have stopped there, but as I cooled down at
the water fountain, I saw a woman twenty years older
than me set to work on the Nautilus machine. She carefully reset the weights to the lowest level, settled herself on
the bench, and without a bit of self-consciousness began
to slowly raise and lower the weights while the Arnolds
and Buffies around her heaved the world up onto their
straining backs. Thin and frail-looking, she went about
her workout with all the solemnity of someone perfecting the human form. Watching her, I suddenly felt that
what we were all doing was more than just a cultural
obsession with youth and beauty. There was something
almost *Apollonian* about it all, a striving for physical perfection through slow, grinding labor, as if one could approach those ancient gods only through suffering. Don't
ask me why that thought struck me so clearly, watching
her. It would have made more sense to think that about
the young gay man in the corner, perfecting his already
perfect body by doing situps on a steeply sloping board,

or the movie-star-beautiful young woman practicing her kickboxing moves. But for me, it was watching that frail woman slowly raising and lowering her tiny portion of the world's weight that made it all seem beautiful, something expected of us by older gods than ours.

I stood there by the watercooler, towel draped around my neck, sipping my water and watching her. When she finished with the first station on the machine, I tossed my cup in the trash and went over to take her place. If I could follow her, then I wouldn't feel self-conscious. She seemed so completely serene, so unconcerned about the looks she got as she moved slowly from one piece of equipment to the next.

I found that I could lift her weights too easily, so I studied the way the weights were set, then moved the pin down a few notches. That seemed more challenging. Not difficult, but I was aware of the weight now. It was kind of pleasant to realize I wasn't the weakest person in the room. I allowed myself to go slowly, matching my pace to that of the older woman beside me. She gave me a smile as we got up to move from one station to the next.

"It's a good idea to go easy," she said. "Especially the first time."

I smiled, nodding my agreement. Maybe we weren't Atlas, carrying the world on his shoulders, but we were doing our share. By the time we finished, I realized that the crowd had changed. I glanced at my watch, surprised. It was nearly eight o'clock. I'd been there almost two hours, long enough for the after-work regulars to finish and head out for dinner, replaced by people coming from restaurants, ready to work off their meals.

I changed quickly, then walked up Broadway with a feeling of accomplishment. That wasn't so bad, really. A little awkward at first, but like anything new, you just needed to find your feet.

"Well, I was starting to wonder," David said, glancing at his watch when I came in. He was stretched out on the couch with a manuscript. "I thought maybe you'd run off with a weight lifter."

"Took me a while to figure out how to use everything." I dropped my gym bag in the entryway beside the coat closet, where I wouldn't forget it in the morning. "But I can see why you like it down there. Lots of young lovelies."

"And the girls aren't bad, either. Especially if you like 'em sweaty." He tossed his manuscript aside and sat up. "Have you eaten?"

"No, and I'm starving. How about you?"

"I made some chicken. It's in the refrigerator."

I could have eaten cardboard at that point.

David brought his manuscript into the kitchen and sat with me while I ate. "Did you know that the average married couple spends almost twice as much time each day commuting as they do talking to each other?"

"Another uplifting study of the American marriage?"

"Cultural history of the freeway."

"That sounds exciting."

He shrugged. "It's got its moments. He makes a good case that the building of freeways was what most shaped postwar American life."

"Hasn't that book been written already?"

"Several times. But that's never stopped us before."

He laid the manuscript aside. "Edie Boyarski is trying to dump this on me. She wants to trade me for *Great Sex the Kabbalah Way.* Apparently she knows somebody who knows somebody who can get it in front of Madonna. That's what they call marketing, these days."

After dinner, I stood in the shower for twenty minutes. First hot, to soothe my muscles, then cooler, like a warm rain. Is the rain warm in California? That's how I'd always imagined it. Falling gently across the parched hills and the eucalyptus groves, making the air moist and fragrant. Long days of rain that make the desert bloom. Until the ground slowly softens and begins to slide, carrying houses away, sending whole hillsides crashing into neighborhoods and sweeping beach houses out to sea . . .

I shut off the shower abruptly. Was it Noah's wife who caused the flood, fantasizing about some shepherd boy?

David was sitting up in bed, reading the newspaper. "Here's an interesting bit of information," he called out as I toweled off. "A recent survey of the bedtime habits of more than fifteen hundred adults found that eighty-seven percent usually watch TV in the hour before going to bed, forty-seven percent usually have sex, and sixty-four percent read." He lowered the paper. "As a publisher, I'm encouraged. We're doing better than sex."

"Well, they're not doing math."

"What do you mean?"

"Their numbers don't add up. Shouldn't the total come out at one hundred percent?"

He looked down at the newspaper. "I guess you could choose more than one."

*That would be nice.* We usually read. David with his manuscripts, while I usually picked up whatever caught my eye on the "Our Staff Recommends" shelves at Barnes and Noble, or something Liz had bought and gotten bored with after a few chapters. One year, she bought the collected works of Jane Austen after reading an article in a women's magazine entitled "Jane Austen's Tips for the Single Girl." After a few weeks, she'd handed me the whole set, saying, "I'll rent the movies."

It was odd, reading Jane Austen in bed with my husband beside me. Men are evasive in those books. Always dancing away at parties or riding off to see to their estates just when the heroine is expecting a proposal. And the ones who aren't evasive are absurd. A bird in the hand, Jane reminds her reader, is *never* better than one in the bush. So what should you feel about the husband dozing off beside you? No estates to see to, sadly, and the dances you know never carry him away.

When I came to bed, David laid his newspaper aside. "Feel like making love?"

Later, when I got up to go to the bathroom, I found I could barely straighten up. The muscles in my lower back felt like a coil of twitching snakes. And suddenly I knew it was my punishment: I'd been thinking of Michael while David made love to me. My mind kept going back to those nights I'd spent in his bed in Palm Beach, and on the Cape, our bodies still young and fierce in their arousal. When I closed my eyes, it was Michael's hands that touched me, Michael who strained toward his own pleasure above me. I'd come three times in quick succession, feeling each time like I'd tumbled down a flight of stairs. And each time, there he was, waiting at the bottom, ready to lead me back up.

"You okay?" David asked sleepily as I made my way back to bed.

"I think I did something to my back."

"While we were making love?"

"I guess."

"You need a heating pad?"

"Maybe just an Advil."

He sighed, got out of bed, and went out to the kitchen. I eased under the covers gingerly, hearing him opening and closing cabinets. He came back with an Advil and a glass of water, stood beside me while I put the pill in my mouth and reached carefully for the glass.

"I feel terrible," he said.

I looked up at him as I swallowed the pill. "No, you don't. You're proud of yourself." I handed him the glass and lowered myself carefully down into the bed. "Isn't that a basic male fantasy? Leaving a woman so worn out she can't move?"

"Maybe when you're twelve." He set the glass down and got into bed. "When you're in your forties, it's a little harder to see back pain as an erotic experience."

❧

This morning it's not my back. It's *everything*. And somewhere in the back of my mind, I realize it wasn't David who did this to me.

He comes into the kitchen and finds me leaning against the counter, unable to move. "Still in pain, huh?"

I give him a look that suggests he's unlikely to get bonus points for that question, and suddenly he's all concern. He helps me to a chair, lowers me into it like I've suddenly turned into his aged mother.

"Maybe we should get you to a doctor."

Ladies, let's face it, this is what marriage is. Not the romantic weekend in Paris, but the five days you spend in bed with the flu. Your husband, for all his faults, is the guy who brings you tea and toast, when all those glamorous career girls with their fabulous legs and flirtatious charm can only weep into their lonely pillows or call their mothers in Iowa for comfort. Your husband, bless him, is the guy who says, "You want me to call Ron, tell him you won't be in today?"

I spend the day in bed. Once the Advil kicks in, it's actually kind of pleasant. In fact, once I accept the idea that I don't have to get up, it's almost a guilty pleasure. I flip through the TV channels, feeling the muscle pain slowly ease like a tide flowing out until I'm left in a state of mild soreness and low energy. The bottle of painkillers is on the bedside table now, along with a large glass of water. I'm allowed to take more every four to six hours, and in the meantime, there are old movies, lurid soaps, and a surprising number of exercise shows. Most prove to be extended commercials, selling the latest piece of equipment to work your abs, buns, and thighs—"a complete workout in one!" I watch in fascination as a model shows us her daily routine, using every one of the machine's surprising features. It's actually kind of delicious to lie here watching her work her perfect body. She glistens; she glows. All she needs is a scoop of vanilla ice cream melting on her rippling abs.

Later, there's a workout show filmed on a Caribbean beach. Three svelte young women and a beefy male body-builder chatter gaily through a sundrenched morning of weights, aerobics, and stretching as sailboats glide past on the ocean behind them. They seem not to notice the beauty around them, completely absorbed in their own perfection.

*Like Michael's buildings,* I think. And the thought of Michael catches me up short. God, I haven't answered his email.

I get out of bed slowly and creep down the hall to David's study, where I switch on his computer and, as it warms up, lower myself carefully into his chair. What can I possibly say? It's embarrassing, like having to make conversation with someone after a one-night stand.

I open my email. There's a pile of new work stuff, but David's made me promise not to do any work today, so I scroll down until I get to Michael's last message, then hit Reply.

*Dear Michael,*

There's so much I'd like to say to him, but none of it seems right. So why not the truth?

*I'm home sick today. Actually, not sick. I think I pulled something in my back at the gym last night.*

Okay, so it's not the whole truth, but close enough. And at least I don't come off sounding like the total idiot I really am. I'm tempted to go back and add *lifting weights,* but that seems to be pushing it too far. Let him use his imagination.

> *Not very "a-musing," I'm afraid, but then I'm still getting used to this new role you've given me. What sweet things you said!*

Now I'm starting to feel guilty. Don't I owe him something for all those sweet words? Some truth, maybe?

> *I wish I could be that girl on the beach who inspired you. I'm so flattered that you were able to see me that way, even if I didn't deserve it. The truth is . . .*

And there I pause. Does he really want the truth? Would it even be fair to shatter this image that he's clung to all these years? What's it matter who I really am? He's built amazing buildings thinking about some girl from his past. Wouldn't it be selfish of me to insist that he see me as I am?

Okay, so I'm just another journalist trying to use him to boost circulation. But would he really need to know that, if I never ask him for the interview? I could tell him anything: I'm a teacher or a lawyer. After we've exchanged a few emails, he could go back to his buildings and his elegant wife with his dreams intact. And I'd go back to being that girl on the beach, turning my back on the sea.

*The truth is, everything you've accomplished you owe to your own talent. Believe me when I say that any "amusement" I was able to give you was its own reward. And it's nice to think I had a role in your work, however small.*

*Eva*

I feel selfless as I hit Send, and watch the screen vanish. I haven't asked him for anything, not even a reply. He can write back or not; it's his decision. No flirtation. (Or at least not much. That line about "amusing" him being its own reward could probably be read as a *little* flirtatious.) Ron will have to live without his interview. Or let one of his writer girls flirt with Michael if he wants the interview so badly. Should be right up their alley.

I make my way back to bed. It's strange to be home alone in the middle of the day; the apartment is so silent, I almost feel like a stranger who's broken in to spy on our lives. I'm rarely alone these days. Either I'm at work, surrounded by people, or I'm spending time at home with David and Chloe. And even when they're out, I'm doing things for them: running laundry, making dinner, shopping for groceries, straightening up. For a woman, having a family means not having a life of your own. It's worth it, of course, but there's something luxurious about all this silence. I leave the TV off and just lie there, feeling the silence surround me. It feels like sleeping on silk sheets.

But that's a dangerous thought.

I reach for the phone. Liz is out of the office this morning. David's in a meeting. Chloe's in class with her phone shut off, so it rings straight through to her voicemail. Her message is in French now. "Bonjour, c'est Chloe . . ."

"Bonjour," I say. "C'est your mother. You take off that beret this instant, young lady! And call your *mère.*"

How pathetic is it that I'm calling *her* at this moment? I vow to myself that when she calls, I won't mention my sore back. I'll just tell her I took a mental health day so I could get some things done around the apartment.

I suddenly realize that I haven't eaten anything since last night. I'm famished, but it seems a shame to ruin such a good start on the day, so I go into the bathroom and run a tub full of steaming water and, gasping, lower myself into it for a soak. Once I've settled back, I realize that this is what I've needed all along. Forget food, forget phone calls, even forget old boyfriends. All I need was a tub full of hot water for my pains to dissolve.

The phone rings and I hear Liz's voice on the answering machine. "Well, that's just perfect. I get this message that you're home sick and I call up, ready with my most sympathetic voice, and you're not there! So where are you? Out playing hooky? Should I start calling the hospitals? And all this time I thought you were the stable one." There's a pause, and then she says, "Seriously, call me, okay?"

I close my eyes, letting my sore arms float on the surface of the water like kelp. I can almost forget my body, spreading out below the surface of the water in a way that must look strangely childlike. When I was a girl I always imagined women's bodies as thin, defined by curves and contrasts. My body looks like a baby's to me now, pudgy and undefined, ready to protect me against hunger and cold. If we lived in water, weight wouldn't be an issue. In fact, we might prefer to be fat, with its buoyancy and warmth, slick as seals in our dense coats of blubber.

An hour later, I climb out of the tub feeling much improved. I wrap myself in a towel, go into the kitchen, and eat a cup of yogurt. It's become a lovely day; what a shame to spend it moping around the apartment. It's too late to meet Liz for lunch, and I have no interest in shopping. But when was the last time I just spent the day walking?

When I was young and broke, I'd wake up on a Saturday morning and head out into the city to explore. Some days, I walked almost the whole length of Manhattan, straight down Broadway from my apartment near Columbia, until I hit the Village, where I'd spend a morning wandering. If nothing caught my attention, I'd keep going, down to Battery Park to stand looking out across the harbor, feeling like some windswept movie heroine, watching for her lover to come sailing in. Then up the East Side from bagels and a schmear to five hundred-dollar sandals to wear at your beach house in the Hamptons.

In those days the city seemed like a huge battery that made the light burn brightly within me. Sometimes, in the excitement of that wandering, I'd forget to eat, until the flame suddenly began to flicker as I strode along. I'd duck into a Korean grocery, buy an apple and a pint of milk, and consume them sitting on the front steps of some investment banker's Chelsea brownstone. If it looked like rain, I'd slip into a museum or spend an hour browsing in a bookstore. And that could be an adventure in itself. In New York, a pretty girl alone in a bookstore is like an animal cut from the herd, and the skillful hunters quickly start to circle. On some days, when the hunters were particularly skillful, that was as far as I got in my wandering. But just as often, I'd make my way back uptown, cut back across the park in the eighties, and get home to my apartment weary but exhilarated just before dark, giving me a few hours to rest before going out for the night.

Hard to believe now that I ever had that much energy. Or the right kind of shoes. I find an old pair of running shoes in the back of the closet, but who am I kidding? This isn't going to be that kind of marathon. Maybe I'll head down Broadway to Columbus Circle, come back up through the park. Just a stroll to loosen up my legs.

It's almost seven when I get back to the apartment, carrying bags of takeout for dinner. David's in the shower. His gym bag lies on the floor of the entryway, next to mine. Side by side, they look like a pair of lazy, overfed dogs. The answering machine on the kitchen counter is flashing with messages from all the people I called in my moment of desperation. David hasn't played them. Does that mean he's angry, or did he just go straight into the shower when he came home?

"Hello," I call from the bathroom door. "Just letting you know I'm home."

The shower shuts off. Silence. He's angry.

"I was feeling better around eleven, so I went for a walk," I say quickly. "I guess I should have called."

"Liz called me this afternoon," he says quietly, reaching for a towel. "She had my secretary pull me out of a sales meeting. Apparently she got a message from you this morning saying that you were at home, dying of the plague, but when she tried to call you, she didn't get an answer. She got worried, so she called Chloe. Don't ask me *why* she called Chloe, but she did. By the time they decided to pull me out of my meeting, they were both convinced you were lying on the floor here with a ruptured spleen. She made me leave work early to come home and check on you. Then I get the pleasure of calling up Chloe to tell her, 'Don't worry, honey. Your mom's not dead. It seems she's gone out shopping.' " He rubs his hair roughly.

"I'm so sorry. I didn't think anybody would worry. I just went for a walk and got caught up looking at buildings."

He looks at me over his towel. "Looking at *buildings?*"

"Yeah. I pass these wonderful buildings every day, but I never really look at them. And it suddenly struck me that since I didn't have to be anywhere today, I could take my time and really look."

He stares at me for a moment in silence. Then he sighs and goes back to toweling himself off. "Well, call Chloe, okay? And Liz. I think she's getting ready to accuse me of dumping your body in the East River."

Chloe seems completely unfazed when I reach her.

"Okay, Mom. I'm glad you had a nice day." Liz, on the other hand, seems to have spent the day Paxilating. "Thank *God* you're okay," she exclaims when I finally reach her on her cell. "I was so worried."

She's talking to me from the ladies' room at Pastis, where she's having dinner with a tax lawyer she met in the waiting room of her massage therapist's office that afternoon.

"We haven't even ordered," she tells me, "and he's already solved my withholding problem."

"Enjoy your dinner," I tell her, and hang up. Any man who can solve Liz's withholding problem deserves an uninterrupted meal.

I find David in the kitchen digging through the take-out bag. "I think they shorted you," he says.

"What do you mean?" I push him aside and unload the boxes of Chinese food, opening each one and lining them all up on the counter. "No, it's all here."

He looks at me. "Where's your kung pao shrimp?"

"I wasn't very hungry. I just got some steamed vegetables."

He gives me a concerned look, reaches up to feel my forehead. "You sure you're feeling okay?"

"Yeah. I just wanted something light. I bought an apple at a Korean deli on my way back from Midtown."

I catch him sneaking glances at my plate as we eat, and he keeps trying to offer me some of his Hunan beef.

"David, I'm fine," I tell him. "There's plenty of food. I won't go hungry."

For some reason he seems to find this disturbing, and we pass the meal mostly in silence. He doesn't seem angry, but when I ask him about his day, he just shrugs and says, "Nothing to write home about, really."

Suddenly, all the energy drains from my body. I lay my chopsticks down on my plate and sit back.

"What's the matter?" David's staring at me again. "You okay?"

"Tired." I push my chair back and get up slowly. "You mind if I just go to bed?"

"Go ahead. I'll clean up."

I climb into bed without even brushing my teeth. For a moment, I lie there savoring the sensation of the sheets against my body. It's early still, and I can hear the traffic on Broadway. It's a strangely comforting sound, as if the city is going about its life and will be there when I wake up, ready to start a new day. As sleep takes me, I hear a quiet clatter of dishes in the kitchen, where David has begun cleaning up.

# 174
## (Really?)

wake up early. I've been dreaming that I'm on the top floor of a tall building, looking out the window as a crowd gathers below. Police have the block cordoned off, and the crowd stands behind barriers at a distance, gazing up at me with wide, expectant eyes. Then I hear a thud, and the whole building shakes. A crane has begun to swing a wrecking ball against the side of the building, and with each crash, the crowd cheers. I cry out, waving my hands wildly to show them that I'm still inside the building, but nobody sees me. They're all watching the ball crash into the building, showering glass and debris onto the empty street below.

For some reason, I don't even try to escape the building. I know the doors are locked, the stairways crushed by the wrecking ball's first blow. I'm stuck there, waiting for the building to crumble beneath me.

I can see the crane's operator working the levers that slowly swing the ball out wide, then send it hurtling back toward me. And in the crowd below, I see David and Chloe, laughing excitedly as the ball smashes into the building.

I wake up just before the final collapse, relieved to find myself in my own bed. What is it they say about falling dreams? All the magazines tell you they mean something, but I can't remember what. Something about sex, no doubt. Or its lack.

David's still sleeping heavily, and the alarm won't go off for another hour and a half. But I'm fully awake so there's no point in staying in bed. I get up and go into the bathroom. They tell you not to weigh yourself every day if you're trying to lose weight, but they don't say anything about if you've given up trying. It's become a daily ritual of self-punishment, and I accept the results with resignation—one more weight to carry through the day.

This morning, the results are encouraging. I should know better than to get my hopes up by now, but the heart's a blind and simple animal. You can't stop it from leaping in joy at the first hint of good news.

I go out to the kitchen to make coffee. It was the exercise, probably. Almost two hours in the gym, and then the long walk yesterday. And I didn't eat much. This morning I'm starving, but I force myself to stick to two cups of black coffee and a yogurt. I'll take an apple to eat at the office later in the morning, get a salad for lunch. But it's hours still until I have to be at the office, and I find myself standing before the open freezer, eyeing a box of frozen waffles I'd bought for Chloe when she came home from school in May. She never touched them; I've eaten three.

*Get out,* my heart cries. *Save yourself!*

The gym. They open at five, so all the young lawyers can work out before they get to the office at seven. I'll take it easy this time: twenty minutes of fast walking on the treadmill, then a few minutes on the stairclimber just to get my heart rate up. No weights.

To my surprise, I find the gym is actually kind of pleasant in the morning. People greet each other with nods as they go into the locker rooms, and there's no wait for a treadmill. I walk steadily for my twenty minutes, looking out at the building opposite. I can't imagine what it would be like to have an apartment facing a heath club. Every time you looked out your window, no matter the hour, you'd see a row of people running on their treadmills, like a race with no finish line. Would you always feel guilty? Or would there be some pleasure in it, the bodies perpetually changing but the motion always the same, like watching trees move in a wind?

It takes me a few minutes to get the hang of the stairclimber. No stairs I've ever climbed give way beneath you, requiring this strange hip-swinging gait. A woman climbs onto a machine in the row ahead of me and I try to imitate her rhythm. It's more like riding a bicycle standing up than climbing stairs. I close my eyes and remember pedaling along the street where I grew up, the day when I found that precise balance that allowed me to ride along standing on the pedals like the older girls, three quick pumps and then up on the pedals and glide. There's no glide on this machine, no thrill of perfect, soaring balance, but when I get the hang of the motion, it reminds me how it felt to master a physical skill—the sense of freedom and public accomplishment as you rode proudly past the groups of kids, showing off nonchalantly what it took months to achieve. You don't get many moments like that as an adult.

Is that what it would be like to walk into the gym without feeling self-conscious? To toss your towel casually across the bar of a machine, punch in your exercise program on the control panel, and start working out with an air of certainty? Would you have to look like one of those thin, muscular women who glide toward beauty every evening on the elliptical machines?

I get back to the apartment just as David's coming out of the shower. He looks at me strangely. "Where've you been?"

"I woke up early, so I thought I'd go to the gym." I pull off my T-shirt and sweatpants and toss them into the laundry hamper. "It's less crowded in the morning."

He stares at me in open astonishment. "What's gotten into you?"

"I guess I'm just ready to start working out." I climb into the shower and turn the water to the hottest setting. I let it run down my back and shoulders, enjoying the shivery feeling it sends through my skin.

I dress quickly, and by the time David's finishing his breakfast, I'm out the door. It's strangely exciting to have this extra time in my day, like I'm ahead of myself: I catch an earlier, less crowded subway train, and when I get to the office there's only a small group waiting at the elevator. But I'm feeling impatient. It's only six flights of stairs; I probably climbed twice that at the gym this morning. I turn past the newsstand, where the old man behind the counter sells granola bars in the morning and chocolates after lunch. He nods to me, a regular customer, but I keep going.

Momentum is the key, I decide. By the time I reach the third floor my legs begin to complain, but unlike at the gym, these steps don't give way beneath me, and I can feel that I'm getting someplace. Is it too early to decide I'm on a diet? That I've begun exercising? I push the thought away. Just get to the top of the stairs. One step at a time.

Then it's just work, work, work. Nothing from Michael. I can feel the day passing under me like a treadmill, but I just have to keep putting one foot in front of the other. I'm hungry at midmorning, but I'm a woman of strength and character: nothing can break my will unless I allow it to. At 11:30 I walk downstairs, past the newsstand, and go two blocks to the corner market, where I buy a tart green apple and a cup of lowfat cottage cheese. I walk back, climb the stairs, and sit at my desk, just in time to hear the phone ring.

"You free for lunch?" David asks me. "My lunch meeting just canceled, and I thought we could grab a bite."

"I just bought an apple and some cottage cheese."

Silence. I can hear the question forming in David's mind—*Are you on a diet?*—but after twenty-three years of marriage, he thinks twice before asking.

So he just says, "Another time, then," and we both hang up.

Here's a little secret I've learned: husbands want their wives to look good, but they *hate* it when we diet. They take it personally, like we're somehow pushing them away. Really, though, it's because they like to feed without consciousness. Dieting is an awareness of cause and effect: *cause*—food; *effect*—gross, unsightly fat, and half the closet off-limits. By their nature, men dislike this kind of reasoning. They prefer to live in a world in which beer leads to supermodels, and the game can be won by the miraculous catch. If their wives stop eating, it's as if we've withdrawn the breast. Then there's sulking until you let them drag you off to Ray's for pizza, where they sit smiling happily at you as you swallow their little diet hand grenade.

Just last year, I was buying him chicken breasts and salad. Did I complain that we couldn't get takeout when I had a taste for mu shu? (Okay, but aloud?) Before men dieted, too, the rules were clear: men ordered steak, and their wives ate salad. Then the men had heart attacks, and the wives moved to Florida and ate whatever they wanted.

These days, men have bodies, too. And women have eyes. So why can't they accept that this is *hard work*?

Fortunately, every diet includes coffee. It has no fat, no carbs, no calories. Only the devil could have created a food this perfect. When the apple and cottage cheese

are gone, I go downstairs for a coffee the size of my first
apartment.

I've got nothing to look forward to this afternoon but
an editorial conference and a printer's proof. And then,
no doubt, a sullen dinner with David.

Maybe I'll stop at the gym on the way home . . .

# 168

*Dear Eva,*
    *I hope your back's feeling better. Sorry not to be in touch this last week, but I had to fly to Tokyo on short notice . . .*

!

    *. . . to deal with the latest crisis on our project there. Have you ever been there?*

Please. My dry cleaning is better traveled than I am. At least it goes to Jersey every few weeks.

    *Apparently they run* Lost in Translation *packages now for American tourists. You can stay in the same hotel where Bill Murray had insomnia, and visit all the places where he had his midlife crisis. In*

*my case it would have been a waste of money, since I
seem to be having one of my own.*

Is he being ironic and self-deprecating, or is he trying
to tell me something? The coincidence is striking, since
David accused me of having a midlife crisis last night.
We were arguing in the kitchen, though I wasn't entirely
clear what the argument was about. Apparently I've been
spending too much time at the gym, and too little attend-
ing to my wifely duties. He'd made dinner three nights
in a row, and I'd done nothing but complain. I tried to
point out to him that I'd actually been *very* grateful and
that I'd said so each night. And as for complaining, all
I'd said was that if he didn't mind, I'd make myself a
salad instead of eating the three-cheese lasagna he'd just
taken out of the oven.

"It looks delicious," I told him, "I just feel like something a little lighter."

"But I made this for you! It's your favorite!"

My favorite? Since when? But the expression on his
face was hurt, so I just said, "Thank you, that was very
thoughtful. But you don't have to cook for me, okay? I
can just grab something when I get home."

"So we eat separately."

"If you don't mind waiting, I can make something for
both of us."

He shook his head. "Am I missing something? I
thought we were trying to have a marriage here."

"And you feel I'm doing something that calls that into
question?" I was starting to lose patience. "I'm going to

the gym and watching what I eat. *You're* the one who told me I needed to go on a diet."

"When did I tell you that?"

"When you said my pants were too tight."

He stared at me. "That's what this is all about?"

"Yes." *Liar.*

"So you're punishing me by not eating my lasagna?"

"It's not punishment. I just don't want to eat all that cheese."

That seemed simple enough to me, but we kept going around and around for another twenty minutes. In the end, David glared at me, tossed his oven mitt into the sink, and said, "Fine. I'll eat the lasagna. You eat whatever you want."

The way he said it, it sounded like the height of selfishness. He grabbed a spatula, served himself a piece of the lasagna, then carried his plate over to the table. "Just let me know when you're finished with this midlife crisis of yours, and we can go back to having dinner together."

So we sat there together, eating our separate meals in silence. How was this different from having dinner together? And since when does being married mean you have to eat the same food every night? Before Chloe was born, we'd sometimes be so busy with work that we'd each arrive home at 9:30 carrying a bag of takeout. If we felt like it, we'd share, but just as often, he'd eat his Firehouse Bar-B-Que while I ate my porcini and feta risotto.

After we had a child it seemed important to have family dinners, so one of us would come home early to cook

and the other would do the dishes. Eventually we included Chloe in the arrangement, and in her final two years
of high school she'd make dinner a couple of times a
week. Nothing fancy, just hamburgers or an omelet, but
it was nice to come home and find her in the kitchen.

"Wash up, you two," she'd call out. "Dinner in five."

But now? Chloe's in Paris, and we're adults with active lives and different tastes. Can't you be married *and*
live your own life?

❧

Now, reading Michael's words, I wonder if David wasn't
right. Am I having a midlife crisis? Why can't women
have a midlife crisis?

> *It's funny that all of this comes now, with an award
> for my work, because I've begun to look at all my proj-
> ects with a kind of weariness. I'm proud of the build-
> ings, but I keep asking myself, "Is this all?" I always
> assumed there would be a moment when the weight
> of what I'd accomplished would be greater than what
> I still hoped to accomplish—but the projects I get to
> build are almost never projects I imagined. They're re-
> sponses to a specific client's wishes, or to the demands
> of a site. There's no such thing as pure architecture,
> obviously, but I always hoped that someday I could
> finish a project and say, "That's my vision."*
>
> *Have I mentioned that I'm building a house? I*

*used to say "We're building a house," but my wife wants nothing to do with it anymore. I think she's starting to sympathize with my clients. When I complain about their lack of vision, she says, "Well, they have to live with whatever you build." She's right, of course, but it's a little annoying to hear it at home.*

*What bothers her is that when I say, "I'm building a house," I mean it literally: every stone, every piece of glass, the wiring, the plumbing. I bought a piece of land up by Ojai about ten years ago, and I spend weekends up there working on it. I'm using only renewable materials. My wife laughs when she hears me use that phrase. "Other people call it garbage," she says. I sometimes wonder when our marriage stopped being about sharing each other's dreams and started being a state of mutual impatience. But you don't want to hear about that.*

Is he serious? Does he really think I wouldn't be interested in the state of his marriage, or is that just his way of letting himself off the hook for saying it?

*Anyway, I mention it because I've been thinking about taking some time off after this whole prize thing to work on the house. I find it clears my head, and I don't have to spend as much time wrestling with my impure soul. Unfortunately, we're supposed to break ground on a project in Stony Brook in two weeks, so it doesn't look like I'll get to do that anytime soon. In fact, I'll be spending some time in New York while we get that project off the ground. Any interest in meet-*

*ing for lunch at some point? It would give us a nice
chance to catch up.*

    *You never answered my question about what you've
been doing with yourself all these years. I'd hate to
think we're going to spend all our time talking about
me.*

    *Michael*


A wave of panic goes through me. Is he serious? He
wants to get together for lunch? *How can I put him off?*
He'll be expecting an older version of the girl he once
knew, not some bloated mid-forties hausfrau.

And he clearly wasn't going to let me slide on the
question about my work. He really wanted to know.

How do you tell a man who's building a house from
renewable materials that you work for a magazine that
specializes in real-estate porn? Centerfolds of overripe
Victorians with flirty bedroom windows and pouty front
porches. Barely legal Georgian new-builds with interior
detailing from Restoration Hardware. Coastal cabins
built from raw stone and redwood for Wall Street bankers who "retreat" to the wilds in 6,400 square feet, with
cedar saunas, entertainment rooms, and automated cli-
mate control. Connecticut farmhouses for Manhattan
Marthas, with stables and greenhouse herb gardens.

What kind of house could Michael be building? One
with no right angles, maybe? A postmodern hobbit hole
of wattle and mud, with windows made from old plastic
seltzer bottles? Ron would be salivating if he knew about
it. He'd want a four-page photo spread, along with an
interview. What a coup for *House & Home*! Something

to amuse and outrage our subscribers in their carefully groomed suburban mansions, like the raw ginger some high-end restaurants have taken to serving between courses—not to cleanse the palate but to snap it out of its blissful stupor.

Michael would break off all contact in disgust if I let Ron get his hands on this secret. But I can't just ignore his question about my job, or his invitation to meet for coffee when he's in New York. Why do we have to meet, anyway? Why can't we just go on exchanging vaguely flirtatious emails, at least until I've had a chance to lose some weight and get a better job?

Well, he took a week to answer my last email, so I get a few days before he can start to feel offended. That gives me a little time to think of an answer that's both encouraging and noncommittal.

Still, his emails are starting to pile up in my in-box, and it's begun to make me uncomfortable to see them sitting there, where Ron might see them if he came in suddenly and glanced at my screen. *Or David,* I think in sudden panic, if I ever left my account open at home. I create a new folder, then pause as I think about what to call it. Something that won't arouse curiosity if anybody happens to be looking.

*Diet Group,* I type, suddenly inspired. Who'd look at that? It sounds embarrassing, a bunch of overweight women sending each other encouraging messages. And in a sense, it's not far from the truth. Michael's emails lift my spirits, so I don't notice so much when I'm hungry. There's nothing wrong with that, is there?

After all, I'm just exchanging email with an old friend,

talking with him about our lives. And it only makes sense that it's led me to think about some things I'd like to change about my life. Watching my diet, going to the gym—that's a good thing, right? Even David would recognize that, if he weren't in such a foul mood these last two weeks.

I mean, it's not like I'm going to fall into bed with this guy. I don't even want to see him. (At least, not until I've lost some weight.) See, I'm moving his email out of my in-box with no intention of answering him very soon. Would I be doing that if I felt excited about his visit?

So there's nothing to worry about.

I go back to my work, my energy renewed. Flirtation, the married woman's cocaine.

Forty minutes later, I set aside the proofs I've been reading and turn back to my email. To my surprise, there's another message from Michael.

*Is this you?*

Below, there's a Web link. My heart rises to my throat. Did he Google me? What has he found?

The link opens to a column I wrote last year entitled "The Allure of Slate Floors," which has been reproduced on a tile manufacturer's website. It's not my best work, and my heart sinks as I read it over. How could he have any respect for me now? At the bottom, a brief bio says "Eva Cassady is a regular columnist for *House & Home* magazine" and they've included the photograph that accompanies my column: a smiling head shot in which I'm turned slightly to one side, so that I seem to be looking at the reader with one glinting eye like Rosalind Russell in *The Front Page*. Eva Cassady, ace girl reporter. The good news is, the photograph's almost ten years old, so at least I don't look fat.

But now I'm out of the closet. Better just to confess and throw myself on the mercy of the court.

I hit Reply and type, *Busted. I write for a home magazine. Can you forgive me?*

I send it and sit there, feeling depressed. And hungry. I'd kill for a chocolate chip cookie right now. The soft kind, like they make at the bakery on Fifty-third, where the chocolate melts inside the cookie as it bakes. It's a ten-minute walk, but that seems like a small price when you get there. And you almost feel like you've earned it, if you walk fast.

It takes a profound effort of will, but I stay at my desk. The afternoon drags past. No answer from Michael by the time I leave the office at five. So that's it: he's decided I'm just another media whore. Or the photograph made him realize how old I've gotten. Either way, the girl on the beach is gone forever.

One slice of pizza, and I feel like a slut.

I couldn't face the gym last night, so I went straight home. When I opened the refrigerator, I remembered I'd meant to stop for groceries. All that remained was one crusty slice of David's lasagna from last week, which even he couldn't bring himself to finish, some sliced ham, and five eggs. Neither of us wanted to throw out the lasagna: David had left that last slice as an accusation, while I was pretending it had nothing to do with me. So it just sat there, curling up at the edges, like some sea creature that had crawled up onto the beach to die.

The eggs were a possibility. I could slice up the ham and make an omlet for us to share. Maybe throw in chopped onion to give it some bite. There was a half bag of salad in the vegetable drawer, along with some rubbery mushrooms and a tomato that will never see its salad days again. I tossed out the tomato, and I was just taking out the rest of the ingredients when I heard David's key in the lock.

"Hello?" His voice sounded surprised. My gym bag was lying on the floor of the entrance hall. I'd been stopping at the gym for an hour every evening to work out these last two weeks, so I almost never got home before him.

"I'm in the kitchen," I called out.

He found me taking the cutting board out of a cabinet to start dicing the onions. "How are you?"

"Okay. You?"

He shrugged. "You making dinner?"

"There's not much. I meant to shop, but I forgot. You mind having an omelet and salad?"

He looked at the mushrooms and the half bag of salad on the counter. "We could go out."

"What do you have in mind?"

"Nothing fancy. Why don't we just grab something in the neighborhood?"

Pizza, barbeque, Chinese-Cuban. There's a macrobiotic place a couple blocks up, but we've never tried it. "Sure. Whatever you like."

I put the food back into the refrigerator and we walked up the street to a pizza place we used to go to with Chloe. They had the usual chicken caesar salad on the menu, but David said, "You want to split a salad and get a couple of slices?"

It seemed like a test. Was I going to stick rigidly to my diet, or could I loosen up and just spend time with him? For some reason, it seemed like an offer I couldn't refuse. Or maybe I was just feeling weak. "That sounds nice."

We sat in awkward silence at first, like two people on

a bad first date, but when I took that first bite of pizza, it was like a great love had returned. David looked at the expression on my face and smiled.

"Nice to see you enjoying something."

Something about the way he said it made me feel sad. I wanted to tell him that I'd actually been enjoying lots of things over the last two weeks, but I swallowed the words back and just smiled. "What would Maribel Steinberg say?"

His smile vanished. He picked up his pizza and took a bite, chewing thoughtfully. Then he swallowed. "I guess she'd say that you have to be true to yourself." He nodded at the slice of pizza in front of me. "One slice of pizza won't kill you."

"Not quickly, anyway."

Silence descended again and we both looked out the window at some young couples passing on the street.

"How's her book selling?"

He shrugged. "Diet books always sell well. It's the perfect product: when one doesn't work, it just creates a market for the next one. Hope springs eternal. So all you need is a marketing hook and a supermodel to endorse it. It's like porn for women."

"You don't think her plan works?"

"As well as any other, I guess." He looked at me. "There's only one way to lose weight, if you ask me. Food is fuel. If you burn more than you consume, you lose weight. So work out and watch what you eat. But you can't sell books telling people that. Everybody wants a secret for losing weight without having to break a sweat. So we publish these books telling them to eat all one thing, or to stay away from something else, when it's really pretty obvious: eat green stuff instead of gooey stuff, and get some exercise."

"That's what I've been doing." I looked down at my pizza. "Until today, anyway."

We walked back to our building through the warm evening. David was quiet, as if he had something on his mind. I slipped my arm through his and said, "Tell me what you're thinking."

He just shrugged. "Work stuff. Nothing important."

We used to talk about everything, from the simplest things to our most complex feelings. When Liz asked me how I'd known David was the man I should marry, I'd told her, "I can talk to him about anything. I feel like we really communicate."

But somewhere along the way, we seem to have lost our trust in each other. You talk to people honestly only when you feel confidence that they'll understand, that they'll listen to you with sympathy and won't use your words against you. Lately there are so many things we don't seem able to say to each other, areas of our marriage that seem too dangerous to talk about, and are better left unspoken.

I went to bed feeling sad, and as any woman who's ever tried to lose weight can tell you, pizza and sadness is a lethal combination. When your spirit's heavy, so are your thighs. I got on the scale this morning, and winced at the results. How could one slice of pizza make you gain *two pounds*? But that doesn't count the sadness, which spreads over everything you eat.

And so, this morning I make my way to the office with

a heavy heart. What's worse, I'm running late, for no reason I can see. It's not like I got up later than usual, or lingered over my breakfast. Big and slow, that's what I've become. As a result, there's no time to go to the gym or walk to work. I have to push my way into a packed subway car, sweltering with the rest of the herd as the train screeches and sways down to Columbus Circle. I walk the last few blocks in a hurry, then force myself to take the stairs, even though I'm already sweating and late for a staff meeting. Not the same as a workout, but at least it's a down payment.

I just have time to drop my stuff in my office, grab a pad off my desk, and hurry into the staff meeting. Ron's in a lousy mood, and he takes it out on everybody. The designs are tired, the photographs are boring, and he'd expect better writing from a third-grader. When he gets to me, he demands, "What's happening with Foresman? Are we getting an interview or not?"

"I got in touch with him," I say uncomfortably. "He's been swamped with interview requests, as you can imagine—"

"All I *can* do is imagine," Ron snaps, "since you've decided it's not important enough to keep me up to date on it."

I feel the blood rise to my face. Ron and I have always gotten along, mainly because he's always treated me with respect. I'm not willing to renegotiate that in front of his entire staff.

"You've asked me to take advantage of an old friendship," I say, my voice tight. "If you have a problem with how I'm doing it, maybe you'd better ask somebody else to write to him."

Ron looks at me, surprised. Then he glances quickly around the table. His staff stares back at him sullenly, like a ship's crew just before they set their captain adrift in a tiny boat with three days' worth of water and a rusty knife.

"What?" he says. *"What?"*

Nobody says anything.

Ron sits back with a sigh. "Okay, you think I'm being a bastard. I can see that. But it's my name on the masthead, which means I'm the one who's embarrassed if we put out a lousy issue." He looks at me. "Let's put the Foresman interview on hold for now. If we can get one for a future issue, that's great. If not . . ." He shrugs. "It's not like our readers will know they've missed out."

The meeting breaks up shortly after, and we return to our offices in silence. I don't feel that I've won a victory, although it's clear to everyone that Ron came as close to an apology as he ever would. So why do I feel bad? It's like when I win a fight with David but I end up feeling like I'm the one who should apologize.

Back at my desk, I turn on the computer and log on to my email with resignation. It's been a bad day from the moment I got out of bed and onto the scale. Why should it change now?

Waiting in my in-box is an email from Michael:

> Dear Eva,
>     So you've stayed interested in architecture. I'm glad.

His tone's more restrained, but it's nice of him to put the best spin on it.

> *Do you have a particular interest in restoration issues? I seem to remember that's the focus of your magazine. I've never taken much of an interest in restoration, but then it's not really an architect's nature to leave things as they are. An architect's natural impulse is to build, the way a surgeon's is to cut. And sometimes we both leave scars.*
>
> *Maybe you can educate me about restoration someday.*
>
> *Michael*

I *don't* have a particular interest in restoration issues. I've got a job at a magazine that's designed to sell home-renovation products, and we write these articles to give our readers ideas and to fill the space between the ads.

Generally, I'm okay with that. But how do I say that to somebody like Michael, who's spent his whole life living his principles?

By being honest, I decide.

> *Dear Michael,*
>
> *What can I say about my work, except thanks for understanding? It's a job. There are times when I like it, and other times, like today, when I'd just like to walk away. I enjoy writing the column, although I can't say that it reflects any deeply held belief in the principle of restoration. Like most magazines, we sell a consumer fantasy. It keeps the wolves from the door,*

*and there are moments when we're able to stretch our*
*readers' imaginations by throwing out new ideas.*

I close my eyes, take a deep breath, then I type, *I'd*
*love to challenge them with your ideas someday.*

Whore! Slut! *Editor!*

But now it's done. I've written the words, and my
conscience feels lighter. Now I can face Ron without the
constant feeling that I'm disappointing him, and Michael will know exactly the kind of lost soul I've become.
He'll understand why I wrote to him, and he'll be able to
break off contact with a clear conscience.

But after staring at the screen for several minutes, I
realize that I can't leave it at that. I have to say something
to show him I'm not a complete career whore.

> *I know you're very busy now, so I didn't want to*
> *join the crowd of journalists clamoring for your time*
> *and attention. And I'm enjoying our conversations*
> *too much to have any desire to hit the Record button*
> *on my tape recorder. Do you mind if I keep you to my-*
> *self for now? It's selfish, I know. My publisher would*
> *be angry to hear me say it, but let our readers find*
> *their own genius.*

I sign it, send it, and then spend a few minutes staring out the window as I twist a paper clip in anxiety. Why
is sending an email always more exciting than receiving
one? It's easier to say scary things in an email, so I always seem to go further than I would if I were talking
to someone in person. But when they write me back,

it's just words on my screen. You can't feel the emotion somebody has invested in their words when you read them on your computer screen, but your own words fly off into cyberspace loaded with a dangerous cargo of risk and hope.

And the worst thing is that some part of you always expects an instant reply. Was that the pleasure of letters in the nineteenth century? You'd send off your long-distance words of love or anger, then you'd get to brood on them for days—even weeks, or *months*—before you could start peering expectantly into the mailbox, hoping for an answer. But then, if you read Jane Austen, her characters are always receiving notes carried by servants, who then wait in the kitchen while you write your reply. And until World War I, fashionable areas of London had three mail posts every day. You could send a love letter in the morning and see your hopes dashed before you sat down to dinner.

In working for a magazine devoted to home renovation, I've learned that modern life is just a style: new ways of doing what we've always done. Add up all the computers and the cables, nets full of ether and nets full of work, all the hardware and software devoted to flashing digits all over the world, and it must come to billions of dollars. And what do we use it all for? To make money and make friends, get in touch with old lovers, and look for ways to escape our boredom. If renovation is putting old stuff to new uses, what should we call putting all this new technology to the same old uses? And to make it even stranger, somewhere there's a computer saving it all: our flirtations, and our cybersex, our "See you at 6:00?" notes, and our

"Sorry, I can't tonight." If there's anything new about all this new stuff, it's how little privacy we get, and how much of ourselves will remain when we're gone. Every affair, every abject flattery or outright lie, gets stored away somewhere. Nothing we do is invisible anymore. But does that really matter? If anybody took the trouble to read it, would they see anything new or surprising? Just the same old desires, but in a new shape.

*Like you,* I can't help thinking with a smile.

Which reminds me: I need to get some work done, so I can leave on time and go to the gym.

Whic does a diet become a diet, and not simply "watching what you eat?" There's a moment when that resolution, which has come and gone so many times, takes root in the thin soil of your character. For a while, you can't bring yourself to speak it aloud, even to yourself. But the thought is there, growing within you. And then a day comes when you're tempted and you resist, saying, "No, thanks. I'm on a diet."

Is this what happens when you begin a love affair? Does it grow within you silently, not even a conscious thought until the moment you realize that you can't say no? Or is it marriage that's like a diet, and the idea of another man is the double chocolate torte that tempts you?

Three days go by with no reply from Michael. But at least the scale has begun moving. The two pounds I put on seem to have been an illusion; gone the next day, and the numbers keep on dropping. Two more pounds now.

I spend my lunch hour in Barnes and Noble, looking through diet books. David's right: they've all got a gimmick. There are the destination books: Scarsdale, South Beach, Beverly Hills. Then there's the quick-'n-easy model: *Lose 10 Pounds Now! Twenty Minutes to Thinner Thighs. The Once-a-Day Diet.* And finally, the vaguely magical: *The Zone, Loving Yourself Thin, Pray the Fat Away! Eat More, Weigh Less!* Most have either a doctor or a supermodel on the cover, white coat or bare thighs. Maribel Steinberg, the skinny bitch, poses in a white lab coat (she's a licensed dietician, it seems) that ends at mid-thigh like a miniskirt; she's appealing to both markets. Nice legs; I'll give her that.

Inside, it's all exhortations and mysterious medical lingo: eicosanoid balance, protein-to-carbohydrate ratios, lipids, insulin resistance. Phases 1 through 4, with meal plans to match. It's a cult, building confidence through repetition of key phrases. The faith keeps you focused, so you stay on the straight and narrow. Heaven is a half-size; salvation can be gained in a sugar substitute.

But does the diet itself do anything that you can't do with salads, fruit, and exercise? All that science sells the book, but is it ever really anything more than an act of faith?

So I work, go to the gym, return home to my husband. David and I have made love twice this week, which isn't bad for us. And I've managed to keep to my diet, mainly by eating the same thing every day: low-fat yogurt and half a banana for breakfast, an apple at 10:30 as a snack, carrot sticks and cottage cheese for lunch at my desk, a Diet Coke at midafternoon to get me through the dog hours, and then a large salad with broiled chicken breast or a lean burger made from ground turkey—no bun, no cheese—for dinner. It's boring, but I've resisted the boredom by doubling my time at the gym. I now go both before *and* after work, forty-five minutes each session. And I make myself go up and down the stairs at work—from ground floor to roof exit—at least twice every day. That way, I end every day with a feeling of accomplishment, and most days begin without disaster on the scale.

Is this the long-delayed moment I've always sworn would come, when I take myself in hand and change my life, becoming one of those determined, organized women I admire? Or am I (as I suspect) just frantic to get in shape to meet Michael, so he won't be disappointed?

Not that he seems in any hurry to come see me. But it's been only three days. As I bounce away on the stair climber, I assure myself that it really doesn't matter if he never writes again. I'm doing this for *me*. Secretly, though, I have my doubts.

I met Liz for drinks last night, and now she's suspicious, too. Or it could be disgust. We met in a sleek restaurant bar near her office on Fifty-seventh, and she ordered a martini, extra filthy, and "as dry as a nun on Easter Sunday." I asked for a sparkling water.

"That's all you're having?"

"I'm dieting."

She stared at me in horror. "Honey, so am I. I'm *always* on a diet." She waved a hand around the restaurant. "Everybody in this *city's* on a diet. But that doesn't mean you have to stop living. Anyway, olive juice is an excellent source of vitamins."

"And vodka?"

"Vodka's an excellent source of languid grace. I've always wanted to be Elizabeth Ashley."

"I thought you wanted to be Holly Golightly."

She shook her head. "I never go lightly, sweetie. Anyway, I'm too old for that. It's Tennessee Williams from now on. I've decided to become blowsy."

I laughed. "Well, the boys will be glad to hear that."

"Do pass the word." She looked at me. "Seriously, you look like you've lost weight. Which one are you doing?"

"I'm just making it up as I go along. Low fat, lots of raw fruits and vegetables. And I go to the gym twice a day."

She made a face. "How disgustingly low-concept. You need a catchy name, or it doesn't qualify as a diet." The bartender brought our drinks, and she brightened as he set the martini in front of her. Two olives the size of cow's eyes floated in a broth of vodka and olive juice. "You should call it 'The Martini Diet.' You eat like a monk all day long, and then in the evening, you get to have a martini to fulfill your minimum daily requirement of languid grace. That's a diet I could live with."

"I was hoping for slightly faster results."

She took a sip from her glass, eyed me over the rim. "Yeah? What's the hurry?"

I hesitated. "I want to surprise Chloe when she gets home." I fished my slice of lime out of the sparkling water, squeezed it, then dropped it back in.

Liz looked at me with a slight smile. "You've always been a terrible liar."

"It's true! I thought it would be nice for Chloe if her

mother didn't look like an old woman when she got home from France."

"Mmm." She sipped at her martini. "Because every young girl wants her mother to wear the same size she does."

"You think she'll be upset?"

"I guess that depends. Do you plan to start dating her boyfriends?"

"Liz!"

She set her glass down on the bar, leaned forward, and rested a hand on my arm. "Sweetie, no woman ever goes on a diet for her *daughter.* The only reason women lose weight is to screw a man or to screw with a woman."

"That's not true!"

"No? Ask yourself why all the single women you know are skinny, and—" She stopped, picked up her drink, and looked quickly away.

"And the married women aren't, right?"

She sighed. "I'm sorry if that sounds insensitive, honey, but it's a fact that married women gain weight because they *can.* They don't have to worry about impressing men. And if you see a married woman who's suddenly obsessed with her weight, that means one of three things: she's cheating, she thinks her husband might be cheating, or there's a wedding coming up and she wants to stick it to the cousins from Philadelphia by looking fabulous." She looked at me, raised an eyebrow. "Somebody getting married that I don't know about?"

*Was* I just trying to impress a man? It's true that marriage could make you lazy. But who can keep up with the demands of always looking fabulous when you've got a career, a child, and let's face it, a husband who'll be there every morning, like a pair of worn bedroom slippers that fit you perfectly.

Liz set her drink down with sudden determination and turned to face me. "Are you worried that David's cheating on you?"

I couldn't help it: I laughed. "No! *David?* Really, Liz, that's crazy. I've wanted to take off some weight for a couple of years now. You've heard me talk about it. I was starting to feel like my weight was some kind of prison sentence. But with Chloe, and my job, I just never managed to stick with anything long enough to make a difference. I'm hoping this time will be different."

She considered me. "Why this time?"

"I don't know. Maybe it's because David was doing it last year. Maybe it's because Chloe is getting older, and I've started thinking this might be my last chance."

"That's my line. I'm the girl in the Last Chance Saloon."

"What are you talking about? You're skinny as a bone."

"I don't have a choice. When was the last time you said, 'Table for one'? Or, wait, here's a fun game we could play." She ran her eyes expertly around the restaurant. "Quick, how many single men are there in this room? Not counting gay guys, cheating bastards, or married men eating alone."

I looked. There was a table full of businessmen near the entrance, and two guys were sitting on barstools at the other end of the room, watching sports on the TV over the bar. I saw the glint of a ring as one lifted his beer. Two tables with men eating alone, but how could I know if they were single or married? One glanced up at me as I studied him, and his eyes seemed to weigh both me and his chances before he smiled. "That guy," I said to Liz.

She looked over. "Married," she said dismissively. "Cheating bastard. You'd just be a notch on his belt."

"How can you tell?"

"He takes a minute to decide if you're worth the trouble. *Can he fuck you* comes before *would he fuck you*. Single men have choices, so one look and they've made up their mind. This guy's looking for trouble, but not too much." She sipped her drink. "Try again."

"One of those guys at the table by the door is checking us out."

Liz looked over, then gave a little wave. "That's my broker. Probably be over to sell me something in a minute."

"The waiter. The one by the fish tank."

"Gay."

"How about the bartender?"

She looked. "Straight, too young, and technically single. But he's got a live-in girlfriend over in Brooklyn; she's got a lease with an option to buy."

"How could you possibly know that?"

She smiled. "That's Chad. I know every bartender in the city. Trust me, when you have to sit at the bar waiting for your date to show up, it's nice to have somebody to talk to."

"Okay, I give up. How many?"

She shook her head sadly. "See, that's the thing. You

can't give up. Not unless you want to spend the rest of your life alone. So you go to the gym and you get to know the bartenders and you try not to think about the odds."

I put an arm around her shoulder. "I'm so sorry. You're right. I'll just shut up about my diet."

"I don't want you to shut up about it. But it's not your last chance. You're married, so you get lots of chances. That's what marriage is about."

Funny, Liz always talks about my marriage to David like it's an exile on some barren shore, from which I can watch the ships passing on their way to love. But now she was making it sound like the only safe harbor on a rocky, storm-whipped coast.

"Life is full of second chances," I told her, ashamed of the lameness of my words even as I said them.

"Is it?" She forced a smile. "I'm not sure I've had my first chance yet." Then she laughed suddenly. "Listen to us. We're a fun pair."

I pushed my sparkling water away. "Screw it. I'm getting a martini."

Liz laughed and called out to the bartender, "Chad, make my friend a filthy one, just like mine." Then she turned back to me, raised her glass, and said, "Here's to second chances. For everyone."

# 166

Two days with no change. Must be the martinis. From now on, I'm not returning Liz's calls.

# 166

Okay, so I didn't get to the gym last night. And my period's coming. But still, this is frustrating. I've been really good ever since the martinis, eating my hamster salads and drinking my eight glasses of water every day. I should be seeing *some* difference.

No email from Michael for several days. He must have written me off.

# 166

'm hungry. My period still hasn't started.
   I want to die.

# 162

My definition of joy: walking briskly up Broadway on a perfect late October afternoon, talking to your daughter in Paris on your cell phone. The only thing that could be more perfect would be walking up the Champs Elysees talking to your daughter in New York. Still, there are autumn days when it's hard to imagine anyplace more perfect than New York, when the whole city seems to fill its lungs with the crisp air and awaken to its own perfection, so that the women seem more beautiful and the men more driven with energy and purpose. Or is it the other way around?

"Liz told me you've lost some serious weight," Chloe says. "She called me last night, said I wouldn't recognize you."

"She's exaggerating. I've lost a few pounds, but nobody's confused me with a supermodel yet."

"She said she can't ever get hold of you, 'cause you're always at the gym."

For some reason I find this embarrassing. "That's just

silly. After work I spend some time on the stair climber, and then I go home. Like everybody else."

"And in the mornings?"

"Sometimes in the mornings. If I can get myself out of bed early. But, really, it's no big deal."

"It sounds like a huge deal. You should be proud of yourself. I'll bet Dad's thrilled."

She's right, I am proud of myself. I've become a gym regular, there every morning at six and back on my way home from work. I'm still not the most graceful gazelle in the herd, but I no longer feel like everyone's staring at me. I've made peace with even the most complicated machines, so the people beside me no longer need to feel endangered by my awkward flailing. It's almost become relaxing at times. My mind wanders. I daydream, imagining what it will feel like to be slim and muscled, slipping into—or out of—a cute little black dress.

And, yes, I think about sex. Not the act, but the excitement that surrounds it. Walking into a party, and men turning to look. Seeing desire in a man's eyes and knowing that he'll wake up later that night thinking about me. Michael looking at me that way. Maybe it's simply all the attention I've been paying to my body. I've ignored it for years, and now it's woken up hungry and restless. The hunger I can fight; I do that every day. But the restlessness is more persistent, like a current running through me.

He's in New York. He flew in last night for meetings on the project about to break ground up in Stony Brook, and another project in the design phase for an office building in Midtown. He sent me an email to let me know that he was coming, and that he'd be staying at an apartment his firm owns in the East Sixties. Would I like to meet for coffee?

It sounds harmless enough, so why couldn't I bring myself to answer him? Is it just vanity? Secretly, I'm scared that if he sees me now, he might be shocked. *What happened to her? She's really let herself go.*

I know I shouldn't care. I'm happily married, right? Besides, people change—what's he expect after twenty years? Still, I couldn't take seeing that flicker of disgust in his eyes when I walk in the door.

But if I don't answer him, he'll be hurt. And I'm the one who wrote to him. Can I really stand him up, now that he wants to meet?

"Mom, are you still there?"

I realize Chloe's been telling me about her trip to Normandy, and I haven't heard a word she's said. "I'm sorry, dear. A bus was going by."

"Where are you?"

"Broadway and Seventy-ninth."

"Oh, God. Would you go into Zabar's and send me a rye bread with the big black seeds?"

There's no way I'm going near Zabar's; I'd gain four pounds just from the smell alone. I've taken to crossing the street and walking down the east side of Broadway, just to avoid it. "You really want me to send you *bread*? You're in Paris. There are amazing bakeries on every block."

"Yeah, but you can't get the real New York rye bread with the big black seeds. And peanut butter. I'm dying for peanut butter."

"Liz told me there's an American grocery store in Paris where you can get stuff like macaroni and cheese or instant mashed potatoes. They probably have peanut butter."

"Yeah, some of the kids in my dorm went there. You'd be amazed what people miss when they're over here. This one girl came back with all these cans of Campbell's tomato soup."

"They don't make tomato soup in Paris?"

"She says it's not the same. It's spicy, more like gazpacho."

Six hours and an ocean separate us, but we chatter away about foods her friends miss like nothing could be more important. If I were back at the apartment, I could make notes and send them a care package filled with Oreos, M&Ms, and Campbell's tomato soup. I'll try to get to the grocery this evening and make up a box.

Food is important: David's wrong when he says that it's just fuel. Chloe's craving for peanut butter is much more than hunger. It's a safe form of homesickness, a way to talk about all the things you miss without having to admit that living in Paris can make you feel like a child as easily as it can make you feel like the heroine of a romantic movie. Telling your friends how much you miss mac and cheese is easier than saying you miss your parents, or admitting that sometimes you cry at night without knowing why. It's hard to live the life you dreamed about, and there are times when all you want is to go home.

Just two days ago Chloe was telling me how much she loved Paris. She was already trying to figure out a way to move back after she finished college. "That's fine," I told her. "As long as I can come visit."

Next week it'll be something else. She'll call me to break the news that America is an imperial power, and I should be ashamed of myself for the amount of the world's natural resources I consume.

"Listen," I tell her as I cross Eighty-fourth Street, "I have to go. I'm at the gym, and if I don't hurry, I'll have to wait twenty minutes for a machine."

"You go, girl," she says, and hangs up.

At the gym, most people wear iPods, a tiny cord running up from their pocket to their ears. Their eyes are distant, alone in the world of the random shuffle, where no song ever comes up too often. A music critic was telling me about it at one of David's book parties last year. I mentioned that we'd just bought one for Chloe, and he started explaining with great enthusiasm how random shuffle was changing the way people listened to music. You could load your iPod with hundreds of songs, from Coltrane to Bach to Metallica, and every time you turned it on, you'd get a different collection of music—all of it suited to your taste, since you loaded the songs in the first place, but in strange and interesting combinations. Sinatra opens for Mozart, with Hendrix playing the encore.

"In a way, it's like living in New York," the music critic said. "You just have to find a neighborhood you like, and after that, you never have to worry about being bored."

Or like being single in New York. If you're married, there's only one song playing . . .

But that's not fair. A marriage is more like a concept

album, with its own complex drama and textures. You might get sick of "Doctor Jimmy," but you can always look forward to "Love Reign O'er Me."

I haven't gotten around to buying an iPod yet, so I'm stuck with my thoughts. It seems like they're always set on shuffle lately, especially when I'm on the treadmill. One minute I'm looking out the window, watching the people passing on the street below, and the next I'm thinking about Michael in his apartment on the East Side. He's probably working late into the night on his design proposal, surrounded by assistants who run out for coffee and takeout.

When would he have time to see me, anyway?

# 161

*Dear Michael,*

*I'm so sorry, but I just got your last message. I'm out of town for a few days, checking my email on the run. I can't believe you're in New York, and I won't get to see you! How long are you here . . . (block, delete) . . . there?*

David's watching baseball in the bedroom and I'm on the computer in his study, driven to it by guilt for letting almost five days pass without answering Michael's last email. Is this what adultery is like? Lying to your husband, lying to your lover? An hour on the StairMaster wouldn't be as exhausting.

Who knew it could be easier to lift weights than to shoulder all these *feelings*? David's feelings, Michael's feelings, mine. No wonder I'm losing weight. It's a daily workout.

I should just tell everyone the truth. I haven't done

anything wrong, so why do I feel so guilty? Like I'm trying to get away with something, because I *don't* want to
have coffee with an old boyfriend! I'm just not ready. I
shouldn't have to explain that to anyone.

*Would you be ready if you weighed 120?*

Yes.

And that's the problem. It's vanity, not solid moral
character, that's keeping me safely at home. I'm a fat
wife, not a good one. So I sneak off to the computer while
David's caught up in the National League playoffs, lie to
Michael, and feel terrible about the whole thing.

*Will these projects bring you back to New York? I'd
really love to see you!*

That's true—when I'm ready to be seen. It's the reward I've promised myself, when I reach my goal. Every
diet needs a clear goal; all the books tell you that. Mine is
the moment when I walk into the coffee shop on the Upper East Side and I see him waiting for me. I stand there
for a moment near the door, and he looks up at me. Then
he smiles. He recognizes me. I'm the girl on the beach,
the girl in his bed. For just a moment, with the sun behind me, I'm the girl who's been haunting his dreams.

And suddenly, I'm Audrey Hepburn. Big hat, tiny
dress, bright smile. Okay, so I know it's a fantasy. If we
ever meet, it'll probably be pouring out, and I'll come in
soaked and dripping. My hair will look like a wet mop,
and we'll both have headaches. I'll drop my wallet while
trying to pay for my coffee, and loose change will spill
everywhere. Since I won't have eaten all day out of ner-

vousness, I won't be able to keep my eyes from wandering over to the pastry case as we talk. But it's not like we'll have anything to say to each other, anyway. He'll get silent from nervousness, and I'll chatter. After an hour, we'll part, hurrying out into the rain, both relieved to get away.

But I send the message, then spend some time restlessly surfing websites about diet and exercise. Had other women tried my method? I type in "diet" and "old boyfriend," and several pages of sites appear. *Will You Get Fat After 40? Should You Reconnect with an Old Boyfriend? Is a cup of coffee with an old boyfriend really worth an unpleasant atmosphere at home?* (Ouch.) And then a reader's poll:

*Who is the one person you'd most like to say "LOOK AT ME NOW" to once you've met your weight-loss goal?*

| | |
|---|---|
| *Yourself* | *57.2%* |
| *Husband* | *19.8%* |
| *Old boyfriend* | *17.1%* |
| *Old school rival* | *5.8%* |

Can so many women really be that self-affirming, or do they just not want to admit that no goal is achieved until you see it in someone else's eyes? I scroll down through the rest of the poll.

*How do you feel when you look in the mirror?*

| | |
|---|---|
| *I cringe* | *43.7%* |
| *I see some pinchable inches* | *27.6%* |
| *I'm afraid to look* | *25.5%* |
| *Quite comfortable* | *3.2%* |

Okay, so maybe they're not so self-affirming. Do they really think they'll enjoy looking in the mirror when they reach their goal, or will they still cringe and see pinchable inches?

*What best describes your relationship with food?*

| | |
|---|---|
| *Love affair* | 56.3% |
| *Platonic friends* | 26.7% |
| *Enemies* | 17.0% |

There's something called *The Better Sex Diet*. Soy binds estrogen receptors, which helps the vaginal area remain lubricated. Chili peppers and ginger improve circulation and stimulate nerve endings, which could improve sexual pleasure. Who knew? All that Chinese food didn't go to waste. ( Just to my waist.) *From an erection standpoint, anything that's good for your heart is good for your penis,* says the article's diet doctor.

From an erection *standpoint*? Good lord, where was their editor?

Fat is good for sex, at least until it starts to get in the way. Fat helps to produce hormones. Women with low body fat may stop menstruating, find arousal and lubrication more difficult, and even lose their capacity to achieve orgasm. The curse of the supermodel: lots of lovers, but no arousal. Only the Greek gods could have thought that one up. So was Venus *fat*? I'd never considered that possibility, but she is the goddess of timely lubrication.

The article lists foods that are good for sex: oysters (high in zinc, good for testosterone production), champagne (but only in moderation), chocolate-covered strawberries (oh, the cunning devils!). And walnuts. Walnuts? It seems the Romans threw them at newlyweds as a symbol of fertility, instead of rice. Whole grains, especially oats, help to produce testosterone.

I'm beginning to detect a pattern here: all these foods are good for *men*. Because they can eat anything, the bastards.

But at last they come to honey, rich in the mineral boron, which helps the body utilize estrogen. Finally, something for us ladies. *It's likely,* the author writes coyly, *that creative minds will also think of other ways to milk honey of its potential libido-boosting powers.*

Oh, my. I've always loved honey. It's the primal ooze factor. There's something evocative about that golden flow. David and I once rented a porn movie in the days before Chloe, and there was a scene in which two women poured honey all over each other and then licked it off. At the time, I thought, *How do they get it off the sheets?* But the scene has stayed with me, something sweet and low to set the imagination working. Anything that combines sex and dessert is okay in my book. I mentioned it to David once, and a few nights later he suggested we try it. He went out to the kitchen and came back carrying a squeeze bottle of honey in the shape of a bear. The bear was smiling and rubbing its tummy, and I couldn't help laughing. "It's like having sex with Winnie the Pooh!"

Needless to say, the honey turned out to be more exciting as an idea than it was in practice. By the end of the evening we were sticking together in unexpected and awkward places, and the sheets were ruined.

I go back to surfing sites, but nothing else seems worth

my time. *Star says she's lost that weight, and rediscovered love with an old boyfriend, through diet and exercise . . . Demi and her 27-year-old boyfriend, Ashton Kutcher, are infanticipating, and she manages the weight with a diet of . . . My old boyfriend is the chocolate I'm no longer interested in eating . . .*

Old boyfriends wind through these diets like the faint scent of baking bread that haunts you on your way to work. There's an untold story here. How many diets begin in humiliation, after a cruel remark during the breakup fight? The diet becomes a revenge fantasy: "I'll get in shape, and then you'll wish you hadn't broken up with me."

Nothing so interesting on the fitness sites. Mostly it's exercise strategies and equipment you can buy, sports bras, Lycra workout clothes. It seems exercise is just another excuse for shopping. How many women buy the gear instead of using it? One site advertises a *fat-burning dance party* on four DVDs. Do you invite your friends over to burn fat together, or is this something you do alone, like eating Oreos at midnight in front of the television?

Is it all just about loneliness? I read somewhere that men surf the Web for sex, while women do it for hope. Vacation bargains, collectibles, medical advice from others who share your symptoms. However you describe it, it's about breaking through the loneliness, finding somebody to tell you it'll be better tomorrow when your order arrives or when you leave for Bermuda or when you tell strangers about your pain.

It's time to shut off the computer—eventually, it always leads to despair.

But first, a quick email check. Not that I really expect anything, but . . .

*FORESMANM*. He must be feeling lonely in his apartment just across town.

> *Dear Eva,*
>
> *No need to apologize. It was short notice, I know. These projects always hit a crisis just before we break ground, and they're easier to resolve face to face. It feels a little like we're breaking ground on a project of our own—or am I just imagining that?*
>
> *It's always exciting when you break ground, but also terrifying. It's the moment when things that have just been imaginary become real. You've been making decisions in the abstract, but now you see the consequences of every decision you've made.*

Is that a warning? He's talking about us; that's clear. But all we've done is exchange a few emails. I didn't rush off to have coffee with him; I'm the one with my foot on the brake. Maybe that's what he's saying: that he understands if I'm feeling cautious.

> *Nothing's ever built the way it's drawn. You think it'll look one way, but when you get to the site, it all looks different. Do you know what I mean?*

Is he still talking about us here? From down the hall I hear a roar from the crowd on the television, and David groans. Apparently Boston has hitting this year. David tried to explain it a few weeks ago, but it didn't mean very much to me. I'm not a sports wife. I'm a movie wife, a dinner-out-with-friends wife, a Sunday-paper-in-bed wife.

And now, I'm a furtive-email wife. Michael's right: when you get to the site, it all looks different.

> *Are you traveling on business? I spend a lot of time in airports and hotels lately, and I'm still not used to it. You wouldn't call me a homebody, but I can't get used to not having someone to talk to. Actually, most of the talking my wife and I do recently isn't all that pleasant. We seem to spend most of our time arguing. When I'm at home, I wish I was back in a hotel room, where I can get some peace and quiet. But when I'm on the road, the silence starts to get to me pretty quickly. Even an argument seems like human contact.*

I'm not sure how to feel about this. It's sad to think about a marriage crumbling that way—two people who once felt so intimate losing the capacity to be patient with each other. By comparison, David and I have a decent marriage. We may be going through a rough patch, as people say, but it's not like we're cruel to each other. We're not Ozzie and Harriet but we're not George and Martha, either.

On the other hand, I find myself a little excited at the idea that Michael's marriage isn't perfect. The elegant wife has a temper. Everything isn't perfect in the California sunshine.

> *This apartment's not bad. It's nothing fancy: one bedroom, prewar building. More view than charm. My firm bought it a few years ago, when I was in*

*New York a lot for the Deutsche Bank project we*
*were building. For a while I thought about moving*
*here. I thought a separation would do us good. But I*
*couldn't leave my daughter, and most of my work was*
*on the West Coast anyway, so I moved back home.*
*When things get rough, though, I still think about*
*spending some time here. It looks out on the park, and*
*sometimes I just stand at the window and stare out at*
*the lights, like Gatsby in his mansion.*

*Where in Manhattan do you live? East Egg or*
*West Egg? Is there a light at the end of your pier?*
*Michael*

My heart's racing. He's joking, I'm sure, but the image is powerful. What woman doesn't want a man to
gaze longingly at her window from across a crowded
city? I'm tempted to answer him right away, but that
might seem like I was waiting for a reply. And now the
crowd in David's ball game gives another roar, and he
switches off the TV in disgust. As he comes down the
hall, I quickly exit the email program and pull up a
game of Minesweeper just before he pokes his head in
the door.

"You coming to bed?"

"In a minute. Your game over?"

"Bottom of the ninth. I couldn't bear to watch the
rest."

I click a button, and the screen explodes. I'm terrible
at this game. I know where the mines ought to be but
never where they are. It always blows up in my face, and
I'm left with a feeling of terrible guilt that I've killed the

little man with the yellow smiley face, who looks so terrified whenever I click a key.

"Come to bed," David says again, and I realize he's got something other than baseball on his mind. I close the game, reluctantly shut down the computer, and follow David to the bedroom.

Across town, Michael is gazing out his window in my direction. I can't help feeling that I'm betraying him.

# 160

So, what are we doing today?" Carlo considers me in the mirror. "Same as always?"

He gives a little sigh, as if he's given up hope that the answer might change after four years. I'm an easy client: I'm in every six weeks for a trim, not changing the basic shape, with a little color restoration every other visit. I smile, make conversation, and tip well when it's done. So why does he always greet me with what sounds like despair?

"Something's different," he adds. "Have you lost weight?"

"A little." His question makes me strangely uncomfortable. Why can't I be proud of having lost eighteen pounds? But just having to acknowledge it makes me aware of how far I still have to go. "I'm trying to get more exercise."

"Exercise is good," Carlo takes my head in his hands, turns it one way, then the other, as if he's considering the possibilities. "We could go short, if you want a change."

He catches my hair between two fingers, just below my ear. "What do you think?"

Do I want a change? I've worn my hair the same way since Chloe was small: down to the collarbone, lightly layered to accentuate the waves, combed back from my face and parted on the right. It's the same haircut I see on lots of women my age every day, wives and mothers with jobs to get to and errands to run and no time or money to keep up with fashion. I've worn it without feeling ridiculous through endless changes in Manhattan coif-culture, from Laurie Anderson spikes to the buzz cut and the femme-mullet. Yet lately, when I look in the mirror, I see a librarian or a Sunday school teacher; someone who lives on a dairy farm and brings hot dishes to her elderly neighbors.

When I was young, I wore my hair very short. I was thin then, with big, dark, waiflike eyes and a swan's neck. I could get my hair cut in barber shops: just walk in and tell the man to cut it like he would a little boy before his first day of school. That's how I looked when Michael knew me. If I lost all the weight, could I look that way again?

But that's a long way off, and the thought of cutting my hair short is a little terrifying. You need delicate features to carry off that kind of haircut, or else you just look bovine.

I sigh. "Let's just shape it today. I'm not ready for a dramatic change yet."

Carlo sighs, too, and reaches for the scissors. "Okay. You know where to find me when you get your courage up."

We've got to get you some new clothes." Liz shakes her head. "You look like five pounds of groceries in a ten pound bag."

We're walking up Fifth, headed for the Aztec and Noguchi exhibits at the Guggenheim. Michael's safely back in Los Angeles and I'm seizing the moment to do some quick culture-loading before he comes back. Things aren't great in L.A., according to his emails: he's arguing with his wife daily, his daughter's suddenly become sullen and spiteful, and nothing's going smoothly at work. He can't wait to get back to New York, where everything's simpler.

*Simpler?* For him, maybe. When he's in town, Midtown is a no-man's land filled with minefields. I can't keep making excuses, telling him I'm out of town or buried under work. Every day at my office I live in dread that he might suddenly appear. He told me that he picked up a copy of the magazine at a newsstand near his apartment. Our address is right there on the masthead, so how long until he decides to pay me a surprise visit?

Meanwhile, Liz has a point. I need a new wardrobe. Not a full wardrobe, just a few outfits to get me through this stage when all my old clothes hang on me like sacks and the wardrobe I dream about—size 6, or even 4—still hangs on a distant rack. My weight has changed and I'm putting on muscle in unexpected places. If I have to open a jar in the kitchen, I no longer automatically hand it to David. The other day I wrenched open a jar of kosher pickles without hesitating, and he looked at me as if I'd suddenly turned into a broad-shouldered farm girl, jerking the heads off chickens to get them ready for the pot.

"What?"

He just shook his head and went back to chopping peppers for our salad.

What could I say? *Sorry, I'll let you open the jars for me from now on?* I don't have time for that kind of ego-stroking, especially given the number of pickles I eat lately. Kosher pickles are my new true love. Low-cal, low-carb, high salt. What could be more perfect for a woman who spends an hour in the gym and drinks eight quarts of water a day?

But the muscles also throw off the weight-loss equation. Muscle weighs more than fat, so if you're burning fat and building muscle, it's harder to tell if you're on track to meet your weight goal. I look at my body in the mirror and I can see the difference: my thighs and hips have gotten smaller, and there's muscle definition in my calves and abs. I can run up the stairs at work without getting out of breath, and many afternoons I walk home from work, cruising past the legions of exhausted-looking office workers. I could probably move even faster if it weren't for my clothing, two sizes too large now, billowing out behind me like a sail.

It's hard to believe that these clothes were *tight* on me back in September. Now it feels like I could walk right out of them, the way a snake sheds its skin. And that's not far from the truth: when I imagine a new wardrobe, it's not just smaller versions of what I wear now but a whole new self, leaving the old one behind to be blown away. What are clothes anyway, but the skin we show the world?

"Maybe a few things," I tell Liz. "I'm just passing through this size."

"But you want to feel the difference, right? Something to remind you where you're going."

"I'm not buying Prada," I warn.

Liz sighs. "At least let's brighten your palette a little. You dress like a Sicilian widow."

"They say black is the new black."

"Not if you're still wearing the old black."

We're an odd species, changing our colors daily. Dark colors for serious business, bright for mating. Lately, I'm drawn to red. Every morning I pass a Victoria's Secret on my way to work, and it's the bright red lingerie in the window that catches my eye. Not that I dream of fitting into that kind of thing yet. It's aspirational shopping: looking for the thing you'll buy the day your dreams come true.

But who would I wear such a thing for? David? Michael? It seems absurd to imagine putting it on, like a costume for a Halloween party. Do women really wear that stuff? The stores are everywhere, so the merchandise must be selling. I know some women who swear by their bras, but let's face it, that's not what's put them in every mall in America. Wearing tiny fragments of silk and lace is a private pleasure, like driving a luxury car. Something to make you feel special under your office clothes, a secret to remind you that the self is made of secrets. And never mind that they're selling that same naughty secret to women in every suburb and city across America. Every one of them can feel special when she wears it.

After the museum, we go shopping for my new middle-weight wardrobe.

"Nothing too expensive, okay?" I beg Liz in the cab. "I don't want to invest in this size; I'm planning to trade it for a smaller one."

"I've got one word for you," Liz says. *"Resale."*

"You're not serious."

"It's the finest in fashion at a fraction of the original price." She sends the cab driver to Madison. "Where do you think the East Side fashionistas unload their shameful fat sacks?"

Chanel, Prada, Donna Karan—it's all there, some of it actually in my size. I buy five outfits; three that fit me now and two more that should fit me on my way down. Between these and the few items I can still wear, I should get through the fall without embarrassment. Considering what I've been wearing to the office in the last few years, I'm moving upmarket.

When I get home, David's stretched out on the bed reading. He looks at the bags and his face goes white. "You went shopping with Liz?"

"Yeah." I set the bags on the foot of the bed. "And wait'll you see the fabulous Philippe Adec suit I found."

He watches in silence as I take out my new outfits, hold them up, then lay them across the bed. By the time I get to the Elie Tahari, he's looking at me like someone he barely recognizes.

When I'm done, he swallows hard. "So how much did all this cost?"

"It's all resale," I tell him triumphantly. "We got some unbelievable deals."

"Yeah? We're going to be able to pay Chloe's tuition?"

"If we don't eat much." I gather up my bags. "But then I'll need more clothes."

Later, he comes out to the kitchen as I'm slicing up veggies for salad. "The clothes look nice," he says carefully.

"Thanks." I go on chopping, not looking up.

"You're mad at me for asking about the cost."

I shrug. "It's not like I've given you any reason to think I'd break the bank. I need new clothes, the old ones don't fit me anymore. But you don't really seem to have noticed how much weight I've lost."

"I've noticed," he says. "You look great."

"I *will* look great when I'm done. Right now I look better. Until then, I'm making small daily improvements.

And while I don't expect you to acknowledge them all, it would be nice to think that you're not blind to the entire process."

He regards me over his glasses, which gives him a surprised, owlish look. It's the look he used to give Chloe when she was little and she'd say something that made him pause and consider that she might not always be a child. I give him a moment, waiting to see what will come out of this contemplation, but he only says, "I'm sorry. I didn't think you'd want me to make a big deal of it." Then he goes over to the refrigerator and takes out the salad dressings.

*Two* salad dressings. It's been weeks, and he hasn't noticed that I've stopped using mine. Every evening, I put a small teaspoon of olive oil on my salad and some ground pepper. Yet whenever he sets the table, he takes out his bottle of caesar and my untouched bottle of herb vinaigrette.

"I don't use that anymore," I say testily.

He gives me that surprised look again. "What?"

"The salad dressing. I haven't been using that for six weeks."

He looks down at the bottle in his hand. "Okay." And he puts it back in the refrigerator.

# 148

*Dear Michael ...*

Because I'm bored and my column's going nowhere, I've done what I always do these days to raise my spirits: started a message to Michael. We write every day now. Nothing important or profound, just how the day's going, what's happening in our lives. We sound like an old married couple talking over dinner, except there's a hint of flirtation to excite the mind. Michael's picked up the game quickly enough, returning my shots and adding his own interesting spin.

I've told him about my diet. It took courage, but when he started asking about my day, it seemed ridiculous to leave out the one thing that most defines me at this moment. I've been careful not to give any specifics; just a casual reference to working out and tightening my belt. Okay, I may have hinted, vaguely, that I was training for a marathon—but that was in a moment of weakness when Ron brought in pizza for the office and I could smell its aroma drifting in from the conference room down the hall.

Anyway, to my surprise, he's taken an interest, occasionally asking, *How's the training coming along?* He calls it "the training," which might suggest that he's taken me a little too seriously on the marathon thing. He's started talking about his own running—eight miles a day, mostly along the beach at Santa Monica—and I'm starting to get a little worried that if I don't clarify this particular point, I could end up trying to gasp through the New York City marathon at his side. He's begun to talk as if we're kindred spirits (his wife talks about his running dismissively, as a symptom of a midlife crisis), and I'd really hate to disappoint him.

So I've invented an old knee injury which necessitated arthroscopic surgery last year, from which I'm now trying to come back. It's amazing what one can learn from the internet. I've talked in detail about my surgery, the healing process that followed, and my dismay at the weight gain that accompanied my immobilization. But I'm back in the gym now, doing strength training to build up my knee, and the weight is slowly coming off.

It's a little scary, how easily the lies come. Yet the lie has had one real benefit: I've raised my cardio workout, picking up my pace on the treadmill to a thumping, heavy jog, and two mornings a week I skip the gym and go out running. It's a little humiliating, since the early morning runners on Central Park Drive are all very serious, and they flash past me as I trudge along, walking as much as I run. I'm gasping for breath, and the muscles in my legs quickly start to feel like rubber bands that have lost their stretch. But I keep going, driven by the fear of exposure and humiliation, and gradually I start to run more and walk less. It's cold in the mornings now, and the trees are mostly bare. Still, there are moments when it's actually pleasant, and these hours gasping in the crisp air bring my body back to life.

But questions haunt me as I follow in the wake of the other runners: What exactly am I running toward? Do I really think Michael and I will go running together, or am I just anxious to make sure that when he looks at my legs, he sees a runner's calves, not the thick legs I've squeezed into my stockings these last few years? But how closely do I expect him to be looking at my legs? Am I imagining a quick glance as I enter the café where we'll meet for coffee, or a close inspection as he slowly removes my stockings and glides his hand up my inner thigh?

Both, I'm ashamed to say. I can't help it, but the fact is that I've begun to imagine myself in bed with him. I find myself picturing the movements of our bodies, his arousal, my surrender. It's more vivid than I'm used to imagining. For me, sexual fantasy is usually like movies made before 1968: everything is implied by the expressions on faces, or the sudden tensing of bodies. At most there's a flash of breast or thigh, but the real action takes place under silk sheets, out of the camera's eye. For years, I've even used body doubles: the body moving under that sheet isn't my own heavy flesh but a leaner, more graceful model, maybe the body I was so eager to share in college and my first few years in New York, or the generic superbody of the movies, the universal object of all our desires.

So what's particularly surprising about these new fantasies is that they feature an unideal me: it's not the perfect body of my twenties, but the body I imagine having when I've finished my diet—leaner, but older. Not the perfect body of youth, but one that Michael can still enjoy, and that I can enjoy through his reflected pleasure. And there's the problem: I'm not remembering the pleasures of the past but anticipating pleasures I'm hoping will come. I've lost control of this flirtation, and now, like an animal that's broken out of its cage, it's turned on me, sinking its claws in deep.

Am I really this weak? Would I really need Michael's desire to take pleasure in a body I've worked so hard to restore? Why can't it just be *mine*?

But if it's mine, then can't I enjoy it any way I want? Besides, it's Michael who's inspired this change. David seems to take no interest in my diet, except when it gets in his way. If I reach a point where a man can take pleasure in my body again, I can't help feeling that it's Michael who deserves it.

But my mind's wandering. Like my desires. That's happening a lot lately, and it's not helping me get my column written. I have to get back to work!

*Dear Michael . . .*

December 2005

# 139

*I*s Chloe coming home for Christmas?

Michael and I have moved on to instant-messaging now. Chloe taught me how to use it in early November, sending me a page of instructions by email and setting a time when we could meet online. But we screwed up the time difference and I ended up on my computer an hour earlier than planned, typing "Chloe? Are you there?" into a busy chat room. Eventually, some guy with the screen name XTC32 wrote back, "Yeah, this is Chloe. What are you wearing?" I quickly got off the computer.

Eventually we figured out the timing, but it never really worked well. I had to rush home from the office to get online by 7:00 p.m. while she had to rush home from the Parisian club scene to meet me there at 1:00 a.m. I got the distinct impression that I was cramping her style, and was relieved when we went back to emailing. I could write her a quick note at any time, and she could answer when she hadn't just finished off a bottle of cheap merlot with a boy named Jean-Pierre.

When I suggested IM-ing to Michael, we ran into the

opposite problem. I couldn't stay awake long enough to start a conversation at midnight, and he couldn't get home out in Santa Monica early enough to be free to slip away to his computer before nine. We tried it at work a few times: I'd get online right after lunch and he'd meet me there when he got to the office, but our conversations were distracted, and one of us was always hurrying off to take care of some work crisis.

*I think this is a local technology,* I tell him one evening. *It's great if you're both at the same point in your day, but it doesn't work so well with a three-hour time difference. With email, you can answer whenever you've got a free moment. You just have to wait a little longer for a reply.*

I waited a few seconds, and his reply came back. *I'm actually a big fan of delayed gratification. Everything's more fun when you take your time.*

I smiled. *Everything?*

*Wait and see.*

I got a little shiver along the back of my neck. What did he have in mind for me?

*Patience is an impressive quality in a man,* I wrote.

*I enjoy the feeling of anticipation—when you both know something's going to happen, it's just a matter of when. . . . And how many times.*

Oh my. At that moment, I couldn't help thinking there was something to be said for instant gratification, too.

*Anyway, we can try this again the next time I'm in NYC,* he wrote. *At least we'll be in the same time zone then.*

*When are you coming?*

*End of January, probably.*

I did some quick math. If I continued to lose steadily,

I'd be close to 130 by then. Would I let him see me at that weight? Probably. But only with clothes on. If he wants to see more, he'll have to be content with the pleasures of anticipation for a while longer.

Weight loss always gets harder after the New Year; all the magazines say so. The cold weather makes your body want to hold on to its layers of fat like a coat. That's why the New Year's weight loss resolution almost never works. In January and February you become an arctic seal, not surrendering a pound without a battle.

March, then, or early April. If we make it that far, I'll be seeing weights I haven't known since my twenties. Then he can claim his reward for all this patience.

*Maybe we could actually get off the computers and get together in person the next time you're in town,* I write. *You still owe me a cup of coffee.*

*I just like keeping you in anticipation.*

I can't help it: I *like* this guy. We both know I'm the one who's been avoiding the meeting, but he turns it around and makes it sound like his fault. Lots of men would start accusing me of playing games, without thinking about what kinds of anxieties might lie behind my reluctance. But Michael accepts me as I am. Who knows? If we met, my weight might not even bother him. Not that I'd want to risk it. Anyway, it would still bother *me*.

*What are you doing for the holidays?*

*Not sure yet,* he writes. *Maybe I'll go to the beach and watch Santa arrive on his surfboard. Is Chloe coming home for Christmas?*

*No, she's going to Venice for Christmas. Then Florence over New Year's.*

*Sounds lovely. Tell her to bring rain boots. Venice often floods over Christmas. You have to walk on boards to get across St. Mark's Square.*

*Must be nice for the gondoliers. Have you spent much time there?*

*Enough to ruin a few pairs of shoes. A friend of mine has an apartment in the Cannaregio that he lets me use, away from all the tourists. I go there to draw the buildings every couple years. I've got sketchbooks full of palazzi in my desk.*

*That sounds idyllic. I've never been.*

*Maybe I'll take you someday.*

I stare at his last words with a breathless feeling. Is that what we're talking about? Running off to Venice together, waking up in his apartment to watch the sun rise over the rooftops?

I realize suddenly that several minutes have passed. He's waiting for my response.

*I'd like that.*

It must speak volumes—my delay, and then my answer. I feel like we've crossed a bridge into new territory, and I don't have a map where this path leads.

We've agreed that we're going to be lovers. I've told him I'd go to Venice with him if he asked me, and we both know what that implies.

It's just a matter of time now.

❦

"What's gotten into you?" David lies on his back, catching his breath.

*Nothing, yet.*

And that's the problem. The anticipation is driving me crazy. Not that I can say that to David, but I doubt I'm going to hear any complaints from him. At the moment, he's getting more sex than a frat boy. His wife's suddenly become insatiable; I can't get enough.

"It's the diet," I tell him. "All this hunger's got to come out somewhere."

That's a lie, of course. The last thing you think about when you're starving is sex. Even if you do manage to put aside the thought of food for a while, in the middle of passion your stomach starts growling.

But food isn't what's on my mind these days. I sit in my office staring at my computer, my mind in Venice. That apartment in the Cannaregio has kidnapped my imagination. (It's a residential district of eighteenth-century buildings, a ten-minute walk from the Rialto. I looked it up.) I picture myself drinking espresso in tiny coffee bars while Michael sketches buildings, then shopping for fish and produce in the outdoor market, taking my purchases back to the flat to make a simple dinner. Afterward we leave the plates on the table, unwashed, as Michael leads me into the bedroom, his eyes lit by desire.

My column's late again, and I've got a pile of copyediting on my desk. But all I can think about is sex. I burn with it, like a teenager. At the gym it drives me mercilessly, until I'm pounding away on the treadmill as if someone's chasing me. I can sense the woman on the treadmill next to me trying to match my pace, but it's too fast for her. She gasps, catches the handrails to keep her balance, then quickly slows to a walk. When I'm finished,

I do sit-ups and ab crunches on a steeply sloped board.
I'm like a boxer training for a championship fight, working every muscle until it's tight as a fist. But where the
boxer images fist-pumping victory, all I can think about
is surrender: I tighten all my muscles so they'll please
Michael's eyes, and then slowly loosen under his touch.
*Just ten more crunches,* I tell myself, gritting my teeth. *It's
a small price to pay.*

But David is getting the immediate benefits. You'd
think with all this exercise I'd come home worn out and
stiff, but to my surprise, it's exactly the opposite. It's as
if once I've fired up my boilers, I can't stop until I've
burned off all the steam. We leave the dirty dishes in the
sink, the phone messages unplayed. Even if it's Chloe
calling, we let it ring, pausing only to listen to her voice
on the answering machine—Is she okay?—and then go
back to fucking on the couch, the kitchen table, the bathroom floor. I like to be on top lately, riding him like a
horsewoman taking the fences at a gallop. I throw my
head back, close my eyes, and growl. Since when do I
*growl?*

David appears to enjoy it. At first he seemed to find
the urgency of my desire disturbing, especially when I
started growling. But he went along with it, even started
to enjoy the changes. That's one thing about husbands:
they rarely need much convincing when it comes to sex.
Husbands know which side their bread is buttered on.

The only problem is that all the fire and urgency
seems to be mine: he's happy to lie back and let me run
the show. I know I shouldn't complain. Lots of women
would be thrilled to be allowed to steer the boat from

time to time. Too many men tend to confuse their wives with cars: drive 'em fast until you get where you're going, then put it in park and go watch TV. At least David's trying to be sensitive to my needs. But what I want, deep down, is for him to wait until I start growling, then flip me on my back and demand my unconditional surrender. It's not that I want a man to bully me into orgasm: I'm just looking for a little passion to match my own. It's exciting to be desired, to look into a man's eyes and see that he's got to have you, *now*.

That's what's got my fire burning. Michael's emails are full of desire, although he's careful to keep it friendly. He finds me interesting. My job, my diet, Chloe's dreams—he's ready to hear it all and he responds thoughtfully, as if the details of my life really matter. But just below the surface, there's a wolfish gleam in his eye. We don't get explicit, but I can imagine the things he'd like to do to me.

Which is probably what makes it so exciting. Sex with Michael takes place only in my imagination, which means he's the perfect lover, ready with the slow caress that builds my arousal, or the unexpected surprise to carry me over the edge. What chance does your husband stand against a dream lover whose touch is always just the way you'd like it and never exactly the way you'd *expect* it? Husbands are old hands at running up the sails and getting the ship moving, even when the wind is failing. But the lover in your dreams is the pirate who boards you and claims you as his prize.

Later, when it's all over and David dozes off beside me, I slip out of bed and go into the kitchen to clean up the dishes. *None of this is real,* I assure myself guiltily as I scrub the broiler pan. *You're just enjoying a vivid fantasy life. Nothing wrong with that.*

But when the dishes are done, I go into David's study and switch on the computer. Might as well take a moment to check my email . . .

# 136

Then, suddenly it's all real, and I'm terrified.

*I'm back in New York,* Michael writes in an email that's waiting for me when I get to my office. *We had a small crisis on the Stony Brook project over the weekend, so I flew out to take care of it. But it looks like they may have it solved, so it seems I may have flown all the way out here for no reason.*

*What are you doing for lunch?*

Well, I was planning to have an apple and a small container of lowfat cottage cheese at my desk, like I always do. I still haven't figured out how to handle lunch in a restaurant. Ron wanted us to take our designer out last week, so I ordered a caesar salad with chicken, dressing on the side, then spent most of the meal avoiding the croutons as if they were tiny icebergs that could sink my diet if I got too close.

But how can I do that with Michael? I'd be too self-conscious, picking at a salad like the chaste food martyr I've become. I'd rather burn at the steak, or plunge my spoon defiantly into a chocolate orgasm, than let him see me as a devout diet nun. I've told him I'm on a diet, so he knows I'm not at my perfect weight. And the truth is, I look better than I have in years. I'm only twenty pounds from my goal, and all the exercise has given me muscle where everything used to be at the mercy of gravity. And it's only lunch, right? We'll sit and talk, just the way we've been doing for months, only without the computers between us.

That thought makes me panic. We haven't even talked on the phone! In a sense, we're total strangers. Sure, there are things I'd like to ask him about—his work, his daughter, the house he's building, his wife—but it's easy to ask personal questions at a computer screen when he's three thousand miles away. Will I really have the courage to look him in the eye and ask about his marriage?

It's tempting, if only to see the look in his eyes as he tries to talk about it. In an email, it's easy to shade the truth in ways that hide the fact that your marriage isn't perfect, but only because you've become bored with having everything so *easy.* I never mention David's good points—his thoughtfulness, his consideration, the fact that we rarely fight—and I can't help wondering if Michael isn't leaving out things like that, also. If his marriage is so painful, why hasn't he left? Could it be that, like me, he's just enjoying a flirtation?

Not that I would ever hold that against him, but it would be interesting to watch his eyes as he answered my questions. Would he get that furtive look so many men have when they talk about their marriages? Or would he try to hide it by getting aggressive, turning the questions back at me? Let's face it, I don't really know a thing about this guy. It would probably be a good thing for me to sit across a table from him and talk about our lives. It might even cool things down between us, and I could go home to David with a clear conscience.

*Lunch sounds nice,* I type. *Did you have someplace in mind?*

❦

I see him through the window, sitting at a table in the corner, his chair turned slightly so that he can face the window. But he's talking to the waiter now, so I get a moment to look at him unobserved. He's older than the photograph on his firm's website, with a bit more gray in his hair. But still good-looking in that thoughtful way I remember. His face looks like it's been carved by a sculptor, and his hair manages to be both neat and windblown all at once. He's handsome. My memory hasn't lied about that.

There's a nervous feeling in my stomach that's been growing all morning, getting stronger during the walk over from my office, that nervousness you get before job interviews and first dates. It's not a feeling I've ever enjoyed, which probably explains why I'm still married and still working at *House & Home*. When I was single, I often just skipped the first date altogether and slept with the guy I'd just met, simply to avoid this feeling.

*It's not a date,* I remind myself. *We're just two old friends having lunch.*

Still, I back away from the window and walk up the

street to collect myself, to cultivate the serenity of the married woman.

*I am a wife and mother,* I recite, picturing the Madonnas of medieval paintings with their placid smiles. *I am in control of my life.*

I can't keep standing here. Michael will be looking at his watch now, wondering if I'm coming. (He should know better. He never had any trouble making me come.)

I take a deep breath, walk back to the restaurant, and push the door open. He recognizes me as soon as I walk in. Maybe I haven't changed as much as I think. He gets to his feet, smiling, as I cross the restaurant toward him. He comes out from behind the table with his arms open—not *too* wide, as if he's expecting full-body contact, but relaxed and welcoming—and I'm happy to follow his lead, right through the quick kiss on the cheek that seems to acknowledge past intimacy without making any assumptions about the future.

He smells nice. No cologne or aftershave, just a faint scent to awaken a distant memory of sunlight and sea spray and bodies moving together in the night. Then he's taking my coat as we simultaneously say, "How *are* you?" and both laugh at the awkwardness of it, and he drapes my coat over an empty chair. It gives me a moment to sit, take a deep breath, and steady myself to face the full force of his gaze.

For a moment, neither of us says a word. We look at each other, and then we both smile, and he reaches across the table to squeeze my hand. "It's good to see you, Eva. You look fabulous."

And that's all it takes. I feel myself relax, and all my self-consciousness melts away. "You look pretty good yourself."

His hand is warm holding mine and he looks deep into my eyes, and I feel like we've picked up right where we left off years ago—a touch, a hungry look, and my heart racing.

We order, we chat. He asks me about Chloe, and I ask about his daughter, Emma. She's doing fine, he tells me. Then he smiles. "Emma and Chloe. Our young Victorians."

"I know. Her dorm at Smith is full of Noras and Elizas. There's even a Tilda. You think we've scarred them for life?"

"They'll survive. Anyway, who really thinks about their name? It's just a word people use when they talk to you."

"You don't feel any connection to your name?"

"There are too many Michaels for it to mean anything. How about you? Do you feel like your name describes you?"

"Eva?" I consider. "I don't know. Maybe. I guess you could say I'm easily tempted."

He smiles wickedly. "I'll keep that in mind."

I blush, and suddenly there's a feeling in my stomach that I recognize as desire. But not the "Mmm, that would be nice" desire you feel with your husband. It's different, more primal. *Burn the house down,* it whispers to you. *Scatter the flocks. He'll be waiting for you in the dark woods.*

I barely touch my lunch, too excited to eat. He doesn't seem hungry, either. We both lean on the table, our plates untouched, talking in quiet voices. We must look like a couple of spies.

"Tell me about your house. Have you had a chance to work on it?"

He laughs. "If you knew how long I've been waiting for somebody to ask me that! Most people start to avoid the subject after a while. They don't want to get me started."

"I'm interested. I like hearing you talk about it."

He tells me, sketching the design on a napkin so I can see how he's contoured the house to the surrounding hills. At moments, he sounds like a little boy who's building a fort in the woods. But then his voice grows serious, and I can see how he must look when he's working on a job site. The house itself is like nothing I've ever seen before: all oblique angles to catch the sunlight in summer, and channel rainwater along a series of gullies through a filtering system to a cistern at a low point in the center of the roof. "There'll be a well since the rainfall isn't high enough to sustain the house's water needs in the summertime," he says, "but this way we use as much renewable water as possible without any substantial energy use."

"So you'll be showering in rainwater?"

He looks up at me and smiles. "Ever tried it? It's really soft water. Makes your skin feel like velvet. That's what we'll use in the hot tub, too."

*We*. Does he mean his wife? He keeps saying that she has no interest in the project, but maybe when it's finished, and there's chilled wine in the cellar and a hot tub full of rainwater to enjoy, she'll let him drag her up there for a weekend to sit in the small Buddhist temple he's designing on a high cliff and watch the sun set over the Pacific.

Or does he have somebody else in mind?

"Chloe went to a climbing camp in Vermont where they showered with rainwater," I tell him. "She loved it."

"She's got good taste. So you let her climb mountains? I'm impressed."

"When Chloe gets something in her head, there's no stopping her. She's been that way ever since she was a baby."

"Determined, huh? Does she get that from you?"

I look at him, surprised. "Me?" Suddenly, without warning, my eyes fill with tears. Is that how he imagines me? You'd never call me determined. Not in that sense, at least. It's my job, my daughter, my husband that determine me. I'm determined by my diet, and by the foods I dream about but don't eat. My fat determines me. And the machines at the gym, on which I spend hours sweating to rid myself of the fat, they determine me, too. So, yeah, I guess I'm determined—but not in any way I'd ever wish on Chloe. *Let her stay in Paris. The French don't seem nearly as determined as we are. Must be all the wine.*

Michael's looking at me with concern now, watching me swallow hard and blink back the tears.

"Chloe's her own person," I tell him and he nods, probably relieved to think it's mother love that's made me well up this way.

He just smiles as I wipe my eyes. "Kids do that to us. They're like mirrors in which we see ourselves, only we wish better for them."

"Do you see yourself in Emma?"

He hesitates. "I see my *best* self in Emma. But that's not always the self I see in me." He looks up at me. "You know what I mean?"

I nod. "That's what I was saying about Chloe. I wish I had her strength of spirit."

For a moment we're both silent. Then he reaches across the table, gives my hand a squeeze.

"Don't kick yourself, okay? You've got an injury. You'll be running marathons again before you know it."

I look down at my plate, suddenly filled with self-loathing. "I guess you're right."

An awkward moment. He glances at his watch. "What time do you have to be back?"

I look at my own watch and realize with shock that we've been sitting here for almost two hours. "Oh, God. I completely lost track of time! I've got a two-thirty editorial meeting."

"Then you'd better go." He stands up to help me with my coat. "Can I see you again sometime?"

"I'd like that." I'm feeling breathless now, anxious to get back, but when I turn to face him, it's suddenly hard to leave. "How long are you in town?"

"I fly back the day after tomorrow. But I'll be here for a week in late January. Maybe we could get together then?"

"That would be great." Without planning it, I lean in and kiss him on the cheek. Just a quick kiss, but I find myself reluctant to pull away, my eyes closed, breathing in the scent of him. His arms come up and draw me against him, and we stand there for a moment, the sounds of the restaurant fading around us. Then I'm gone, walking quickly toward my office in a blur of traffic and sound.

Only later do I realize that I've left him with the check. I ate almost nothing, yet I don't feel hungry. Can a woman survive only on desire? I catch myself smiling in the middle of my meeting. *You should write a diet book.*

oliday parties, a big dinner with David's parents in Connecticut, along with his sisters and their families, Liz's traditional bacchanal for all her friends and clients—I drift through them all placidly, not losing weight, but not gaining either. It's the most one can hope for during this season of plenty. It seems like I'm at the gym half the day, and so are most of the women I know. We seek forgiveness for our sins—the extra helping of turkey with dressing, the tiny sliver of pumpkin pie—on these merciless machines. The bathroom scale is our stern confessor.

"You look great!" David's colleague Edie Boyarski cries out as we come into his firm's office party. She hasn't seen me since I began my diet, and now she rushes over to examine me more closely. "How'd you do it?"

I just smile. "Diet and exercise." "Really?" "That's it, no secret." But still, women crowd around me. There *must* be a secret!

Once the drinks get flowing, I notice David's male colleagues eying me, too. Several approach me to ask how I've managed it, hinting that their wives could lose a few pounds. A few are more honest, admitting that they're asking for themselves. One, very drunk, makes a broad pass, which I sidestep easily. Off in the corner, I see David smiling, surrounded by men.

I'm not doing badly. The pies at these festive gatherings don't tempt me, and I take only the leanest slices of turkey, with vegetables to make it look like my plate is full. Not that it fools Liz. At her party, I see her eyeing my plate with suspicion. She senses that there's something going on here, some secret that she doesn't know, and it offends her very soul.

"That's all you're eating?"

"You got a problem with carrot sticks?"

"Not at all. Melt some cheese over them, I'll eat the whole bag." She reaches over, takes one off my plate. "Did you see my mistletoe?"

"Hard to miss it." She's hung sprigs in every doorway, and there's a forest on the headboard of her bed. "How's that working out for you?"

She sighs. "I've spent most of the evening loitering in doorways. I feel like a hooker."

"So how's business?"

She shoots me a look. "I haven't seen you and David making use of it. I thought the whole point of being married was to have someone to kiss whenever you want."

She reaches for another carrot stick, and I have to resist the impulse to jerk the plate away. She can eat anything she wants! Why does she have to steal from my plate? But I suppose she could say the same about me. I've got a husband, a comfortable marriage; she's the one who's going hungry. So why am I stealing off someone else's plate?

"I hate carrots," she says glumly. "They make me think of rabbits."

"What's wrong with rabbits?"

"They spend all their time eating and screwing. It's depressing."

I look down at my carrots. "You think there's a connection?"

"Between eating and screwing? Definitely. The only time I don't feel guilty eating is when I've just finished screwing."

"Or else rabbits are hungry all the time, so they screw a lot to keep their minds off it."

She looks at me. "Is that your secret?"

I can't help it; I blush.

She raises her eyebrows. "Maybe you don't need the mistletoe after all."

I eat another carrot and glance over at at the row of pies she's lined up on the sideboard. "You've got enough pie there to break anyone's determination."

"That's the plan. You feed them, you fuck them, then you hide their clothes so they can't leave." She looks away suddenly, and I can see her eyes filling with tears. "You want to hear something ridiculous? Lately, when I order Chinese takeout from the place at the corner, I get two meals so they won't think I'm eating alone."

I reach out to lay a hand on her arm.

"And when I order pizza, I pretend to have a conversation with my boyfriend so the guy taking the order won't think I'm ordering a large pizza just for me." She looks at me. "You don't know how lucky you are to have someone, Eva."

"Liz, I'm so sorry."

"So will you eat something?" She waves a hand at the table vaguely. "I've got all this food . . ."

❧

"Well, that was fun," David says as we head home. "Liz really outdid herself this year."

I say nothing, annoyed by his sarcastic tone but secretly grateful to have escaped the scene without pie on my conscience or my hips. I've had it with parties. I'm impatient to get past this oasis and back to my long trek through the desert.

At night, I dream of numbers changing. I'm in an elevator and I've pressed the wrong button, going up instead of down. All I can do is stand there, helplessly, watching the numbers climb. But then I realize that if I push all the down buttons at the same time, and throw my weight against the straining machinery, I can slow the elevator's climb. Gradually, it comes to a stop, groaning, and then slowly begins to descend. My heart races as the numbers above the door start to go down. I've beaten it! I've made this happen! But then the elevator starts to pick up speed, and I realize that this isn't a slow, controlled descent but a free fall, and

I'm trapped inside an elevator that's hurtling toward the ground. I wake, sweating, just before it hits bottom.

"You okay?" David asks sleepily, and I realize I've come awake with a jerk, as if I'd been about to fall out of bed. The clock on my bedside table says 3:20.

"I'm fine. Just a bad dream."

"You've been having lots of those lately." He turns over, pulls the covers up over his shoulders, and goes back to sleep.

Have I? It's not like I remember them. That's what makes this one so unusual. I get out of bed, go into the kitchen, drink a glass of water slowly, looking out at the dark city.

*You've got a guilty conscience.*

That's what a shrink would tell me. Either that, or I'm secretly scared of what will happen when I reach my goal. How can you want something so badly and then find that you're afraid of getting it just when it's within your reach? It seems like a cruel joke, as if we're genetically designed to be miserable. What evolutionary good could our misery serve?

Stupid question, really. We're animals, built to desire. Hunger and sex, that's what keeps us going. Happiness isn't built into the design, except as a temporary reward. A good meal, a satisfying fuck, a moment with your child when it all seems worth it. Desire has become a habit, stronger than exhaustion or hunger. It pushes me out of bed into the bitter January morning, so that I'm at the gym long before the first hint of light in the cold, gray sky.

What's nice about the gym is that you can make the numbers go *up*. Minutes on the treadmill, rate on the stair climber, and weight on the Nautilus. More weight on the machine equals less weight on me; my body's changing faster than the numbers on my scale. I've got clearly defined biceps, and I can detect ab muscles emerging under the remaining fat. My legs, after all the running and stair climbing, look like I'm ready to climb Everest in a pair of cute shorts. I pause in front of the full-length mirror in the weight room every morning to consider these changes. I'm still not as thin as I'd like, but at least everything's starting to look firm.

Gym mirrors aren't instruments of vanity or self-loathing, like those in our bathrooms; they're reality checks. You work up a fierce sweat and your muscles feel like they're carved from stone, so you study yourself with almost technical self-assessment as you catch your breath. The mirror in the gym shows you that what you feel is only an illusion: your muscles may feel cut from granite, but you still look like Gumby. Yet I can what see what I've accomplished in this mirror. Every day I look at myself, turning one way and then the next to get the full effect. And little by little I can see more of the weight room emerging behind me, like an island slowly coming into view at the end of a long journey.

I could say the same about Michael: I feel strong now, but that hasn't always been true. Four days passed after our lunch without a word. *Okay,* I thought in despair when I checked my email on the fourth day and found nothing. *He got a look at you, and he's lost interest.*

I tried not to think about it, but I found myself checking my email every few minutes throughout the morning, getting more depressed with every hour. At last, I couldn't take it anymore. What could I lose by writing to him? He had probably dumped me already, and at least I'd know.

> *Dear Michael,*
> *It was so nice to see you. I hope your trip back to L.A. wasn't too exhausting.*

In case, say, he was too tired to send an email. It's thoughtful to give somebody an excuse, but I'd be disappointed if he were lame enough to use it.

> *We're up to our necks in our holiday issue—enough Christmas cheer to bring out the Sylvia Plath in any woman.* (Whatever that means.) *If you're ever tempted to pick up a copy, I'd suggest mild depressants to balance out all the sugar.*

Actually, it's not so bad this year. I wouldn't have mentioned it, except that I'm searching for a way to keep the tone light. Ron's been more restrained than usual, just a few shots of families gathered around the hearth, candy canes and stockings hanging from the mantle, and a gratuitous wreath on the front door of the house we're using on the cover. Never mind that we took the shot back in March, during the last decent snowfall up in Connecticut. Our art director thought it had a Christmas feel, so she drove over to a craft shop in a mall near Waterbury, bought a plastic wreath, and hung it on the door. The photograph's been hanging on a bulletin board in her office for seven months, until Ron gave in, let her use it as the December cover. The worst thing is that we had to start thinking about Christmas back in September, so that by the time everybody else is getting into that holiday spirit, I'm ready to grab an axe and take out a few elves.

Feeling self-conscious, I couldn't think of anything to say that wouldn't sound stupid. That's the problem when somebody goes silent on you: it makes all the easy conversation suddenly seem lame, and you start casting about for a good reason to write.

> *I made the mistake of mentioning to my publisher that I'd had lunch with you. He asked me to find out if I could get an interview with you the next time you're in town.*

In fact, Ron hadn't mentioned the interview in weeks. But I was feeling desperate, and talking about business made me feel less exposed to personal rejection.

> *I'm sorry to mention it, and feel free to say no. I know how you feel about interviews. But I promised him I'd ask, so now I've gotten that out of the way.*
>
> *I really enjoyed our conversation over lunch and would much rather do that again. See you in January?*

Too desperate? It was a little early to start coming off as clingy. But I never have been able to pull off the tough dame bit, so I contented myself with changing the question mark to a period.

*See you in January.*

Much better. More confident, with an assumption of equality. Like we were *both* planning to meet in January; it wasn't just up to him.

I sent it, then did my best not to think about it for the rest of the day. Meetings, copyediting, the desperate search for a subject for my column—life goes on, with its way of diverting us. In the evening, I went to the gym. There's a man who's begun making eye contact with me in the weight room, smiling in that "misery loves company" way as we go through our workouts. If I smiled back, he'd start talking to me, and we'd become gym buddies. He wears a wedding ring, but that may not mean much. He's not bad looking and he's clearly been at this for a while, since he's lifting substantial weight and his muscle definition's good. But he's not one of the bodybuilders, just someone who stops in after work. A lawyer, I'd guess. I'm a little wary, but it's nice to think he might find me attractive. The weight room regulars have seen me at my worst, watched me grow in confidence and shrink in size. His smile strikes me as an acknowledgment of this, as if they're starting to accept me as one of them.

David was keeping late hours, but I found it kind of pleasant to have the apartment to myself in the evenings. I made a salad for dinner, then read or emailed Chloe until I dropped off to sleep. David usually crept in around ten, and I'd hear him moving around in the kitchen before he came to bed.

"Tough day?"

"Just long." He stretched out, groaned slightly. "I'll tell you about it in the morning."

Not that he ever does. Mornings are rushed. David sleeps until seven, but I'm up at five thirty and in a hurry to get to the gym. We might pass in the bathroom when I get back, as I grab a quick shower and dress for work, but there's no time for talk. It's an intricate ballet between sink, shower, and full-length mirror as we assemble ourselves for the coming day.

For me, the big question is always clothes: What's clean? What still fits? Can I get away with wearing this fat sack one more time, until I can get to the cleaner's? My size keeps changing, which is thrilling, but I wish my clothes would shrink with my body.

❧

The next morning, when I checked my email, there was Michael's reply:

*Dear Eva,*
    *Sorry, sorry, sorry. I should have been in touch, but I got back to find chaos breaking out everywhere—a crisis at the office, craziness at home. For a while, all*

*I wanted to do was turn around and drive back to the*
*airport and catch the next plane back to New York.*
*But I guess the best pleasures are deferred pleasures,*
*so I'll have to content myself with the thought of see-*
*ing you in January.*

*So your publisher wants an interview? Tell him*
*I'll do it, but only if he flies you out here. We can drive*
*up to the house, and I'll show you around. How does*
*that sound to you?*

*Michael*

I could feel my heart racing like I'd just finished thirty
minutes on the StairMaster. Has anyone ever studied the
aerobic value of arousal? Maybe that's the cure to America's obesity epidemic. We just need to go around exciting
each other, and we'll all stay thin. That would explain
how French women manage it.

I got up and walked down the hall to Ron's office,
found him tacking up photographs on a large piece of
cork board on the wall of his office so he could stand
back, look at them from across the room. I asked him,
once, why he did that. Don't people look at the photographs from about eighteen inches away? That's the
average distance from their eyes that a reader holds a
magazine. I could understand why he'd want to make
sure that the cover looks good from a distance, since you
want to make sure it'll catch people's eye as they walk
past the newsstand. But he does this with all the interior
photographs, too.

"You ever watch a couple read magazines in their

living room?" He picked up an old edition, opened it to a photo spread of a young movie star's New England retreat, held it up to me. "Honey, what do you think of this couch?" He tossed the magazine on his desk. "My ex-wife used to do that to me all the time. I'm in the next room, it's like from here to Staten Island, and she wants my opinion on the furniture. Anyway, if it looks good from a distance, chances are it'll look good up close."

Actually, in my experience that's rarely true. Things that look good from a distance can betray your hopes when you see them up close. Women know this from clothes shopping, and men. But I didn't want to burst Ron's bubble, especially when I was about to ask him for money.

"You still want that Foresman interview?"

He looked over at me, raised his eyebrows. "He's agreed to do it?"

"I'd have to fly out there, but he's offered to walk me through the house he's building."

"Can you bring a photographer?"

I hesitated. "I'll have to ask him. He's a private man. But he knows the kind of magazine we are, so I suspect he'll understand that we want photographs to go with the interview."

"If you can bring a photographer, then let's get you on a plane. We can scare up some file photos of his other projects."

I walked back to my office feeling a strange hollowness in my belly. It's excitement, but at this moment it feels oddly like the desire for a fresh-baked blueberry muffin sliced down the middle with butter melting on both halves.

> *Dear Michael,*
>     *Time for a reality check. Are you serious about the interview? If so, my publisher is ready to put me on a plane tomorrow.*
>     *Eva*

Actually, now that I think about it, what's the hurry? Ron wouldn't want to put it in our holiday edition, and we've got several weeks to our deadline for the January issue. I'll need to book a flight, find a hotel room, rent a car, and get some decent clothes that actually fit me. God, when was the last time I bought new underwear?

That thought brings me up short. Am I really thinking about buying new *underwear*? Lunch is one thing, and even acknowledging a mutual attraction could be harmless if we never acted on it. But if I'm buying sexy underwear, it can only be because I expect him to see it.

I sat at my desk thinking, *So that's it. You're going to sleep with him.* And I couldn't help feeling strangely relieved that the decision had been made. My mind and body seemed to have gone ahead without me.

Wasn't this why I'd been working my body so rigorously at the gym twice a day? So, go buy the silky nothings that California requires. Hide them away in a corner of your suitcase, where your conscience won't see them. By the time you put them on and stand before the mirror in your hotel room, picturing the excitement in Michael's eyes as, later that evening, your clothes fall away to reveal them, your excitement will silence your conscience. And when those silky nothings are tiny piles of fabric and lace on the floor beside the bed, it will be too late for anything but surrender.

The answer came back within minutes.

> *Dear Eva,*
>     *I've got an architectural photographer out here I like to use. Can I have her shoot the photos?*
>     *Book the flight. I can't wait to see you.*
>     *Michael*

But I'd like to lose a little more weight before getting on the plane. Am I being obsessive? Michael seemed to like what he saw, enough that he can't wait to see more.

Suddenly, it struck me with dreamlike clarity: *Don't go. Not yet. Let him come to you.*

Or go in January—and don't sleep with him. Do the interview, shoot the photos, but if he gets romantic, tell him you need to take it slowly. Then come home and finish your diet. Save the silky nothings for when you can buy them with confidence and take pleasure in wearing them. After all, look how far you've come just by flirting! You feel happy and energized. You've stuck to your diet, and you barely notice the hours at the gym. So why would you want to ruin it all by sleeping with the guy?

*Dear Michael,*
*Realistically, it'll have to be after the holidays. Everything's crazy here. Lots of last-minute changes . . .*

Like my mind—but I feel like I've thrown a huge weight off my shoulders.

Winter descends on me, cold as lost hope. Five days with not a pound lost. I'm working out like a madwoman, practicing enough fierce self-denial to qualify for martyrdom, and still the scale won't budge. Whatever I ate at those parties is sticking to me like batter on a baker's knife.

But I have much less body fat than last year, so I'm shivering all the time. I go to bed in two pairs of woolen socks, sweatpants, and an old Cornell sweatshirt I bought Chloe when she was looking at colleges. I wish I could hibernate: crawl into bed for the next three months and live off my stored body fat as I sleep through the winter months. Wake up in April, skinny and starving, ready to build that layer of body fat back up for next winter. It's a great system, if you think about it. No StairMaster or treadmill, no brutal self-denial. You lose weight as you sleep. And when you wake up, you can have pancakes.

It's bitter out and gray. I go to work and to the gym. As I sit at my desk, I fantasize about the sunlight in Los Angeles. I'll bet nobody thinks about hibernating out there. But how can I go? I'm a holiday cow.

No point in whining. Off to the gym.

# 134

Slow, painful progress. January still bites. And meanwhile I'm eating like a rabbit. The gym, which was crowded in those first days after the holidays, has thinned out. Last week I had to wait for a machine at six in the morning, as the holiday chubbies painfully tried to work off their guilt. But the New Year's resolutions are fading fast, and we're back to the hard-core fanatics.

Strange to think of myself in that club. But I catch myself glancing around, nodding at the other regulars with that smug expression that says, "Just us, again." And they nod back. The whole exchange takes place without a word, but it's clear to everyone what's being communicated: mutual acceptance, even respect. Your body may not be perfect, and you still couldn't be called an athlete, but you've put in your time. You're pure in your obsession, disciplined and self-denying. There's steel in your will, and you flex your muscles against the temptations of sleep and food and mindless television, like a guerrilla fighter crouched in the jungle watching the cities burn.

That's how it feels, anyway. But it would be nice if the scale moved.

# 132

had a dream last night that you were in bed with another guy."

I look up at David, surprised. It's the timing that surprises me, as much as anything. We're in bed, his hands moving over my body in the darkness, as if getting used to its new feel and shape.

I feel my body tensing up in the silence that follows. He's waiting for me to say something. So I ask, "How did that make you feel?"

"Excited."

Okay, that's not what I expected. Is this a trap? His way of feeling me out (while feeling me up) about whether I'm having an affair? Is this an anxiety response to my losing so much weight? Or is this really a fantasy he's exploring?

I've read that some husbands like to think about their wives with other men, but David's never mentioned it before. Is this something new? The way he's touching me, it's like my body feels strange to him. Maybe the unfamiliarity is exciting for him, like being in bed with a stranger. So he confirms it by imagining me with another man, whose pleasure in this new body reflects his own.

"Tell me about it," I whisper.

He does, in detail. The man's a stranger, somebody I've met on an airplane. Drinks, a hotel room. I'm a bad girl. Shameless. But it all pays off in the end.

It's exciting to listen to him whispering. I can hear the arousal in his voice, feel it in the urgency of his touch. I can't help but respond. But the violence of my response surprises me. It's like something that's been pent up within my body has suddenly been released, a confession he's wrung out of me.

When it's over, we lie there in the darkness, not speaking. I feel embarrassed, even a little angry. David gets up, goes into the bathroom. When he comes back, he hands me my flannel nightgown from off the floor.

"You okay?"

I nod. I'm grateful for the nightgown. My shoulders are cold.

David slides under the covers. "Pretty intense."

"Did you really have that dream," I ask him, "or were you making it up?"

"It was a real dream, but I had it last week."

"And you've been thinking about it ever since then?"

He shrugs. "I'm not brooding about it, if that's what you're asking. But it's stayed with me. I thought you might find it exciting."

I look over at him, cautious. "Well, I guess you were right."

He turns on his side and pulls the blankets up over his shoulder. "Sleep well."

And that's it. Within a few minutes he's sleeping peacefully. Was I reading too much into it? Could it just have been a dream? A guilty conscience makes everything an accusation. Still, all I've done is flirt and fantasize. Is that any more real than a dream?

So why can't I sleep?

❧

"You ought to write a diet book." Liz considers me with raised eyebrows, the way she might gaze upon a room whose decor she is evaluating. "You're an inspiration to us all."

I flash her a sharp look, and she smiles blandly. We're sitting with a group of professional women who meet for tea once a month at the Palm Court to network and gossip. Liz calls them "the Schmattas," since so many are in the fashion industry, and she insists that I attend with her. "It's professional development, sweetie. You've got to get out of your office sometimes, or you'll be stuck there forever."

I've never found the group the least bit useful. I call them the Fashion Bitches when I describe the scene to David. (Or to Michael now.) Every woman's outfit is examined closely as she enters, its defects quickly assessed. Mine, in particular, seem to excite sarcastic whispering whenever I follow Liz into the tearoom.

But today, Sharona Hallonnan, the self-appointed spokesperson for the fashionistas, leaned over to me after we'd taken our seats and said sweetly, "We've all just been commenting on how much weight you've lost. You *must* tell us your secret."

Not that any of them needs it. Toothpicks, all of them. When they walk, you can hear a sound like ice cubes in a glass. Liz says it's their bones knocking together.

I smile. "It's just watching what I eat and exercising. No great secret."

Out of the corner of my eye, I catch Liz pursing her lips, like she's not buying any false modesty today, thanks. That's when she's most dangerous, and sure enough, she hits me with the suggestion that I should write a diet book. It's clear she's got suspicions about why I've suddenly decided to lose all this weight. She's been sniffing around the subject for weeks now, like the smell's too sweet and there must be an open sewer grate somewhere.

"Really, it's a natural idea," she tells me now. "After all, your husband publishes diet books. It's like having a public platform, and the audience is always there. Won't you consider sharing the secrets of your success?"

Liz has never bought a diet book in her life. She sups on darkness and the souls of ex-boyfriends. It's a perfect low-carb diet.

What would she say if she knew the truth? It's not like she's ever spoken highly of David—or marriage, for that matter. Yet she's got an edge of the true believer about her, as if underneath all that cynicism, she could turn out to be a defender of the faith. It's not the idea of marriage she hates, just the idea of *other* people's marriages. But she'll never stop believing, as long as she lives alone.

I smile modestly at the Fashion Bitches, assuring them that, really, it's nothing, then sit quietly as the conversation turns to their traditional topics: the latest celebrity couture disaster, friends who've clearly had work done, and why men are threatened by smart, successful women.

It's too early for me to claim success. I've come a long way, but I still have to get through the last ten pounds. Besides, what kind of diet book could I write? One for married women, which begins *First, take a lover?* I smile. Even David would see the sales hook there.

"What are you smiling at?" Liz leans in close, whispering to me. "You look like the Cheshire Cat."

I shake my head: my little secret. But it's fun to imagine what I'd teach my readers. No "glycemic indexes" or "carb busters." I'd tell them how to find that old self hidden under the years of accumulated weariness. You're not just a wife and mom, I'd remind them; you're a woman with dreams and desires. That may not be easy, especially when those dreams and desires conflict with your family's needs, but denying them turns them into a weight around your heart.

Along with motivation, a diet book needs recipes and daily meal plans. Lay it all out for them so that even on their worst days, when they can't stop thinking about triple chocolate fudge cake, they've got an easy map to help them stay on the right path. Except my map would be all about wandering astray.

## Day One

### *Breakfast*
8 ounces nonfat yogurt
½ banana
1 outlandish-size takeout cup dark roast coffee
(with a shot of espresso to help you forget
you're dieting)

### *Midmorning Snack*
1 apple or 1 fresh red pepper, sliced

### *Lunch*
Grilled chicken breast
Salad, with 1 teaspoon low-fat balsamic vinaigrette
1 outlandish-size takeout cup dark roast coffee
(with a shot of espresso to help you resist
the impulse to wrestle the doughnut from
your coworker's hands)

### *Midafternoon Snack*
Skip it. Have more coffee and email your lover.
Think filthy thoughts.

### *Dinner*
1 serving crow, eaten in submissive posture. Ask
your husband about his day.
Grilled fish, no butter or oil
Steamed green vegetables (as much as you
like!)

### *Dessert*
3 prunes (Trust me. You'll need them. And have I mentioned the eight glasses of water?)

## Day Two

### *Breakfast*
8 ounces nonfat yogurt
½ banana
1 outlandish-size takeout cup dark roast yadda yadda yadda
1 Prozac

### *Midmorning Snack*
Celery sticks (as many as you like!), which you, the reader of this diet book, will want to shove up the author's skinny ass

### *Lunch*
6 ounces tuna in water, no mayo
Salad, with 1 teaspoon low-fat balsamic vinaigrette
Will you hurry it up with the goddamned coffee?!?

### *Midafternoon Snack*
Screw the email to your lover. You're too hungry to think about sex. Drink four glasses of water all at once. Pretend they're vodka.

### *Dinner*
A whole pack of raw mushrooms, which you were slicing for salads

Does your daughter still have a bag of Reese's
    Pieces hidden in her desk? (Gone. Shit.)
1 lean hamburger made from ground turkey
    breast, no bun
Steamed vegetables (all you like!)

*Dessert*
    6 prunes (now more than ever)

## Day Three

*Breakfast*
    You're kidding, right? Do I have to spell it
    out for you? And what's wrong with these
    damned prunes, anyway?

*Midmorning Snack*

You get the point: you have no life. Just the diet. Every
day, the same rituals of self-denial.

    Dieting is like a strict religion, which is probably why
Weight Watchers is so popular: without a community,
you're just a hermit having visions of chocolate sundaes
in the desert. But having a group of people who share
your righteousness makes the sacrifice seem easier. They
affirm you; they share your pain. And they help you remember the creed: *Pleasure is bad. Hunger is good.*

And did I mention the exercise? Twice a day, forty minutes each time. That means getting up at five to get to the gym before work, and then stopping on your way home from work, which means not eating dinner until eight. After that, you fall into bed, exhausted, because you've got to get up again the next morning at five.

On the upside, if you can get through the first five days, it gets easier. You have days when you float on a cloud of unknowing, like a mystic. You really can have visions just from hunger. Mostly they're visions of pizzas, but every now and then there's a moment when the world seems sharper, as if every person and object has been lit by some heavenly light. And your sex drive returns. At least mine did, but I give Michael credit for that. Would I really have survived that first week on the diet without his emails?

That's why my diet requires a lover: to keep you distracted from your hunger and focused on your goal: being naked without shame. Actually, maybe the Weight Watchers model could work well with this diet: combine it with a singles group, so that everybody pairs off with a flirtation partner. You'd never have to worry about people cheating on their diets, because everybody would be cheating on their spouses. In fact, that could be our slogan: *Cheat your way to a new you!* You'd have to keep them apart, though, until both partners had reached their weight goals. I'm thinking branches in distant cities, with all contact by email. You could set up chat rooms for those just getting started, where they could find compatible flirtation partners. Or, even better, *hire* trained flirts to pose as dieters in distant cities! One guy with great romantic chat could help thirty women lose weight. Like phone sex with weigh-ins.

Next, recipes. Every diet book includes recipes. That would be a challenge: it's hard to make a chicken breast sexy. Lowfat versions of seduction foods, maybe? Or just give the meals sexy names:

### Intimate Chicken

> 6 ounces Callebaut semisweet (dark) chocolate, broken into pieces
> ¼ cup low-fat milk or water
> 2 tablespoons sugar
> 1 tablespoon chili powder
> 1 teaspoon ground cumin
> 2 boneless, skinless chicken breasts
> 1 tablespoon chopped cilantro
> Lettuce, for garnish

Melt the broken chocolate and milk or water in a small heavy saucepan over low heat. Stir constantly. As the chocolate begins to melt, add the sugar, chili powder, and cumin for passion. Continue to stir slowly until ingredients are incorporated. (Additional liquid can be added as needed.) Set aside. Gaze at it longingly as you broil the chicken breasts, plain, then scatter chopped cilantro over them to give the illusion of flavor. Serve on a bed of lettuce.

And for dessert? Something very sexy needed here, to compensate for the simplicity of the chicken breasts.

### Voluptuous Pears
    7 pears
    3 tablespoons honey
    1 teaspoon fresh gingerroot, grated
    1 cup red wine
    Lettuce, for garnish

Preheat oven to 350° F.

Peel 6 of the pears. Place stem side up in a baking dish. Combine the honey and gingerroot. Drizzle over pears. Pour half the wine over pears. Cover tightly with foil and bake for 45 minutes or until pears are soft. Baste often with the remaining half cup wine. Remove foil and let pears cool in the pan.

Serve to husband on a bed of lettuce with pan juice poured over each pear. Slice the seventh pear and eat four thin pieces, imagining how good they'd taste in honey, ginger, and wine.

Entertaining? Need a quick, exotic, and sexy appetizer that won't ruin your diet? Try:

### Spicy Oysters
    2 tablespoons unsalted butter
    8 mushrooms, chopped
    2 cloves garlic, minced
    16 oysters
    4 ounces dry white wine
    1 teaspoon cumin

½ teaspoon low-sodium soy sauce
Lettuce, for garnish

Melt the butter in a skillet over medium-high heat, sauté the mushrooms and garlic for 2 to 3 minutes. Add the oysters and sauté for 3 minutes. Add the wine, cumin, and soy sauce and simmer for 1 minute.

Serve on a bed of lettuce.

How many calories are in an oyster, anyway? Not that it matters: you'll be eating the lettuce.

If you've got a good fish market in the neighborhood, the possibilities are endless. You can eat your lettuce coated with the juices of tilapia, monkfish, or pan-seared scallops. No fish market nearby? You can always get salmon at your local grocery's fish counter (farm-raised, color added). Then you can look forward to Pan-Roasted Salmon with Ginger, Poached Salmon with Mint, Sesame Salmon with Wasabi, Salmon Stroganoff, Salmon Strudel.

If you can't eat, you can still cook. And dream. Make the recipes sound sexy enough, and maybe you won't be tempted to sneak off to the Waffle Hut in the middle of the night. And eventually, if you can stick to the diet, the final dish might be *you.*

Served on a bed of lettuce.

With enough motivation to exercise, my readers would lose weight, even with the occasional oyster. But then there's the challenge of keeping it off. I'm trying not to think about all the statistics that say that most successful dieters regain all the weight within a year, that diets don't work. You have to change your life. You can't just stop eating, and even if you could, the body would adapt, metabolize more slowly, clinging to the fat like a bankrupt man counting his last few coins.

I've decided it's the exercise that really changes your body. People don't get fat because they eat: they get fat because they eat the wrong things—huge amounts of fat and sugar, the endless Happy Meal of American abundance—and then fail to burn it off. We're built to survive even when food is scarce, and fat is the body's savings plan.

So the trick isn't to starve yourself, or to find some magic formula of foods. It's finding the right balance of food and sweat. Marathon runners eat huge plates of pasta before a race because they need the fuel. That's why serious runners always look so smug at parties. They can eat anything they want, while the rest of us pick at the raw carrots and celery stalks. They find each other by the buffet at parties, where they load up their plates and stand there basking in collective envy while they talk about distance, times, and their endless injuries. Everybody hates them.

But that's because they've found the secret: if you eat it, you have to burn it. The problem is motivation. Running is hard, and the couch is soft. Who has the self-discipline to get to the gym twice a day?

Desire is what got me moving, desire burning like a fever in my blood. It's the thought of Michael's eyes moving over my body. I'm like a woman possessed by merry devils, with energy to burn. It's rare that I have to talk myself into exercising.

Yet I couldn't even tell you if what's happening with Michael is real. At times, it feels like love. Then the next day, I'm just as sure that nothing will come of it. But maybe that's what it takes: Not self-discipline, but self-deception. A mirage we can follow across the desert.

The Fashion Bitches are still chattering, and I glance at my watch, looking for a chance to get away. Several of these women are Liz's clients, and she sees these monthly teas as a chance to scare up business by encouraging the divorced women to tell their married friends what *fun* they're having now that they're on their own, going to all the parties and openings, redecorating their apartments, and just having the *best time*. She drags me along as cover, so we'll look like a couple of professional women out for an afternoon of social networking, rather than the relationship vultures we really are.

"Did you see Helen Delkowitz," she'll say in the cab afterward. "She's got that 'I'm going under' look they all get just before they decide to file the papers. I'll be doing her place this time next year."

And usually she's right. She's got a sharp eye for marriages in trouble; she can scan a crowded party and spot the next season's divorces, like an owl spotting mice from the top of a tree.

Am I starting to look like these women? They're all thin and angular, without the soft middle that happiness gives us. But it's their faces that scare me: hard and shiny, with merciless eyes. There's rage hidden behind those perfect smiling masks. And loneliness. They've achieved the ideal weight, worn the perfect clothes, bought the perfect furnishings for their perfect apartments, and still they can feel it all slipping through their fingers, as their husbands leave them for younger women and they watch their children harden into spoiled Upper East Side party kids. This wasn't what they'd pictured twenty years ago, when they were young women feasting on the city like a banquet. But then they'd fallen in love, and all the dreams turned to facts. That's where the disillusionment begins. Dreams always lie ahead of you; they keep you moving forward. Facts are the jungle firebase you have to defend against age and time and disappointment. And all the while, the sexy young girls keep pouring into the city, with hunger in their eyes. If you're not careful, they'll take your job, your husband, your carefully constructed life. They want to *be* you, not realizing that the dream is a trap, and it'll only be a matter of time before their faces become as hard and empty as yours.

The women have been chattering for almost ninety minutes. It should start to break up soon, and they'll all hurry off to their health clubs to burn off the tea sandwiches. Liz will invite me out for a drink, then rehash the whole event, carving up these women like lambs for a skewer. But I can't help feeling sorry for them today; now I see them as prisoners of their youthful dreams.

"Men all want to think they're the hero of the story,"

one woman is saying angrily. "And it terrifies them to think the story might not be about them."

There's a murmur of agreement. All their lives, these women have written their own scripts. Why couldn't their men respect that? Yet they all married investment bankers or litigators, heart surgeons or media moguls. Secretly, they want a man to cast a long shadow, so they can rest in his shade when it suits them. Then they complain when their men lie or cheat or simply don't listen. And now that most of them are single again, I don't see any of them dating public school teachers or poets. They like their men type A, because that's what they were taught to admire.

I lean over, whisper to Liz, "I'm going to take off."

She shoots me a look, like I've promised to watch her back and if I leave now, the knives will come out. But Liz can take care of herself. I've seen her blade work: it's quick and lethal. I pity the poor Fashion Bitch who takes her on.

I grab my coat and slip out from behind our table. "Bye, ladies," I call, with as much false cheer as I can summon. "Happy holidays!"

While they're still protesting that it can't be *that* late, I bolt for the door.

"Eva!" Liz calls.

She's gathering up her stuff: a bad sign. If she's leaving a prospective client, it means she's got something on her mind. With Liz, that's usually an interrogation.

I'm tempted to make a run for a taxi, but she's coming toward me now. I wait at the door.

Liz slips her arm through mine. "Let's go get a drink."

"Cranberry juice with sparkling water," I tell the waiter. Liz rolls her eyes at me, but I'm not going to let anything blow my weight back up, now that I'm getting so close. Liz has a martini.

"Look," she says when the waiter leaves, "there's no way to say this that won't sound ridiculous, so I'm just going to say it. David asked me to talk to you. He's worried about your marriage."

"Wait. David came to *you* to talk about our marriage?"

She nods solemnly, but I can see that she's enjoying this.

"How come he couldn't just talk to me?"

"I gather that's part of the problem. He feels that the two of you aren't talking enough lately."

A wave of irritation rushes through me. "I appreciate that you want to help, but he should know better than to go behind my back. If he's got something to say to me, he should say it to *me*."

"That's what I told him." She rests a hand on my arm. "Look, I don't think he was hoping I'd get involved. He just wanted to know if I could help him understand what's going on in your life at the moment." She looks at me closely. "Is there something going on I should know about?"

Now I'm angry. "Liz, if I thought there was something you should know about, I'd tell you. There are things about my life that I've been unhappy with for years, and I'm trying to change them. If David's finding that difficult—of if *you* are—then I'm sorry. But this is important to me, and I'm not going to let anyone sabotage it."

She stares at me, surprised. But just then the waiter arrives with our drinks, so we're left in an awkward moment of silence as he lays out two napkins, sets down our glasses, and asks if we'd like anything else.

"We're fine," Liz snaps, with the impatient tone she uses with all aspiring actors. "Just leave us alone." She waits until he leaves, then turns to me. "Do you really think I want to sabotage you? I'm *worried* about you!"

"Why? What am I doing that could make you worry? Losing weight? Exercising?" I shake my head. "When you're fat, everybody likes to tell you that you should lose weight. But when you actually start to do that, everybody wants you to eat. They don't want you to change; they want you the way you were. It's as if people feel threatened by the idea that I'm getting my life under control."

"Your life is under control? I wasn't sure, see, because your husband's telling your best friend that he thinks the marriage is in trouble."

"He really said that?"

She nods. "And he'd have to be really worried to say it to *me*."

She's right. If David's talking to her, it's serious. I've gotten used to their being polite to each other when they can't avoid a conversation, then expressing their distaste when they each get me alone. I'm the common element, the only point of contact. I can't imagine the two of them sitting down for a heart-to-heart.

"So are you going to tell me what he said?"

Liz tries to look somber, but I can see the satisfaction in her eyes. "He feels you're not communicating. That you've become so caught up in dieting and working out that the two of you don't really talk anymore. He says you've become like strangers who share a bed."

"And this is my fault."

"Well, it did sound a little one-sided to me."

"Did you say that to him?"

She smiles. "I told him to stop whining and take you to Paris to see Chloe."

"That might work." But I'm too angry to take any pleasure in the thought. What was he *thinking,* talking to Liz about our marriage? That's my job!

"I can't believe he said all that to you. He makes us sound like some awful Victorian couple passing each other on the stairs. We made love just last night!"

She waves the image away. "Please, that's more information than I need. Anyway, he came to see me on Tuesday. I told him to talk to you about his feelings. Anything after that is outside my knowledge."

So is that what David's dream was? His way of *talking about his feelings?*

"I'm so sick of men."

Liz looks at me, raises her eyebrows. "Yeah? You trying to tell me something?"

"I'm not coming out, if that's what you mean. I'm just

sick of always having to tiptoe around the fragile male ego."

Liz smiles. "I just grab their balls. That always seems to work."

"And look how well you're doing."

I regret it as soon as the words are out of my mouth. She stares at me for a long moment, then slowly lifts her martini glass and looks out across the room over its rim.

"I'm sorry," I say. "That was mean."

"No, darling. That was *bitchy.*" She turns her eyes on me with icy penetration. Then suddenly she smiles wickedly. "Maybe there's hope for you yet."

Church bells ring out across the city; crowds dance in the streets, and fathers lift their babies high to catch a glimpse of the long-awaited miracle. It's the World Series, the Final Four, and the Super Bowl all rolled into one.

David comes into the bathroom, alarmed by my cry. "What's wrong?"

I can only shake my head, tears in my eyes.

David looks down at the scale on which I'm standing. "Ah." Then he turns and walks out of the bathroom.

How long has it been? Well, before Chloe was born. I gained some weight when we first started trying to conceive her, having read that low body fat can inhibit conception. So *Reagan* was in the White House the last time I weighed less than 130 pounds. And, let's face it, I'm not talking about the glassy eyed Reagan of the last couple years. We're talking brush chopping, jeep driving, cowboy Ron, calling out in his best actor's voice, *Mr. Gorbachev, tear down this wall!*

*I weigh 129!* I step onto the scale three times just to confirm it. The numbers don't lie.

I'm not done, mind you. My goal's still ten pounds away, and everybody says the last ten pounds are the hardest. Like trying to peel away the final bits of fat clinging to the inside of your skin, layer by painful layer. So it's back to the gym with new determination: I'm a warrior, a freedom fighter, ready to take a sledge hammer to the last obstacle between me and a size 2.

What seems so momentous in the morning fades as the day goes on: work piles up, last-minute meetings, etc., etc. It's funny, I can't help thinking, what a feeling of accomplishment you get by losing weight, when really you aren't *doing* anything. Sure, I'm working out like a maniac, but I'm not graduating from college, getting a dream job, moving up in the world. It's the opposite of accomplishment, if you think about it. Negative aspiration, the desire to become *less* than you are.

Still, I feel so damn proud of myself. And I know that the number that looks so great today will make me feel like crap in a few months if I see it again on the way back up, so I spend ten extra minutes on the stair climber that evening to drive the terrifying thought away.

David's out tonight, having dinner with an agent. We've avoided each other since my conversation with Liz. If David thought that talking to her would get our marriage back on its feet, he was sadly mistaken. Instead we limp along, both of us pretending we don't notice something's deeply wrong. I catch him looking at me expectantly from time to time, as if he's waiting for me to say something. I let him wait. If he wants to talk, he knows where to find me.

Anyway, we're both busy. We get home late, so we usually end up eating separately. Whoever gets home first makes dinner and leaves a plate in the refrigerator. We're always polite to each other, expressing gratitude for the thoughtful gesture, observing that the dinner is particularly delicious. Still, it's a relief to know he won't be waiting for me at home tonight.

On the way home from the gym I stop at the Korean grocer for more salad greens. The elderly couple who run the place seem to spend their day bickering in Korean, but it's impossible to imagine one of them without the other. Is that what every marriage becomes? A long-running comedy of annoyance?

I bring my bags of salad up to the counter, and the old man looks at me with suspicion. "You not eat enough," he says, jabbing two fingers at me. "You too skinny!"

The woman scowls, then unleashes a torrent of Korean at her husband. Is she telling him to mind his own business, or accusing him of flirting with the customers? They're both shouting as I wait for him to ring up my purchase.

By her tone, I suspect she's telling him he's crazy, to shut up with the *too skinny. Isn't she in here every night buying salad?* What's he trying to do, drive away *all* their customers with his *too skinny?*

Suddenly she drops what she's doing, marches over, and pushes him out of the way to ring up my salad. He's the one shouting now, waving his hands, but she ignores him, snatches the money out of my hand, drops it in the cash drawer, and then slides the change back across the glass counter. Then she hisses something at him, and suddenly they're both smiling at me, as he takes a plastic bag from a roll under the counter, drops my bag of salad into it, and holds it out to me.

"Very good," she says, bobbing her head slightly. "Skinny very good."

And I realize that what I've heard is just a difference of opinion. One man's "too skinny" is his wife's "just right." For all I know, she's been dieting herself, bringing home bags of salad and steaming vegetables until he's almost ready to kill for a clay pot chicken. She starves, and he complains. After all these years, what else is there to talk about?

I eat my salad in front of an old movie: *Holiday*, with Katharine Hepburn and Cary Grant. I come in near the end, as he begins to realize he doesn't love her conservative sister, but rather Katharine, the free spirit who doesn't expect him to spend his life in an office like other men. He's too honorable to admit it, of course. He'll go through with the marriage, but the sister won't have it, won't run away to Europe with him to chase after a dream. She wants a hardworking banker like her father, a man who will buy her a big house where they never see each other except to go to church on Sunday. But he clings to his dream, and in the end it's Katharine who gets on the boat with him, a couple of free spirits whose marriage will never slip into silence and salads.

By the end, I'm in tears. What happens to those dreams of being different? No couple ever thinks they'll lose their way and end up like all those other couples who turn themselves into bill-paying machines and never speak of their dreams. So how does it happen? Is that just where time leads us?

I wash my plate, wander into David's study and switch on the computer. Challenge: Can I write to Michael without (a) going on sadly about the failure of our dreams, or (b) going on happily about my weight? Can I be a sane, caring (if slightly flirtatious) woman for once, and ask about his life instead of obsessing about my own?

*Dear Michael,*

Okay, so now what? While we chat about our lives, our jobs, and our children, we're avoiding the real subject: it's almost three weeks into the new year, and I still haven't booked my trip to L.A. He must think I'm insane. All that excitement about the interview and the photographer, then I back away like a spooked cat.

So why not go? Michael's willing, Ron's authorized it, and my weight's back in the Reagan era. All I have to do is book the flight.

I bring up a travel site and spend a few minutes pricing flights, hotels, rental cars. Ron's paying, so I don't have to take the red-eye or line up for a seat on a no-frills airline. Still, I'll be flying six hours for a two-day visit. Not much time to enjoy the sunshine—or act out some fantasy of a romance with Michael, especially if I'm already exhausted from the trip.

And Michael's coming to New York at the end of the month. Why not wait and see him first on my own turf?

I'm scared, I'll admit it. Not so much about what might happen, but about losing my motivation to change my life. If I let myself get involved with Michael, then he *becomes* my life, or at least part of it. He's no longer the fantasy that keeps me moving. The sweat is real, and the hunger. But it's the fantasy that helps me get through them. If I fly out to L.A., is that real, or is it fantasy?

*Dear Michael,*

The cursor blinks at me expectantly. Will the day come when I have nothing to say to him? Right now, I've got the opposite problem: too much to say, and no words to say it. Or rather, a fear that I'll use the wrong words, get the thought all twisted around so that he misunderstands. What I feel is more complicated than either fear or desire. It's both, and neither. I want to keep losing weight, keep going to the gym. I want to be this woman, thin and healthy, who follows her dreams instead of allowing life to overwhelm her. I'm afraid of losing focus, slipping back into my old self, fat and happy. So while I want to see Michael, that's not the *whole* truth.

*Dear Michael,*
    *I can't help feeling that I've been dishonest with you . . .*

At that moment, I hear David's key in the lock. I quickly shut down my email, and bring up a computer game. And that's how he finds me, the lonely wife playing solitaire.

# 128

And then, suddenly, Michael's back in New York. I knew he was coming, of course, and it became a distant landmark to measure my progress. *By late January I'll be ready to stand before him naked, unashamed.* But now it's *here,* and I realize that that exciting thought wasn't really an act I'd ever perform, but a goal. Shamelessness came to symbolize freedom from my embarrassment about my body as it grew over the years.

Do I really want to sleep with him? No. Okay, yes. But I'm like the man who plans a vacation all year, picturing himself driving a sports car along a coastal road, but when summer arrives, the sports car becomes unnecessary: it's the *freedom* he's been longing for, the wind in his hair, sunlight glittering on the ocean, a feeling of speed as he roars along the winding highway.

We seek ways to deceive ourselves into enduring our endless, painful, boring work, when really, it's the work that matters. *Being* thin isn't as important as *getting* thin: it's the daily discipline of going to the gym and eating healthy foods that's changing my life, not some look of desire in Michael's eyes when my clothes fall away.

So why does that thought leave me so excited? I can't help imagining it, now that I know he's here. We exchanged emails almost every day last week, then on Friday he added one brief line at the bottom of his that sent a wave of fear and excitement through me.

*You know I'll be there on Monday, right?*

We'd talked about his visit in general terms, but suddenly it seemed so real, so undeniable, so . . . well, *timely*.

David's out of town all week, at a book convention in Miami. He goes every year, and it struck me that I'd be taking him to the airport on Sunday night, around the same time Michael would be arriving from L.A. Like a scene from a French bedroom farce, the husband leaves from one gate while the lover arrives at the other. I could ask Michael for his arrival time, offer to meet him and drive him back into the city. But then I start to imagine the embarrassment if his flight came in early, or if David's departure were delayed, and a line of sweat breaks out along my spine. On second thought, maybe it would be better to send David off in a cab, stay away from the airport altogether.

So, on Sunday morning, while David packed, I complained of an upset stomach. I felt a little ridiculous, like a child trying to get out of going to school, but eventually he got the message and said there was no need for me to drive him to the airport; he could just as easily get a cab.

"You don't mind?" I vanished into the bathroom, calling out, "I think that might be best."

I suspect he was relieved; we'd both been dreading the drive. What would we say to each other? *Have a safe trip. Enjoy the warm weather, and try not to work too hard.* (That's a laugh. I've been to these conventions, which seemed to consist of lavish meals, going out for drinks, and talking with old friends among the display booths.)

The irony is that my stomach started to give me trouble as soon as he left. Nerves, probably. What would I have done if this had hit me on the way to the airport? Or, even worse, on the way *back*, with Michael sitting beside me? What if I was coming down with a stomach flu, putting me out of action the whole time Michael was in town? I almost laughed out loud. Just my luck. I'd probably start to feel better on Friday, just in time to pick up David at the airport.

But I was better Sunday evening, and when I got to the office this morning, I found an email from Michael waiting for me:

> *Hi, Eva.*
>    *I'm back in town, staying in the apartment. Any chance we could get together? I'll be busy all day, but I'm free this evening.*

So we're talking drinks or dinner. Or both. No safe escape back to our offices afterward, and no husband waiting for me at home. This is the real thing. I've got no more excuses.

I take a deep breath. *How about dinner? I know a great Spanish place in the Village. On Charles Street, near Seventh. 8:00?*

The Village is neutral ground, as far as we can get from his bed or mine. Then panic hits me: what will I *wear*? All my clothes are too large again. The things I bought with Liz are fine for work, but this is different. I'll have to slip out at lunch and buy something.

His answer comes back within ten minutes: *Sounds great. Here's my cell in case there's a problem.*

I hesitate before replying. Is it smart to give him *my* cell phone number? Am I risking a call at a bad moment, turning my back on David as I hurry to get off the phone without revealing anything? He'd know in a second that I'm hiding something. It's not like he wasn't suspicious already.

But it only makes sense. Michael may be late. Also, it's Monday, so the restaurant may not even be open. If he's got my cell we can quickly change our plans, so nobody's left waiting on the street.

*Thanks*, I write. *Here's my number. I'll be out of the office this afternoon, but I'll have my cell with me.*

I take care of a few urgent things on my desk, then walk down the hall to Ron's office, where I put a look of discomfort on my face then knock on his door.

"Yeah?"

I open the door, but he's on the phone. He covers the mouthpiece, looks up at me. "What is it?"

"I'm not feeling well," I say, trying to look pathetic. "Some kind of stomach bug. If it's all right with you, I'm going to head home."

He waves a hand in my direction, impatiently. "Sure, fine. See you tomorrow." Then he goes back to his conversation.

One more guilt to add to the growing list. That's the thing about adultery: you start to feel like a spider in a silken web of lies. One wrong step, and the whole thing could collapse beneath you.

No time to think about that, though—there's shopping to be done. A short black Reem Acra dress with a matching jacket leaps off the rack at me. There's lovely beadwork across the front, and just the right amount of cling to show off my new shape. Next I buy shoes that flatter my newly muscular calves. And finally, in a last plunge into the waters of my unstated intentions, a pair of lacy black French-cut underpants and a matching bra, the sexiest things I've ever bought. I carry my purchases home, trying not to think about how much I've just charged to my credit card, and try them on before the full-length mirror on our bathroom door.

It's an odd experience, like spying on a stranger. She's braver than me, ready to play the femme fatale in her sexy black underwear. My body's still not fully my own; or it's not the comfortable ready-to-wear body I'd grown used to in recent years. It's leaner, more muscular; a work of craftsmanship.

And I realize, as I unzip the slinky black dress and let it fall to the floor, what exactly this body is: it's a gift I've made, over many months of hard work, for Michael.

It's this moment of removing my clothing that has terrified and thrilled me; imagining the pleasure in his eyes excites me more than anything that might follow as he leads me to his bed.

It's five thirty, so I take a quick shower, then leave a message for David at his hotel in Miami. "Hi, it's me.

Just checking in to see how the conference is going. I'll be around for a couple more hours, then I'm going to go grab some dinner with Liz. We might go to a movie afterwards, so I'll have my phone shut off. Anyway, if I don't talk to you tonight, I'll give you a call in the morning."

Lies, lies. It's scary how good I'm getting at this.

But tonight may end in perfect innocence. We'll have dinner, maybe get a drink, then a quick hug, a kiss on the cheek, and I'll get a cab home. A nice evening, and nobody gets hurt.

*Condoms,* I think, in a sudden panic. *I meant to buy condoms.*

After all, a girl who goes out in a slinky dress and sexy underwear needs protection. I slip on a pair of jeans and a sweater to run out to Rite-Aid, where two young men are making the same purchase. Six o'clock is the condom hour, when the hopeful hit the drugstores before their dates.

I linger a short distance away, waiting until they've made their selection, then I slip into the aisle and confront the bewildering variety of choices. Latex, obviously, but which brand? All have pictures of smiling young couples on the box. There doesn't seem to be a brand for middle-aged adulterers. Lubricated? Probably not necessary, but why take chances? Extra sensitivity? Sounds good. Ribbed? (Hmm.) And they come in *sizes* now. How should I know? It's been twenty years. But then it occurs to me: if you're a woman buying condoms, always buy Large. It's an expression of confidence.

I carry the box up to the counter with the label pressed

against my leg. The clerk scans it without interest, drops it into a plastic bag, and tells me the total in a bored voice. I pay and hurry out of the store with the bag stuffed into my coat pocket.

*It's only six thirty,* I think when I get back to the apartment. *You've got his cell number. You could still call and cancel.*

Tell him you're sick, then stay home and watch an old movie. Eat popcorn. It suddenly sounds nice; safe and comforting. David will probably call when he gets back from dinner. We'd talk for a while, and he'd tell me about how crowded and ridiculous the convention has become this year, just as he does every year. Then I'd go to bed early and masturbate, thinking of Michael. Tomorrow I could return the dress, unworn. But I'd keep the underwear as a surprise for David when he got home. It might help put the spark back in our marriage.

But even as I think it, I'm reaching for the slinky black dress. *I'll just go to dinner. That's all; nothing else will happen.*

But I slip the condoms into my purse, just in case.

❧

"You look amazing."

Michael's waiting in the small entry area of the restaurant when I arrive. He helps me off with my coat then takes a moment to admire my dress. I've never worn something this nice—or this *expensive*—and I'd worried that I was overdoing it. Would he think I was one of those *Sex and the City* women who spends more on shoes than most people do on their mortgages? But it's clear from the way his eyes move across my body that he likes the dress. He's an architect, a man with a strong visual imagination. And for a moment, he's clearly using it.

Then the hostess takes my coat from him, and Michael touches my shoulder gently. "It's really nice to see you. I've been looking forward to this."

"Me, too."

He leans in to kiss me on the cheek and I do the same, only we both go for the same side, so we end up nose to nose. We both burst out laughing, and I say, "Well, that was graceful."

He smiles. "Let's try again. Without all the fancy moves."

And he kisses me. On the lips this time. He lingers just long enough to let me know he means business, then he draws back, and our eyes meet.

"That's better."

Yes, it is. No question about it. A lovely kiss, which I feel all the way to my lacy black underthings. What's surprising is how natural it feels, like something inevitable that's now behind us. I feel oddly relieved. Now we both know what tonight is going to be about.

The hostess reappears; our table is ready. We follow her through the crowded restaurant, everybody glancing up at us as we pass. Is it just me, or do they all seem to *know* I'm out with a man who's not my husband? They've seen him kiss me in the entrance. God, what if there's somebody I know here? It never even occurred to me, this far downtown, but Manhattan always turns into a small town just when you're hoping to be anonymous. Run out to the market for milk with your hair unwashed, and you'll see three ex-boyfriends, the catty receptionist at your office, and the immaculately tailored CEO of a hot media company with whom you just had a job interview. Kiss a man in a restaurant, and you're sure to find that half your husband's friends have developed a sudden craving for paella down in the Village, just in time to witness you tasting the forbidden fruit.

I'm being paranoid, I know. It's the price of being an adulteress. There's nobody we know here, and even if there were, it's not like he had his tongue down my throat. So he's an old boyfriend—what woman hasn't been there?

For me, paella is the food of the gods, served nightly in heaven. (Not that I'll ever get to taste it, the way I'm going.) I haven't dared order anything that rich for months, and it'll take me days in the gym to work it off. But tonight I'm throwing caution to the wind. It turns out Michael loves it also; he has stories of fabulous paellas eaten in Barcelona, Majorca, and tiny coastal villages in Portugal where the wine comes in clay jars with no label, the grapes crushed in great stone vats in the courtyard behind the restaurant. So we order paella for two and a bottle of Pagos Viejos.

"It means 'old debts,'" Michael tells me as the waiter fills my glass. "It's made by a little winery in Rioja. I was there two years ago, and a friend took me out to this little town called Logarno, where they make this." He raises his glass, goes through the whole routine of sloshing it around and then closing his eyes and putting his nose in the glass. Is he a wine snob? That could be annoying. But then he opens his eyes, sees me watching him, and smiles. "I never smell what all those wine guys say you should smell. Do you? My friend did this whole routine of smelling and describing. First in English, then in Spanish, to the vineyard's owner. It's twenty minutes before you ever taste the wine."

"What did he say about it?"

"He was talking about black and blue fruits, espresso, and floral elements. When he got to lead pencil shavings, I had to laugh."

I put my nose in the glass, close my eyes, and sniff. It smells like wine. "I read somewhere that the sense of smell is left over from when we used to go around on all fours. Our noses got small after we got up on two feet, because scent is only important if your nose stays close to the ground. Sitting in the park one day, after I read that, I started watching the dogs. They're all running around, dragging their owners on leashes, following these trails of scents from rock to tree. Think about how different the world would seem if you could smell all that. Like a whole other story going on, which we have no idea about."

"You think we've totally lost it? I don't know about you, but my memories are strongly connected to smells. Like the leather on a baseball glove. Or freshly cut grass."

I smile. "For me, it's suntan oil. I'm just a kid again when I smell that for the first time every summer."

"I always get aroused by the smell of patchouli, because all the sexy girls wore it when I was in high school."

He looks at me over his wineglass. "And I like the way you smell. Very much. What are you wearing?"

Oh my. I'm freshly scrubbed, but I didn't put on any perfume. "Nothing. It's all me."

He looks into my eyes, and I feel his gaze go through me like a jolt of electricity. This could get serious.

We drink our wine. Michael tells me more about his trip to Spain, and it's easy to imagine sitting on the patio of a café in a small country town as the afternoon slowly cools. Or spending the sun-baked hours after lunch under a ceiling fan in a hotel room, the sheets thrown back to let the breeze blow on our naked bodies as we find ever new ways to work up a sweat.

The wine is lovely, and before I know it my glass is empty. Michael refills it, and there's fresh-baked bread to dip into olive oil. When our paella arrives, even Michael is impressed. I'm in heaven. I haven't tasted food like this for six months. We have more wine to go with the paella, and by the time the waiter comes to collect our plates, the bottle is empty. The unaccustomed pleasures of the wine and the rich meal make me feel like my whole body is tingling.

Michael takes the check as soon as the waiter lays it on the table. "Let me get this. It's my treat."

"Not a chance," I say firmly, trying to take it from him. "You paid for my lunch last time."

He hangs onto it, smiling at me. "I'm on an expense account, and I've got a very generous entertainment budget." He gently releases my grip on the check, then laces his fingers through mine, an intimate gesture that sends a warm feeling spreading through me. "But if your pride won't let you accept my generosity," he says, "I'll let you imagine some pleasant way to pay me back."

I can think of a few right away. And from the look he gives me, it's clear he can see those thoughts on my face. He turns to look for the waiter with a new urgency.

When we get up from the table Michael takes my arm, and we walk out to the entry area for our coats.

On the street, the cold air hits me with surprising force. I start to shiver, and Michael puts an arm around my shoulders as he hails a cab. He gets me settled in the back, leans forward to give the driver the address, then sits back beside me. We look at each other without speaking for a moment, and then suddenly we're kissing, deeply, passionately, as the cab makes its way across town, headed for the Upper East Side.

'm so ashamed.

Four days without going to the gym or stepping on a scale. And the meals I've eaten! But, then, sex can be an excellent workout—and I feel like I've spent the last four days training for the Olympics.

For twenty years I've touched no one but David, and no one but David has touched me. It's strange and exciting to have this new pair of hands moving over my body. The tastes and smells are all different, too—like a banquet in an exotic land, where each dish looks familiar but the spices are strange and surprising.

Michael's body was both new and strangely familiar, and my own body felt the same. I heard my own cries as if at a distance, like waking in a hotel and hearing a woman surrendering to her pleasure in the next room. Was that *me*?

Yes, I was tipsy that first night. Filled with wine, rich food, and the excitement of kissing this man I barely knew in the back of a taxi speeding up Madison as all the lights turned green before us. My eyes were closed, and I was lost in the heat of his body. But as we crossed Thirty-fourth, he drew back with concern in his eyes.

"Do you have to get home? I could send him over to Broadway."

"David's away."

And that's all that was said. We kissed some more, and the city flew past. When we got to his building, he paid the cab and led me inside. In the elevator we stood side by side, our hands touching, watching the numbers rise, like two children waiting outside the principal's office. I used to fantasize about making love in an elevator, the way people do in the movies, until I learned that most elevators in New York have security cameras hidden in the ceilings. The last thing I want is some security guard seeing me with my skirt hitched up and my panties around my ankles. For all I know, it might end up on the internet.

When we reached the eighth floor, Michael led me quickly along the corridor to his door. He fumbled with the keys, his hands trembling with excitement. *He's as excited as you are,* I thought with surprise. That made me even more excited. It was hard to resist the impulse to grab the keys from his hand, push him out of the way, and unlock the door myself.

Inside, he pressed me against the wall to kiss me deeply. The keys were still in his hand and I could feel them digging into my arm, but I didn't care. How long had it been since anyone wanted me this passionately?

He started to undress me, his urgency exciting. His fingers found the buttons and zippers and clasps, released them, and my clothing fell away, revealing my sexy black underthings. He smiled. "Very nice," he murmured. Then he bent, picked me up, and I couldn't help laughing as he carried me off to the bedroom.

"Don't hurt yourself," I said, but it was beyond thrilling. Only a few months ago he would have landed in the emergency room if he'd tried to lift me; now I felt light in his arms.

He laid me on the bed, then stood over me peeling off his clothes. I watched him in the glittering light from the city's skyline. It had begun to snow. It felt like time had stopped, and we'd found a world where anything was possible. We could stay in bed for a week, watching the snow fall. We could run away together to some place warm, where the palms bent over a moonlit ocean.

And then he lay down beside me, naked, and we kissed. His hands moved across my body, and soon my sexy black underthings were gone and I stopped caring about the snow or the glittering city, or anything else but the feeling of our bodies moving together in the darkness. I was young again. Not far away, an ocean sang its quiet song.

*೪*

The next morning, I called in sick from Michael's apartment. My head felt like the bottom of a garbage chute, and somewhere under all the excitement, my heart beat unsteadily. I'd broken my marriage vows. What had I been thinking?

Michael was quiet, too. Was he thinking the same thing? Or was it just the wine? He made coffee, then went into the shower while it brewed. I got dressed and went into the kitchen. Nothing in the refrigerator except a carton of milk and a cup of yogurt; he probably ate his meals out. When the coffee finished brewing, I poured myself a cup. Michael was out of the shower now, moving around in the bedroom.

"Can I bring you some coffee?" I called.

"I'll be there in a minute."

I stood at the counter drinking my coffee and thinking about what had happened. The sex had been wonderful. Gentle and playful at first, but growing in intensity as things developed. My response surprised even me. "God, your neighbors must hate me," I'd whispered after one particularly embarrassing crescendo.

"There are no neighbors. Most of the apartments on this floor are owned by out-of-town corporations and professional firms for their executives to use when they're in town. I almost never hear anybody next door."

*Thank God for that.* It was embarrassing enough that Michael had heard me. But he seemed to enjoy it. Each time, he'd smile, kiss me deeply, and then set to work teaching me a new song.

This went on for hours. Just when I thought things might be drawing to a close, he'd find a new position, and we'd begin to build the pleasure between us again like some shining tower that rose until it pierced the clouds. I'd hang on as long as I could, but each time, I'd fall, crying out as I tumbled from that height to crash back into myself, breathless and gasping.

"No more," I finally told him. "It's your turn."

"But I'm enjoying myself."

"Well, it's time for you to let me have some of the fun."

I turned him on his back and took him in my mouth, experimenting until I found the rhythm that made him groan. It was different from David's rhythm, and I felt like an explorer discovering a new land.

Later, I slept naked in his arms. Deep, dreamless, exhausted sleep. And when I woke, it was with a feeling of surprise that there could be a day following such a night.

Michael came into the kitchen as I was pouring a second cup of coffee. He came up behind me, put his arms around me, and gently kissed my neck. "Tired?"

"What do you think?" My body felt like I'd just run ten miles, carrying a rider who kept spurring me to take the fences at a gallop. But there was also a tingling warmth spreading from between my legs as he kissed my neck. I set my coffee cup down on the counter, turned to face him, and found that he was aroused.

"Come back to bed," he whispered in my ear.

"Don't you have to get to work?"

"My first meeting's at ten. We've got a little time."

He led me back into the bedroom, where he removed my dress and my underthings and made love to me again. It was different this time, less languid, more urgent, but the result was the same. We finished together, lying exhausted in each other's arms.

"I have to get up," he said after a while, without much confidence.

"You're going to need another shower."

"Either that, or another box of condoms."

I didn't mention that I had my own supply. I was a little afraid he'd tell me to get them.

He quickly showered again, then offered to buy me breakfast at a coffee shop a block from his building. The idea of sitting there in my slinky black dress like the fallen woman I was seemed more than I could manage, so we parted on the sidewalk, getting into separate cabs. At home, I found a message from Liz on the answering machine. "Hey, sweetie. David's out of town, right? Are you out playing? I'm available if you want to get some dinner. Give me a call."

I hit the Erase button. The other message was from David, saying that he'd just come back from dinner and found my message, but he was on his way out to a club with some people from marketing and would probably be out late, so he'd try to reach me at the office in the morning. There was a strange tone to his voice. Was he upset to have called and found me out? Or was it just the wine he'd drunk at dinner, and I was feeling guilty?

It was too early to call him back, so I stripped off my clothes and crawled into bed to sleep.

A ringing phone woke me. I reached for the one on my bedside table, still half asleep, disoriented to be waking in the late afternoon light. "Hello?"

But there was no one on the line, and I could still hear it ringing. Only then did I realize it was my cell. My purse lay on the end of the bed, where I'd dropped it when I came in. *God, I hope it's not David,* I thought. I grabbed it, but naturally it stopped ringing just as I found it. Then I had to wait for the message to appear in my voice mail.

"Hi, it's Michael. Just wondered how you were doing. Any chance I could see you tonight? Give me a call on my cell. I've been thinking about you all day."

Those last words made something inside me liquefy. God, after all that sex, could I really be getting excited again? But just the thought of him sitting in his meetings thinking about what we did last night, imagining all the things he'd do to me the next time, set the juices flowing. I dug around in my purse for his cell number.

"Michael Foresman."

"Hi," I said. "I got your message."

"Hey there. You doing okay?"

"I'm fine. I slept most of the day."

"Good. So you'll have lots of energy tonight."

"What do you have in mind?"

"If I told you, it wouldn't be a surprise. Can I see you?"

I thought about playing hard to get. But let's face it, I wasn't. "Where do you want to meet?"

"I'll be done here around four thirty. Can you meet me at my place?"

I laughed. "You don't mess around."

"Nope. I'm all business."

"Are we going out? I'm just wondering what I should wear."

"Wear as little as possible." And he hung up.

I lay there for a moment, the phone resting on my

belly, imagining what he might have in mind. But that was too distracting, and I had to get ready if I was going to make it over there in an hour.

I took a shower, then tried to figure out what to wear. *As little as possible.* Easy for him to say. He didn't have three different size wardrobes hanging in his closet, most of them too big. I have a few office outfits that still fit me, and some casual stuff for weekends that I bought last month—jeans and sweaters, mostly—but nothing that seems to fit the occasion.

I stood in my closet, a large towel wrapped around me, gazing at the row of hangers in despair. Could I just go in the towel? That would excite him. But I grinned, imagining getting a cab. And what shoes do you wear with a towel?

I wandered into Chloe's room, to look in her closet. She's got lots of nice clothes, most of which she doesn't wear anymore. Fashion changes at lightning speed at her age, and something she wore constantly last the summer would now strike her as passé. And if she hadn't taken them to France, what were the chances she was ever going to wear them again? They'd be a year out of style by the time she gets home.

But most of them would have looked ridiculous on me. Everything was cut low at the waist and high at the midriff, and the skirts were tiny. I'd have been one of those women trying to look like they're still nineteen—mutton dressed as lamb. I was just about to give up when I spotted something at the back of her closet: a red silk Chinese dress that David had brought back for her from San Francisco. He'd forgotten her size, so he'd gotten it a size too large. It might almost fit me now. I held it up to myself in front of the mirror. It was awfully close.

I slid it off the hanger, unzipped it, then drop my towel and stepped carefully into the dress. It was snug, but not obscenely so, and the zipper went right up. I considered myself in the mirror: red silk and danger-ous curves. The dress was short, catching me at mid-thigh. It'd been a long time since I wanted to show off my legs, but they didn't look bad. *Cheongsam,* that's what they call this style: short sleeves, with a high man-darin collar, and a Chinese symbol impressed faintly in the silk.

That always gives me a little concern. When Chloe was in eighth grade, there was a vogue for these T-shirts you could buy at only one store in Chinatown, with a big Chinese symbol silk-screened on the front. She begged me to take her to get one, and I finally relented. A week later we were walking down Broadway and this Chinese woman stopped her and said, "Do you know what your shirt says?"

"What?"

"It's a slang word that translates loosely as 'stupid white girl.' "

Immediately after that Chloe gave the shirt to a girl at school who was snotty to her the year before. Knowledge is power.

God knew what this one said. For all I knew, it was the shirt's price. Or the size. Still, the dress looked good on me, and it was getting late.

I still hadn't called David. I'd been dreading it, but

to my relief, when I dialed his cell it rang through to his voice mail.

"Hi, it's me," I said as brightly as I could. "I guess you're in a meeting. Just thought I'd try to reach you while I had a chance. Ron asked me to go out to dinner with some of the advertisers tonight, so I'll have my phone off. I think he's hoping they won't ask about circulation figures if I'm there. Anyway, I hope everything's going well, and I'll try to reach you in the morning. Bye."

I hung up feeling disgusted with myself. But I had to hurry or I was going to be late. I found a pair of shoes that worked with the dress, grabbed my coat off the chair in the living room, and went downstairs to get a cab.

Since Michael had told me to wear as little as possible, I hadn't put on any underwear.

He was in for a nice surprise.

❧

The next day, I went back to work. It meant two cab fares as I dashed home to change, then a second cab to get to the office on time. Ron took one look at me and said, "You sure you should be here? You look like you've been through the mill."

I blushed. "I think I can manage. There's stuff I need to catch up on. If I feel sick again, I'll take the work home with me."

He nodded. "Listen, where do we stand with Foresman? You think he'll talk to you? I need to know if we should hold space in the next issue."

I must have blushed even deeper, because he looked at me with concern. "Do you need to sit down?"

I shook my head. "I just need to pin him down. I'll get on it today."

I walked back to my office. I'd spent most of the night trying to pin him down, using all my best wrestling moves. But since he was stronger, I always ended up flat on my back with my legs in the air.

Michael had enjoyed his surprise quite a bit, as I anticipated. And then later, after we ordered in Chinese food and ate it from the boxes in bed, he'd enjoyed it some more.

"Are you taking something?" I asked him at one point, surprised to find him ready so soon after our last wrestling match.

"What? Like Viagra?"

"Is that a bad question to ask? I'm just surprised by your . . . *enthusiasm.*"

He laughed. "Is that a complaint?"

"God, no. I may run out of sexy dresses, though."

"Like you ran out of underwear?" He ran a finger down my belly. "That'd be okay with me. Though it might surprise the doorman."

"You'll have to give him a nice tip."

"Wear whatever you like," he said. "It's not the clothes that get me excited. And I'm only going to take them off you, anyway."

Exactly what a girl likes to hear. So I showed him my appreciation, and generosity was its own reward.

In my office, I went through my voice mail—two messages from Liz, sounding annoyed—then dug my desk calendar from under a pile of papers, pulled up a travel website on my computer, and called Michael's cell. "It's Eva," I said when he answered. "Can I come out to L.A. to see your house next week?"

"Let me call my assistant and make sure that works with the schedule. Can I call you back in a few minutes?"

*An assistant to keep his schedule.* It shouldn't have surprised me; he's a busy guy. But it's easy to lose sight of someone's role in the world when you spend most of your time with him in bed. I looked around at my tiny, cluttered office, and for a moment I felt the world close in around me, like something I'd lost sight of in my desire.

Then my phone rang. It was Michael. "Next week looks fine. Do you want to come out on Friday, and we'll spend the weekend up at the house?"

"Won't your wife have some questions about that?"

There's a pause, then he says quietly, "You really want to have that conversation?"

He's never asked me about my marriage, and suddenly I'm grateful for that. He's respected my privacy, accepted me on my own terms. Shouldn't I do the same for him?

"Sorry. I didn't mean that the way it must have sounded. I just didn't want to create a problem for you."

"I appreciate that. But trust me, it won't be a problem. She has no interest in the house whatsoever. I'll tell her you're doing a story on it, and that'll be the end of it. We'll have the place to ourselves for the weekend. There's a spa in the valley below the house where Clark Gable and Lana Turner used to go. I'll see if I can get us a room. You can get a stone massage to ease the pain after I walk you all over my property."

"Sounds lovely. Can we get your photographer to come up for a few hours?"

"I'll check. She's pretty busy, but she'll usually make time for me."

"Mmm. I'm not surprised."

He laughed. "Don't worry. It's just business. So am I going to see you tonight? It's my last night in the city."

"You haven't had your fill of me?"

"Shouldn't that be my question?"

"I think there might be room for a little more."

"Good, because I've got big plans."

"Yeah? Like what?"

"Let's just say we'll both still be deeply ashamed of ourselves when we're eighty."

"Oh, my."

"Just want you to be prepared. Six?"

"I can't wait."

What could he have in mind? My imagination immediately began to offer up possibilities, each one more outrageous than the last. It was a clever little game he was playing with me. Imagination is half of sex, and mine was now working overtime, leaving me almost breathless with excitement. By the time I saw him, I'd be ready for anything.

As far as being ashamed of myself when I was eighty, that seemed inevitable. How could I *not* be ashamed? I was cheating on David, putting my marriage and family at risk. And it wasn't like I'd just slipped once—I'd spent the whole week surrendering to my basest urges.

But I was ready to live with my shame. I couldn't have stayed away from Michael that night if I'd tried. We'd spent three days having an unspeakable amount of sex, and I wasn't even close to being satisfied. Just the thought of seeing him again sent a wave of arousal through me, making it a challenge to finish the stack of work on my desk.

David called me in the afternoon and we went through the motions of a conversation, but it was clear he was in a hurry to get off the phone. "It's been crazy down here," he told me. "Dinners, cocktail parties, sales sessions. I haven't stopped for a moment."

"That's great," I told him, trying to keep the guilt out of my voice. "It's been crazy here, too."

He had to rush off to a reception for some regional book buyers but said he'd have lots to tell me when he got home.

"And I'll bet they're a wild bunch, those regional book buyers."

"You don't know the half of it."

"Well, have fun," I said. "I'll see you tomorrow."

*What a weird conversation,* I thought as I hung up. Like calling your parents from college. You know you have to call to assure them that you're doing fine, but all you can think about is how to get off quickly without being rude, because you don't know how to handle the fact that you've changed.

*Had* anything changed? True, I'd broken my wedding

vows. Shattered them, to be honest. And then taken a hammer to the fragments, reducing them to a fine powder that the wind blew away. But I wasn't planning to run away with Michael. He had his life and I had mine, and we'd probably just go on that way, finding ways to slip off and see each other every now and then.

Michael would fly home to L.A., David would fly back from Miami, and we'd go back to the way things were before this strange week of passion. No doubt David would want to make love to me, thinking about all those girls on South Beach with their perfect bodies and tiny bikinis as we went through the motions. But who was I to complain? I'd be thinking of Michael, or about the interesting differences between these two men who were so unalike and yet shared a claim on my heart.

I moved some papers around, replied to the most urgent emails, and tried to look like my mind was on my work. A few minutes before five, I slipped out to take a shower before meeting Michael. God only knew what he had in mind for me, but whatever it was, I was going to enjoy every second of it. I was in the shower when I heard my cell phone ring.

"Crap!" I shut off the water, grabbed a towel, and hurried into the bedroom, leaving a trail of wet footprints. What if it was Michael, calling to cancel our date?

"Some friend you are," Liz said. "I've left messages for you everywhere, but you've been too busy slutting it up while your husband's out of town to return my calls."

"Liz—"

"Just because you get the chance to play the party girl

for a few days doesn't mean you can just dump your oldest friend!"

"I'm sorry I didn't call you, but I—"

"And you're not fooling anyone with that innocent voice, Missy. I *know* you've been out on the town, I can smell it, even over the phone. I'm sitting at home like the poor stepsister, waiting for a call, and you're out partying with Puff Daddy!"

"What?" I laughed.

"You heard me, you vile slut! Where's the party? I demand to know!"

"I wish there were one, sweetie. I really do. But there's a famous architect in town, and Ron's been lusting after an interview for months. I've spent the whole week working on that."

"That's the most pathetic thing I've ever heard. Really, you can't come up with anything better than that? Your husband's out of town, and you expect me to believe you've spent the whole week talking architecture? I'm insulted that you think I'd be convinced by something that lame."

"Liz, I just got out of the shower, and I'm dripping all over the floor."

"I'll bet you're dripping. Is he handsome, this architect?"

I hesitated. "Well, yes. But he's got an elegant wife back in L.A."

"And you're dripping here."

"Liz, I'll call you tomorrow and tell you all about it. But right now I've got to get ready for this thing tonight."

"So you've got a *thing*. Is it a big thing?"

"*Bye*, Liz." I hung up, and quickly dressed in one of the few work outfits that fit me. Michael would assume I was coming from the office, anyway.

The amount I'd spent on cabs over the last three days . . . Cabs, clothes, and condoms—I'd been a very bad girl.

I take yet another cab the next morning, hurrying home to shower my ravished body and change my clothes before going to work.

To be honest, I'm relieved that it's all over, that Michael's leaving today. Too much sex, too much rich food, too many nights with too little sleep—I couldn't have kept this up much longer. While I've been getting quite a workout, it's not the same as going to the gym. It took a lot of courage to step on the scale this morning, but there was no point hiding from the truth. Three pounds gained: a setback but not a disaster.

I'm sore, and I feel like I've been stretched on a rack. Actually, that's not far from the truth. I spent much of the evening blindfolded, my hands and feet tied to the bedposts. It turns out Michael has a wicked streak, and I have a taste for bondage games. Who knew?

I get dressed and go to work, just as I always do. I feel strangely calmer now, as if a violent storm has passed over, sweeping the sky clear of clouds. It's funny, but I'm even looking forward to seeing David tonight. I always enjoy the first couple of days when he comes back from a trip. He's tired but also energized by having gotten away, seen other people, gone to parties, remembered what it's like to be alone in the world.

Before a trip, he grows jumpy and impatient: he's

bored with his daily life, and with me, so the thought of
having some time on his own sounds exciting. He can't
wait to get away. By the time he comes home, he's so-
bered up, remembering what it's like to spend all your
time talking to people you don't really know and quickly
start to find annoying. David actually hates these conventions, but every year, he only remembers this after
he's been there a day or two. He finds hotels depressing,
and even the parties start to seem like a bad first date
multiplied by several hundred drunken strangers.

So he's always glad to see me when he gets off the
plane, and he spends the ride back into Manhattan saying how ridiculous the convention was and what a relief
it is to be home. Maybe that's what every marriage needs:
a periodic reminder that you chose this life for a reason.
When you've been married a while, it's easy to convince
yourself that the world is full of attractive strangers and
lively parties. But when you get out into it for a few days,
you realize that's just the shimmer of water in a parched
desert landscape. It's better to stick close to the well, you
decide, where you can drop your bucket and always hear
a splash.

So he'll tell me his stories, and I'll laugh at how ridiculous he makes it all sound. When we get home I'll
make us dinner while he unpacks, and we'll go to sleep
early, enjoying the feeling of curling up together in our
own bed. You can take only so much excitement, and I'm
looking forward to some rest.

That's how I imagine it, anyway. In fact, David's flight
is delayed, and he comes off the plane in a foul mood.
I watch him walk up the concourse in a crowd of other

publishing types, all looking worn out and irritable. Some years they're like kids returning home from camp, all laughing and chatting as they get off the plane, as if the flight back to New York was just another party. This year they look like a group of commuters at the end of a bad day, each silently carrying his own burden of anger.

I feel a sudden moment of panic. *Does he know?* Has somebody seen me with Michael and called him? A ridiculous fear, I know; it's just my guilt coming out. But for a moment, I have to fight off an impulse to turn and run.

I smile and wave, like a good wife welcoming her husband home at the end of his journey. I've been at work at my loom, my bright smile says, weaving and unweaving, my heart faithful to the end.

He sees me and nods sullenly. My heart sinks.

"Hey, there." We exchange a perfunctory kiss, and he sets down his carry-on wearily. "You look like you had a rough trip."

"Don't ask," he says. "It's useful to be reminded sometimes just how little you matter to anyone."

I raise my eyebrows. "What's that mean?"

"Just a delightful flight." He shoots an angry glance down the concourse. "Like riding in a cattle car."

"Well, you're home now." I take his carry-on, slip my arm through his. "It gets better from here on out."

And that's honestly my intention. I'm going to be a loving, patient, understanding wife, devoted to his needs. Suddenly it all seems possible. Why can't I be the ideal wife to David and still slip off occasionally to see Michael? Just knowing that I have a lover waiting for me will make me less impatient and short-tempered with David, and

the guilt after a few days with Michael will bring me
home ready to be the devoted helpmate. It could be a
perfect system, as long as I can keep my strength up.

We take the escalator down to the baggage claim area,
then wait by the carousel with the rest of the passengers
from his flight. David exchanges nods with several people he knows, but nobody seems eager to start up a conversation. *They're all in a bad mood,* I realize with relief. *It's
got nothing to do with you.*

Then I see a familiar face at the other end of the carousel. "Isn't that one of your authors?"

David looks. "Where?"

"Down at the end, there." I point to an attractive
woman of about my age standing very close to where the
bags emerge, staring at the conveyor belt like she's trying
to make her suitcase appear by sheer force of will. "Isn't
that Maribel Steinberg?"

David stiffens slightly. "Christ, I didn't realize she was
on my flight." He pushes my hand down. "Don't point,
okay? I can't face her right now."

"Was she at the convention?"

"Yeah. We had her doing some events to promote the
book. They didn't go so well, and I'd just like to forget
about the whole thing."

"What happened?"

He shakes his head. "I'll tell you later, okay? Right
now I just want to get out of here."

I look over at her. She looks exhausted and depressed.
Like a woman going home to an empty apartment at the
end of a long day, where she'll feed her cats and crawl
into bed to watch TV. I can't imagine that it would be

hard to promote a diet book. Just show up, be thin, and promise that your book will make it easy for anyone to achieve their weight goals. Had she been seen pigging out at a party? Had the Fat Liberation Brigade shown up at her book signing throwing potato salad? Had she just burst into tears with no warning, unable to take the pressure to be thin one more minute?

She glances up at me, then looks quickly away. A moment later she spots her bag coming down the conveyor, seizes it, and hurries off on her lethal heels, the suitcase rolling along behind her like an obedient dog.

"Must be quite a story. She took off out of here like somebody lit her fuse."

"There's my bag." David grabs his suitcase as it passes, and we walk out to the short-term parking. "How was everything here?"

I shrug. "Same old same old. Liz is mad at me because I didn't spend the week partying with her. Oh, and Ron wants me to go to California next week to interview this architect."

"How long will you be gone?"

"Couple of days. I'll fly out there, do the interview, and get a local photographer to shoot some pictures of this house he's building. Right now it looks like Friday to Monday. That's the only time we can get him away from his other projects."

David shudders as we step out into the cold. "I'm glad you'll get a chance to get some sun. I felt guilty the whole time I was in Miami, thinking about you freezing up here."

"I found ways to stay warm."

He looks over at me. "You didn't spend the whole time in the gym, I hope."

I laugh. "No, I'm not that crazy. I spent most of the week in bed. There were some nice old movies on. Fred and Ginger, Hepburn and Tracy. I was fine."

"An orgy of romance." David smiles. "Well, I'm glad you had fun." He opens the trunk of our car and heaves his bag into it. "That way I don't have to feel so guilty about all the great meals."

"I don't want to know," I told him. "I'd probably gain weight just hearing about them."

He's quiet as we drive back into the city, gazing out at the lights. He looks tired. But that's a relief; he doesn't seem to have noticed how tired I look.

He glances over at me. "You hear from Chloe?"

"She's traveling in Provence with a friend this week. She'll call and tell us all about it on Sunday."

He nods and goes back to gazing out the window, so I put on the radio, and we listen to a Billie Holiday retrospective all the way into Manhattan: "This Year's Kisses," "I Must Have That Man!" "Foolin' Myself," "I'll Never Be the Same."

I drop David at the door to our building with his suitcase, then take the car back to the parking garage. It's three blocks away, but the walk feels nice. There's a dampness in the bitter air, so I pull my coat tight, feeling for the first time in days that I know exactly what I'm doing. It's a cold night, and I'm going home. That's an impulse that requires no explanation. A moment later, it begins to snow. Big, wet flakes that come down through the lights like stars falling out of the night sky. When I stop and look up, the stark beauty of it makes me dizzy. For a moment, I feel like I could float away into all that empty space.

Then the light changes, and I hurry across Broadway. David will be hungry, and I need to get his dinner on the table.

# 129

You never told me what happened with your author."

David looks up at me, surprised. It's been three days since he got back from Miami, and he's started joining me at the gym in the evenings. Right now we're taking turns on a weight machine, so he keeps having to crouch down and change the weights before he uses it, then back to the right weight for me.

"What author?" He straightens, grasps the pull-down handles just above his head, and draws them slowly down toward his chest.

"Maribel Steinberg."

I wait while he finishes his repetitions then steps back. "Oh, that. It was just a comedy of errors. We had set up a signing for her at a bookstore in a suburban mall, and the local rep kept telling us what a big crowd they expected. So we drive out there on Wednesday night, and we find that the store has advertised the wrong time.

There's boxes of her book in their storeroom waiting to be signed, but no customers."

"How'd she handle that?"

He resets the weights for me and I grasp the bar, take a deep breath, and pull.

"Fine. She signed some books for them, then we went out to dinner. It's just embarrassing."

I finish my reps, let the weights drop with a clang. "The way she took off at the airport, it looked like she might be angry."

"If she was, she didn't tell me." He moves over to the next machine and sets the weights. "Authors always take that stuff personally. Like it reflects badly on them, instead of on the store. They're always hoping to find a crowd of fans waiting for them, like they just won the Oscar or something. It's hard for them to be realistic about the kind of publicity we can get them."

He's made this speech before; it's one of his favorite complaints about his job. But this time there's something false about it; he's talking just a little too fast. I look at his face, but he's sliding under the weights now, starting his lift. He grimaces, eyes fixed on the ceiling, as if he's trying to read some message hidden among the tiles.

"She's pretty," I say.

He finishes, lets the weights drop. "Maribel?" He shrugs. "Sure, I guess. Not really my type. She takes it all a little too seriously, you know what I mean? It's just a diet book, but she acts like she's written her autobiography, put her heart and soul into it. It's practically a religion for her. She really seems to think she can change people's lives by telling them how to lose a little weight." He looks over at me, realizing I might take this wrong. "I mean, you've lost a lot of weight and you look great, but that's all it is. You're working out, getting in shape. It's not like you've changed who you *are*, right?"

We're standing by the weight machine in a crowded gym, both of us sweating hard. Is this really the time to have a heart-to-heart about changing my life? But I can't let this slide; it's too important.

"I'm not so sure," I tell him. "Can you change everything you do without changing who you are? It's not just that I stopped eating certain things and started coming to the gym. I made a decision to change, and I live that decision every day. So am I really the same person who used to come home from work, order pizza, and watch TV? If you suddenly picked up and moved to Paris and spoke only French and took up painting, would you be the same person?"

"I'd be the same person living a different life."

"What's the difference?"

"I'd have the same body and the same memories. I'd just spend my time doing different things."

A guy in spandex workout gear comes up and, says, "Excuse me, are you two using this machine?"

"Sorry. Go ahead." David moves away from the machine. "You want some water?" He goes over to the watercooler and brings us both back a paper cup full of water. We stand there in silence, drinking them down.

"So you really feel like a different person?" He crumples his cup and tosses it into the garbage.

"It's complicated. In a way, I want to be a different person. But at the same time, that's a really scary idea."

"How different?"

I look at him. "That sounds like a big question."

"Maybe. What are we talking about here?"

"I don't know. We started out talking about Maribel Steinberg."

He's silent for a moment, watching the guys doing curls with the massive free weights over in front of the mirror. Their muscles bulge under their tiny shirts. "Those guys, the serious weightlifters, half of them started out as the fat kids who got picked on in grade school. You think they feel like the same person now?"

"The way people see you affects your personality. Ask any woman who's lost a lot of weight. People respond to you differently, and so you start to see yourself differently."

He looks at me. "I still feel like I'm twenty-eight, but people look at me like I'm forty-six. Didn't you still feel like a thin woman after you got heavy?"

"Sure, but it didn't last. After a while you get self-conscious about your body because you notice how people look at you. There were things I might have said or done when I was skinny that I wouldn't say or do when I got fat. I still thought them, but I would have felt ridiculous saying them."

"Really? It changed what you'd say to people?"

I nod. "And after a while, you stop thinking those things. You think about the things you *can* say, instead. You make more jokes. You don't talk about food or clothes or sex the same way. So if it changes the way you think, isn't that a pretty basic personality change?"

He looks away. "Looks like we can get back on the weight machine now."

We continue our workout in silence. I feel like we got close to something important but both of us lost our courage. It's not that I want to tell him what's been happening to me; the idea terrifies me. But I feel that he should know that *something's* been happening, or what's the point of our being married?

A big question. And also terrifying.

But I also sense that he's got things to say, too. Clearly, my diet has weighed on his mind. He keeps getting close to a serious conversation about it, then backing away. All this talk about personality change can't be just an abstract question. Why can't he talk about what's really bothering him? Why all this dancing around the subject?

The answer is obvious. Whatever he's thinking, he's afraid that saying it will make it real.

And he's probably right. Could we really go back to the way things were if we spoke our minds?

No. Not now, after what I've done.

"So, what are we doing today?"

"Cut it short," I tell Carlo firmly. "I want to look like Winona Ryder."

He looks at me in surprise. *"Really?"*

I can't help smiling. He looks like a little boy who's been begging his mother for a toy for months and can't quite believe it when she finally says yes.

"I'm ready for a change. Let's do it."

He grins, reaches for his scissors. "Honey, you just made my day."

I take a deep breath and close my eyes. I can hear his scissors go to work just beneath my right ear. I imagine the look on Michael's face when he next sees me walking toward him in the warm California sunlight. Will he even recognize me, or will he see—just for a moment— that girl he knew in Florida with her short hair and her easy smile? I hold on to that thought as Carlo works his terrifying magic. When he's finally done, he steps back, switches off his blow-dryer, and for a long moment there is only silence.

"Open your eyes," he says.

✑

"Who is he?" Liz demands when she sees me at lunch that day.

"Who?"

"Nobody makes all these changes for her *husband.*" She purses her lips and studies my new haircut. "It's a whole new Eva. You look like you just ate the apple."

I barely recognized myself when I saw what Carlo had done. My hair, which had hung limp and exhausted that morning, now curled over my ears in a cute bob that ended at the middle of my neck. I couldn't resist touching it, brushing my fingers across the soft ends.

We're sitting on a retro couch in an attitude bar called 1972, on Ninth Avenue. All the furniture looks like it came out of somebody's suburban rec room, and they play music only from that year—"Layla," "A Horse with No Name," "Lean on Me," "Heart of Gold," and "The First Time Ever I Saw Your Face." Later in the evening, Liz tells me, a D.J. will start spinning scratchy old record albums like *Exile on Main Street, Eat a Peach, Can't Buy a Thrill, Catch Bull at Four, Harvest, Close to the Edge,* Nick Drake's *Pink Moon* (which, to my surprise, came back like a shy ghost as a car commercial a few years ago), *Thick as a Brick*, and *Catch a Fire*. Except for us, the customers all look under twenty-five. It's pure cultural nostalgia for them, but I *remember* these songs. It's almost painful.

Liz considers me while the waiter brings our drinks. He's ridiculously handsome, the kind of boy who ought to be advertising underwear on a Times Square billboard, except that his hair is long and straight, like he's just gotten off a bus from Wichita. "So let's have it. Who is he?"

"Have you considered that maybe I'm doing it for myself?"

"Yeah, right. And if you think happy thoughts, you can fly to Neverland." She sips her drink. "Seriously, kid. You look great. Twenty years younger."

I'm thrilled. "Thank you, Liz. I feel it."

"I'm happy for you." She looks off across the room.

"Have I mentioned that I've decided to become a lesbian?"

"You're kidding, right?"

"Let's just say I'm studying the idea. I did an informational interview last week with this NYU student who's interested in a career in design. Cute girl; one of my clients is her aunt. I happened to mention that my clients are mostly recently divorced women who put all their disappointments with men into redecorating their apartments, and she looked at me with complete innocence and said, 'So why don't they sleep with women?' " Liz shakes her head in wonder. "Like it's the most obvious idea in the world. And then it occurred to me, it *is* the most obvious idea in the world. Women my age are stuck in a seller's market if we keep trying to date men. We're all trying to buy the same rare commodity, so the price keeps going up, and pretty soon you can't get your broker on the phone."

"I'm not even going to ask what that means."

"But the city's full of attractive single women," she goes on. "If we could get organized and start dating each other, we'd have the system beat. This girl was telling me that girls her age all sleep with each other now. If you can't find a guy on Friday night, you just call up one of your friends, and the two of you have a lovely time."

I can't help smiling. "The children will show us the way."

"Damn right. I'll bet Chloe's doing it."

"Please." I raise a hand to stop her. "I don't want to know anything about Chloe's sex life. That's her business."

"But you get my point, right? It's simple economics."

"And if you're lucky, you can share clothes."

She looks at me with an appraising eye. "That's a new outfit."

"Yeah, I went shopping yesterday. My size changed again. I seem to spend more time shopping for clothes for work than I do working."

Liz is silent for a moment. "Maybe it's time to stop."

"Almost. I've got a few more pounds to go."

She looks at my cranberry and seltzer, then brings her eyes up to my face. "Seriously, you look great, kid. You can stop now."

"Another month. I've come this far, I might as well finish."

"Does Chloe know?"

I look at her in surprise. "She knows I've been dieting. Why?"

"Could be kind of surprising to come home and find your mother's changed her life."

"I think she'll be proud of me."

"I'm sure she will. Until you start wearing her clothes and dating her boyfriends."

I have to laugh. "A minute ago you were telling me she's gay."

"Not gay, just flexible. Creative solutions to the problem of diminished expectations."

"So when did we start competing for the same guys?" I shake my head, amused. "Anyway, I'm married."

"Mmm. So I hear."

That's how it goes with Liz. Around and around,

nothing ever fixed in place until she decides it's time for the music to stop. I could find it irritating, except that we've been playing this game for so many years. It's almost comforting, unchanging when the world has begun to spin faster.

"I'm going out to California this weekend."

"Yeah? Business or pleasure?"

"I have to interview an architect. But it'll be nice to get some sun for a couple days."

"Bringing our bikini, are we?"

"I don't think I'll get much beach time. Maybe I'll rent a convertible and put the top down."

She makes a face. A dedicated New Yorker, Liz rarely leaves the city, and then only for the Hamptons. One of her wealthy clients will usually invite her out for a weekend, and she'll spend the whole time counting the hours until she can get back. Manhattan is her magic kingdom: it may not make your dreams come true, but there are always new stars to wish upon.

"Do they have architecture in California?"

"Apparently. They have architects."

"And you couldn't find one here worth interviewing?"

"Our readers don't want to know about New York architects. They're only interested in houses."

"And what are you interested in?" She raises her eyebrows. "Or is being thin its own reward?"

They're playing "The Candy Man" now. I pick up a printed card on the table and look at the list of fun facts about 1972. "Did you know that Eminem was born in 1972? And Snoop Doggy Dogg?"

Liz rolls her eyes. "Within three days of each other, I know. It was an epic week. I've read it."

"Other events in 1972 included the opening of the twin towers of the World Trade Center, the first recombinant DNA, Nixon's trip to China, the SALT I treaty, the shooting of George Wallace, the murder trial of Angela Davis, the election of Juan Perón as president of Argentina, the Munich massacre, Mark Spitz's seven gold medals in swimming, the withdrawal of the last U.S. ground troops from Vietnam, Bobby Fischer's chess match with Boris Spassky, the Watergate break-in, Nixon's reelection, and the Dow Jones Industrial Average breaking one thousand for the first time."

"And they found that Japanese soldier still hiding in the jungle." Liz reaches over and takes the card out of my hand. "If you keep reading, you'll get to the fact that the big movies were *The Godfather, Cabaret,* and *Deliverance,* and that *M\*A\*S\*H* premiered on TV. Fascinating stuff, but I'm more interested in what's happening right now."

"Have you ever eaten the same thing every day for six months? It's not that exciting."

"Are we talking about your diet or your marriage?"

"You seem to think they're the same thing."

"That's probably why I'm not married. But, then, I'm not fat, either." She looks at me and her face gets serious. "There's a difference between eating the same thing every day and starving."

"You're saying I should shut up and be grateful for what I have?"

"No, I'm saying you shouldn't take it for granted. There are people out there who are hungry."

We sit in silence for a while. Then "I Am Woman" comes on the sound system, and we both roll our eyes.

"Don't you just hate irony?" Liz asks.

Before I know it, it's Friday. David's got meetings all day, so we say goodbye over breakfast and he heads off to work, leaving me to my frantic last-minute packing: slinky black dress, sexy black underthings, good shoes for the fancy restaurant at the spa. Red silk cheongsam, box of condoms, but also a box of tampons, since my period's due any day—and what could be more inconvenient and inevitable than having it start just as I'm getting off the plane in L.A.? We're also going to be walking Michael's property, so I throw in jeans, T-shirts, and a pair of sneakers. What do you wear to get a stone massage? The spa probably has fluffy robes, like in all the brochures, but I throw in a pair of gym shorts just in case. Maybe they'll have a gym and I'll get a chance to work out between all the architecture, sex, and stone massages. Oh, and a miniature tape recorder, for our interview.

I picture us sitting on some rocks on a sunlit hillside as I ask him the questions I've prepared, a bottle of wine and a soft cheese beside us. Or maybe in bed, both of us naked, Michael stretched out with his hands behind his head, gazing up at the ceiling as he thinks over my questions, gives his carefully formulated answers. I'll be sitting up, leaning against the headboard, my notes open on my lap.

Then it strikes me that maybe that's not the most flattering position for a naked woman in her early forties, even one who goes to the gym every day, so I quickly put robes on both of us. We're just back from our massages. *Interview first,* I insist, *then we can make love.* Michael agrees, but his eyes keep wandering over to me, and his increasing desire adds a playful tone to his answers, until finally he reaches over, takes the notes from my lap, and tosses them onto the floor. But he forgets the recorder, and it captures everything that follows, forgotten until it suddenly clicks off forty minutes later, as we lie there catching our breath.

Michael laughs, says, "Does that answer your question?"

And a few days later, as I'm transcribing the tape, I reach that point in the tape and sit stiffly under my headphones, riveted by the sounds of our lovemaking, reliving it with every moan, every creak of the luxurious king-size bed.

Would I be able to make myself erase the tape? Or would I be tempted to keep it, hiding it away to listen to when I want to masturbate, like some furtive teenage boy with *Playboy* magazines under the bed? The idea is both exciting and terrifying. What if David found it? The first third of the tape would be boring, just an interview.

But what if he kept listening, until he heard my notes hit the floor and all questions definitively answered? The thought fills me with shame, but even more shamefully with excitement. When I was younger I used to have a secret fantasy about being caught in the act, exposed, a curtain suddenly thrown back to let a crowd see everything. In the fantasy, my lover didn't notice or was too caught up in the act to care, and I, teetering right on the edge of climax, couldn't help having a thundering orgasm as the audience of teachers, relatives, and close family friends looked on.

What's it say about me that I've got this secret exhibitionist streak? Is it exposure that excites me or defiance? Would a feminist argue that the fantasy is just a way to claim my desire, my own body, instead of letting the world tell me what to find exciting? Everything about us is a confusing tangle of society and self, including our sexuality. But shouldn't that be ours alone? *Can* it be? Can anything be exciting if somebody doesn't disapprove?

Maybe we'll skip the interview in bed. Better to do it at the site, anyway, so I can have the photographer get pictures of anything Michael points out as important.

I finish packing, with ten minutes left before I need to get a cab. It's midafternoon in Paris. Chloe's probably in class, but flying always makes me nervous, so I try her cell phone. As expected, I get her voice mail, and the thought crosses my mind that if my plane crashes, this will be the message she gets from beyond the grave, like those awful stories of people coming home on 9/11 to find voices on their answering machines of loved ones they'd never see again.

"Hi, Chloe. It's Mom. I know you're probably in class, but I'm headed out to the airport for my trip to California, and I just wanted to say I love you. Oh, and I cut my hair. I'll try you again this evening when I get to L.A."

I hang up, feeling silly. She'll probably roll her eyes and tell her friends, "My mother's so neurotic. Every time one of us gets on an airplane, she acts like we're never coming back, so we have to go through this whole routine of saying the things we'd want to make sure we said if the plane crashed."

But I don't *always* do this. I didn't do it when David flew to Miami. Of course, I had other things on my mind, then.

David seems to be just as distracted now. When I came home with my new haircut, he stared at me open-mouthed, then caught himself and said, "Wow! That's a change!"

"For the better, I hope?"

"It's really cute. Makes you look a lot younger."

Then he went back to his manuscript.

I stared at him. *That's it? Twenty years with the same haircut, and that's all you say about it?*

I went into the bathroom and stared at myself in the mirror for a long time. "Well, I like it."

*And I didn't do it for you.*

I drag my suitcase outside, where I flag down a cab and make the driver's morning by saying, "LaGuardia, please."

I get off in L.A. feeling like a sophisticated traveler jetting from coast to coast on a secret mission of pleasure—and an expense account. It feels pretty glamorous to be striding along the concourse at LAX with my *New York Times* under my arm and a famous architect waiting to whisk me away to a luxurious spa.

Michael offered to pick me up at the airport, but I refused. "You're busy," I told him. "I'll rent a car and meet you up in Ojai."

"You sure? It means driving the L.A. freeways."

Fourteen miles on I-405, then just over fifty miles on 101, up past Ventura, where I turn off on Highway 33 to go up into the mountains. Just over eighty miles total. MapQuest tells me to expect an hour and a half, and I insist to Michael that it's no problem. Why should he drive all the way down from Santa Monica just to pick me up? I'm perfectly capable of renting a car and meeting him in Ojai. Secretly, I can't help thinking he'll find my independence attractive. Or maybe I'm just wary of being stuck up in the mountains if things don't go well.

I start to question my decision almost immediately. The car rental agency doesn't have the Civic I requested, so they upgrade me to a Buick Century, which feels like I'm driving a La-Z-Boy. With the delay it's after three when I get on the road, and the Friday afternoon traffic is already starting to build up. And so that's where I am, sitting in a traffic jam on the 405, when my cell phone rings.

"Hi," Michael says. "Where are you?"

"Well, at the moment, I'm behind a black Hummer and in front of a semi truck. That's about all I can see."

He laughs. "Welcome to L.A. You have a good flight?"

"Not bad. But when did they stop handing out those little pretzels with your drink?"

"It's a cost-saving thing. Just think how much they could save if they stopped taking passengers altogether." There's a pause. "Listen, Eva, something's come up, and I thought I should warn you."

My stomach sinks at those words. He's going to bail on me. I've come all this way, and now he's calling to tell me that he can't make it. For a moment, I wonder if I should edge over to the right for an exit, to head back to the airport. Ron won't want to pay for me to spend a weekend at a spa unless he gets a cover story. I keep my voice calm, as I ask, "What's up?"

"My wife wants to come up to Ojai. She heard you're doing a magazine story on the house, and she thought it sounded fun."

For all my effort to stay calm, I can't hide the shock in my voice. "Your *wife*?"

"I'm sorry. It's fine if you want to back out. I can imagine how weird this would be for you."

No, he can't. His *wife*? Am I really going to spend the weekend smiling like an idiot at the woman whose husband I've just spent a weekend screwing? Is he crazy?

"Eva?"

On the other hand, how would I explain to Ron my turning around and going home now, just because Michael Foresman's wife wanted to join us for the house tour? I'd have to lie, tell him that something came up and Michael canceled the interview at the last moment.

He couldn't blame me for that, right? But if he ever found out . . .

"Eva? Are you there?"

"Yeah, I'm here." The Hummer in front of me edges forward a few feet, and I follow automatically. "Michael, I don't know if I can do this."

"No problem. I completely understand. I'll just tell her something came up and you had to cancel the interview."

So we'll both tell the same lie. I suddenly feel disgusted with myself. Is this what I've come to? Am I going to spend my life lying to everybody?

"Michael, we should go ahead and do the interview. You caught me off guard, but I can handle it."

"Really?" He sounds doubtful.

"Yeah. I've promised my publisher an interview and a photo spread. He's holding space for it in our next issue. I can't just bail on it because I'll have to meet your wife."

There's a long pause, and I sense that he wishes I had just decided to bail. This is going to be hard for him, too. *So live with it,* I think angrily. *I'm going to.*

"Okay," he says at last. "Whatever you want to do. I'll call the spa and see if I can get another room."

"Maybe I should stay someplace else. There must be other hotels in town, right?"

"Are you sure? I feel terrible about this."

"I wouldn't have stayed at a fancy place like that if I were just traveling on business."

"Okay, let me make some calls and I'll get back to you. What time do you think you'll get up there?"

I look up at the endless line of traffic inching along in front of me. "I think we've got some time."

❧

It turns out to be a popular weekend in Ojai, and Michael has a hard time finding me a room. But two hours later, as I approach Ventura on 101, he calls me to say there's been a cancellation at the Best Western, so he's grabbed the room for me.

"It looks like we'll be getting up there around seven," he tells me. "Do you want to meet us for dinner?"

"Would you mind if I just got some dinner on my own and we met in the morning? It's been a long day, and I'd prefer to go into this when I'm not exhausted."

"That's fine." He sounds relieved. "Why don't we plan to meet for breakfast around nine tomorrow? If you come out to the inn, we can get breakfast at the Oak Grill. You want some suggestions on restaurants for dinner tonight?"

"I'll be fine. So how do we play it in the morning?"

"What do you mean?"

"Do we act like we've never met?"

He hesitates. "Would that make you uncomfortable?"

"Not as uncomfortable as your wife figuring out that you slept with me."

He doesn't laugh. "So we've corresponded and spoken on the phone, but we've never met."

"Then how will I know who you are?"

"Well, my photograph was in *Time* a couple months ago. But I'll tell the hostess that we're meeting you. If you get there first, leave your name with her, and I'll do the same. She'll make sure we meet."

I feel my anger return. *This is such bullshit.* But I stay calm. "That's fine. I'll see you in the morning."

I get to Ojai around five. The hotel clerk directs me to a café, where I get a salad, then I walk around the town for a couple hours, going into galleries and shops. I can see why Michael likes it here. It's an artist's town, surrounded by stunning scenery. The name means "Nest of the Moon" in Chumash, a Native American language, and I can see it: the valley in which the town sits has an unearthly beauty, making it look like the kind of place the moon might come to rest after its long journey.

I gaze up at the hills surrounding the town as I walk back to my hotel, feeling depressed. What am I going to say to Michael's wife in the morning? I hate the idea of faking my way through the interview, pretending not to know Michael or that she had no interest in the house until she learned about the magazine feature. I imagine her swanning around the building site, having her photograph taken gazing out over the valley as if she always comes here to find peace.

We've seen this before. Tell a socialite that you're planning a feature on her home, and all the cracks in her life suddenly get closed up: estranged husbands show up to be photographed reading in the library (one actually held the book upside down), and children who usually call only when they need money for their drug habits appear neatly dressed and well groomed, showing off the smiles they learned at Groton or Choate. After the pictures are taken, as the photographer strikes his gear, the smiles vanish and the family scatters to pursue their private vices. They've held it together long enough to be immortalized as a happy family in the pages of a magazine dedicated to gracious living. What more can anyone ask of them?

It's depressing to think of Michael as one of those people. Why couldn't his wife stay back in L.A., I wonder, as I crawl into my lonely bed. Or better yet, why couldn't she have married a man who shared her interests, and leave Michael to those of us who understand his dreams?

 ❧

The next morning, I drive up to meet them at the Ojai Inn. I've barely slept. Around 3:00 a.m. I finally got up and started writing out my interview questions in clearer form than the scrawled notes I'd made. I check the batteries in my tape recorder, organize my blank tapes. I'm going to be brisk and professional. I break out the ironing board and run a cool iron over my shirt to take out the wrinkles from my suitcase. As I'm digging out the clothes I plan to wear, I come across the box of condoms. Feeling slightly sick to my stomach, I toss them into the garbage can in the bathroom. The sexy underwear, I shove down into the bottom of the suitcase, out of sight.

I'll wear no-nonsense cotton today. I'll clear my mind of all thoughts except architecture.

I arrive early at the inn, get a table in the Oak Grill, and order a pot of coffee. I want to be waiting when they arrive, so I won't have to cross the dining room to greet them. I'll just get up from my chair as they approach, smile and say, "Michael?" with my hand extended, as if we're finally meeting after weeks of letters, email, and phone calls.

In fact, when they come in, I've just noticed that there's a small spot on the front of my shirt, and I'm brushing at it with a napkin when I hear footsteps, and Michael says, "You must be Eva."

Surprised, I look up. He's smiling at me, and I can see him taking in my new look. But now his wife comes up beside him, and I can tell instantly from the look on her face that they've been arguing. Does she suspect something? There's no time to get nervous now, so I get up from the table, shake Michael's hand and tell him it's a thrill to finally meet him.

"How was your trip?"

"Fine. Until I hit the traffic on the 405." I turn to face her, extend my hand, smiling. "Hi, I'm Eva Cassady. It's a pleasure to meet you."

With a feeling of physical shock, I realize she's not the elegant blonde I'd pictured, but a dark-haired woman of about my height, and a fair bit heavier than I am now. It's strangely like looking at the self I was a few months ago.

"I'm Mari Foresman," she says, and we shake hands. "Welcome."

We chat over breakfast, and to my surprise, I find that I like her. She'd worked as a special education teacher in East Los Angeles before their daughter was born, and now she's on the board of an organization that provides services for the developmentally delayed. She's not the elegant society wife; she's the social advocacy wife, whose impatience with Michael's work isn't because it's so strange and avant-garde, but rather because it's self-indulgent, unconcerned with the social good. She doesn't *say* that, of course. But as Michael talks about his desire to challenge the traditional notion of the home, which builds out from the kitchen and hearth in layers of wealth-display by mimicking the wings that were added to Palladian villas, I see her face settle into a patient smile. She's clearly heard him give this speech many times.

"Most people still cook in their kitchens," she says mildly at one point. "If the kitchen's at the center of a house, it's because families come together around food and they separate to sleep. But that's a luxury. Go down to Chiapas; you'll find that the peasant farmers cook and sleep in the same room. And most of them haven't heard of Palladio."

Michael looks annoyed at the interruption. He doesn't look at her, just leans forward to make his point directly to me. "There's no reason to restrict ourselves to that model of a house," he insists, "any more than we have to imagine a bank as a stone fortress with big columns out front. Most banks are glass towers now, because they no longer deal in cash—money moves electronically. And the same thing's true about our lives. Food is no longer at the heart of our culture; now it's information. The flat-screen TV is the new hearth. Before long, computer screens will replace windows."

"And is that a good thing?"

"It's neither good nor bad. Evolution isn't a moral process; it's just a response to the real conditions of life. We're a species evolving from individual consciousness to a collective model of information sharing. What the science fiction writers used to call the 'hive mind.' And it's only going to get faster. Already, the internet-ready computer has moved off the desktop and into the palms of our hands. The next step is direct neural connections, where we'll be able to access all the information in every major research library in the world through a wireless connection implanted directly in our brains. The military is already experimenting with this for their fighter pilots, so it's probably less than twenty years away as a consumer product. People hear that, and they get nervous about mind control. But we're already allowing our minds to be shaped by the information that bombards us daily on twenty-four-hour TV, the internet, the iPod you wear while you jog. Imagine how differently our minds will work when information moves instantly from brain to brain. Thought will flow as quickly as money flows now."

Mari gently rests a hand on his forearm. "Maybe you should tell her how all this relates to your house."

And suddenly I realized that she hadn't come along this weekend to get her picture into a magazine. She'd come because she knew how her husband could get when he started talking about his vision for the house, and she wanted to protect him from his own worst impulses. *Stick to the subject,* she's warning him. *You're an architect, not a social theorist.*

But he's off and running now. As we eat our breakfast, he talks about how schools will have to evolve to respond to this age of instant information, no longer teaching and testing on information—historical facts, mathematical formulas—but on reasoning, a return to the Socratic symposium. And libraries! What will they look like when all the books are gone? Mari and I quietly have grapefruit and nonfat yogurt, while Michael excitedly shapes the world of the future.

"Maybe we should head out to the house," Mari suggests, finally. "We don't want to keep your photographer waiting."

Startled, Michael looks down at his uneaten breakfast. I find myself looking at him with affectionate amusement. Is this the flipside of all that sexual energy I'd enjoyed last week? He's almost childlike in his enthusiasm, a little boy who needs to be reminded to eat his breakfast before he rushes out to play with his toys.

I glance over at Mari, and catch the same expression on her face as he takes a few quick bites of his cold omelet, then abruptly pushes the plate away. "Ready?"

We drive up out of the valley in their hybrid car. Michael has fallen silent, now gazing out at the road like a moody child. Mari turns in her seat to look back at me. Where in New York do you live?"

"I'm on the Upper West Side. Broadway and Eighty-second."

"Really? I lived on Seventy-ninth near Riverside for

two years after college. That's my favorite part of the city. You can still feel traces of the old radical, intellectual tradition, even with all the changes. Bagels with Trotsky on Sunday mornings."

"It's mostly Wall Street types and media executives now. But you can still get good bagels, and the Trotsky's delivered fresh daily up around Columbia."

She smiles. "How long have you lived there?"

"Since college, really. My husband and I have been in the same apartment for fifteen years. We've moved only once, when my daughter was five."

"So she's away at college now?"

"Actually, she's in Paris for her junior year abroad. Apparently it's hard to get bagels there."

She laughs. "But the Trotsky's fresh."

"Exactly. So why did you leave New York?"

She looks out the window at the dry California hills. "I got a chance to work with a woman who was creating new programs to help developmentally delayed children in the immigrant community, kids who had the extra challenge of not being native speakers, so I came out here." She smiles. "We get back to New York from time to time, and Michael has to spend a fair amount of time there for his work. But I still miss it."

I say nothing. Just the thought of how Michael gets back to New York makes me feel terrible. I *like* this woman. If I'd met her at a party, I'd have thought it would be fun to get to know her better, go out for lunch sometime. But now I've slept with her husband.

We turn off the highway onto a road that winds up

among the hills. It ends at a locked wire gate, like you'd see on a dairy farm, with a dirt track leading off beyond. Michael gets out; goes up to unlock it.

Mari looks back at me. "Sorry about all that at breakfast," she says, quietly. "Michael gets carried away sometimes. This house is where he invests all the ideas he can't put into his client work." She smiles. "I'm amazed he's showing it to you; it's not something he lets many people see. It's like his mistress."

I feel like something's caught in my throat. "That must be hard for you."

She shakes her head. "He's a passionate man. This is the price you pay for loving a genius. There are some things you just have to accept."

I'm too taken aback to do more than nod, and now Michael's opened the gate and comes back to the car, sliding in behind the wheel. "I've got to get that lock oiled. It sticks worse every time I come up here."

As we drive forward, bouncing along the rocky two-wheel track, I feel like Alice tumbling down a rabbit hole. Friendly wives, sticky locks . . . paging Dr. Freud. And if this house is Michael's mistress, what does that make me? A renovation? The warehouse where he's stored his dreams?

"Take it slow," Mari tells Michael, looking back at me. "She looks a little green around the gills."

Michael looks up at me in the rearview mirror. "Sorry about all the bumps. I need to get a grader out here and get this driveway smoothed out."

"Will the photographer know how to find us?"

"I gave her directions. She should be here by early afternoon. That'll give us time to walk over the place, and you can figure out what you'd like her to shoot."

Off to the right, we pass an array of solar panels set along the hillside. "I can get about sixty percent of my power from those panels. I've also got a geothermal grid, which takes up the slack in the winter. If I put a windmill up on that ridge, I could probably sell power back to the electric company."

The ridge divides the property in half, and as we drive over the top, suddenly there's the house—spread out across a small plateau just below us, with a spectacular view of the valley beyond. It's a dramatic sight, and Michael stops the car so I can get out and absorb it. The house is all sharp angles and sweeping curves, like something a child might build if he'd lost all the straight blocks from his building set. The materials are even stranger to the eye: adobe, corrugated metal, raw woods, and those translucent glass bricks you used to see in dentist's offices and South Florida shopping malls. Each material seems to arise out of the meeting of two other materials at an angle or corner, but I can't tell if that's supposed to suggest conflicts resolved in synthesis, or mating and birth.

Michael rolls his window down. "What do you think?"

How do you tell a man that his dream is *ugly*? Maybe it's only because my eye isn't trained to see beauty in conflict, but the effect he's created is harsh, defiantly resisting my attempts to see it as a coherent design.

"Fascinating," I say. "Very . . . striking."

Up close, the effect is even more dramatic. He's left

raw edges on the concrete and wood, and the connecting bolts that hold the metal sheets to the house's frame look like something sticking out of Frankenstein's neck. The walls tilt out at strange angles above you, and my first impulse is to step back so I won't get crushed when they fall.

Mari sees my response and smiles. "Everybody does that. Your automatic response is self-preservation."

"Interesting effect."

She laughs. "Yeah. Home, sweet home. We've got a house that makes people want to run away."

Michael shoots her an annoyed look. "Come see it from the other side."

We walk around to where the hillside falls away, and a magnificent view of the valley opens up before us. But where I expected to see a wall of windows, there's only a plain adobe wall, with a door that leads out to a path through some rose trellises down to a small wooden deck at the cliff's edge.

"That's a million-dollar view," Mari says, gesturing out across the valley. "If you could see it."

"That's the point," Michael says. "People pay a fortune for a view, so they can sit inside their houses and look out at the world through the glass. You want a view, go outside. Get out into the world. A house isn't a picture frame." He looks over at me; smiles. "It's like building a hotel on the beach, but having all the windows face the land."

Mari sighs. "I'm looking forward to the roses, anyway."

Michael points to the roof, which rises at a series of

steep angles at the edges of the house. "Up there is the rain trap. It all runs down to a cistern on the side of the house, and we can use it for bathing."

We go inside. At the center of the house is a circular solarium with a glass ceiling and glass walls, so that the light spreads out into all the rooms that surround it.

"Here's your wall of windows," Mari says. "They're just on the inside, instead of facing the view."

"The solarium has a retractable roof, so it can become an inner courtyard," Michael tells me. "In the rainy season we can channel the runoff away from the cistern when it's full, and it becomes a series of waterfalls along these windows." He points across the solarium to a glass wall opposite us. "That's the master bedroom. The waterfalls will act as curtains to give privacy."

Mari looks at me. "I'm going to buy some curtains, just in case. Imagine having a houseful of guests, and suddenly it stops raining. You wake up in the morning, and you're all looking into each other's bedrooms. Still, it's a lovely idea, if it works."

All the rooms have skylights to give natural light, and as we move from room to room, I notice that each room has a different color of sunlight streaming down into it.

"You can vary the tone of the glass," Michael tells me when I ask him about it. "I wanted each room to have its own texture." He gestures to the walls. "This is where I cheated a little on the recycled materials. I thought Mari would be happier if the interior walls were more finished."

"I like the idea of the recycled materials," Mari says. "That's probably my favorite thing about the house."

The walls are polished wood, and the floors are slate and tile. It's actually very soothing: warm colors and abundant light. The kitchen is off in one corner of the house, but it's hardly an afterthought. He's installed lovely copper counters and brushed-metal cabinets. Most of the appliances are in place, and when Michael turns on the lights, a series of dramatic spots illuminate the cooking areas.

"Wow," Mari says, impressed. "You've changed the whole design in here."

Michael looks at me. "She thought I was going to have us cooking over an open fire. Big iron pot hanging on a tripod."

I run my hand across the restaurant-grade Viking stovetop. "I'm going to want lots of pictures in here. My publisher has a thing for kitchen appliances. He calls it the money shot."

"He must have seen the bills." Mari opens the convection oven and peers inside. "Did we pay for all this, or did you get it free because Eva's doing an article on the house?"

Michael takes my arm. "Let me show you the rest of the house," he says.

There's still some tile work and fixtures to be completed in the master bath, but I think the photographer ought to be able to work around that. Otherwise, the house looks more finished than Michael had led me to expect. They could move furniture in anytime. Right now, there's only an old architect's drafting table with a set of hand-drawn plans in the living room, along with a battered futon couch.

Michael says, "That's where I sleep when I come up here on weekends to work on the place."

I nod, but say nothing. I already feel awkward enough, without getting into sleeping arrangements. "Where would you like to do the interview?"

"Outside? I could set up some folding chairs down at the temple."

"Where's that?"

He laughs. "Well, it's actually just a deck at the moment, but I'm planning to build a Buddhist temple there."

And now I remember. The Buddhist temple, where his wife will go to drink her chilled wine and watch the sun set. We walk down to the deck, which perches at the edge of the steep hillside, giving you all the view the house denies you. Michael gets four folding chairs from the trunk of his car, carries them down, and sets them up facing the valley.

"I've got a cooler full of wine and sandwiches in the car. Would you like something?"

"Later, maybe. It's still too early for me." I take out my tape recorder and my notes. "Let's do the interview, and then we can eat."

"I should leave you two alone," Mari says. "I don't want to get in the way of your interview."

"Actually, I was hoping you'd stay," I tell her. "It'll make things less formal."

The truth is, I don't want to be alone with Michael right now. Not with his wife wandering around. One of us might be tempted to say something or make a gesture that could arouse her suspicion. More to the point, I find myself feeling uncomfortable with Michael, ashamed of what we've done, but also angry at him for getting me into this situation. I know I have no right to feel that way. I was the one who contacted him, I pushed for the interview. So what had he done to make me angry?

He married a woman I like. If she'd been frosty and elegant, less down to earth, I might not have felt so bad about sleeping with her husband. But right now, I almost like Mari better than I like Michael. So I'm just going to do my interview, get my photographs, and get my skinny butt back on the plane back to New York. Lesson learned.

I start off with some questions about his architectural philosophy, and Michael says some provocative things that he's said in lots of other interviews lately. Still, it's good to have them in our interview. Next, I ask him about the challenges of designing a house according to his principles, and he responds by launching into a lengthy critique of everything that he sees as wrong about the idea of a house in contemporary America: It's boring and bourgeois, empty of any meaning except an outdated notion of the family and the conspicuous display of material wealth. We're still building houses in the digital age based on designs from the steam age; all we've done is update the appliances.

*Our readers are going to hate him,* I think as he goes on about the cult of the fireplace in upper-middle-class homes. *But, then, that's exactly what he wants. What better way to confirm your genius than to be hated by the upper-middle-class?*

Later, I get him to describe some of the innovative design ideas he's included in this house. As he talks, I make some quick notes on the features I want photographed, so our readers will be able to see what he's describing.

"Let me show you," he says at one point, and we get up to walk around the house as he points out what he considers important about the design, while I hold my tape recorder up to catch his voice. Mari stays down on the deck, and when we're on the far side of the house, Michael suddenly reaches out and shuts off my recorder.

"You okay?"

"I'm fine, but I don't want to talk about it here. Let's just go on with the interview." I switch the tape recorder back on and ask him about the solar panels. We're talking about alternative power sources and energy-efficient building materials when we see a cloud of dust rising, and a Jeep appears at the top of the ridge.

"That's Haley," Michael says. "I was afraid she'd had some trouble with my directions."

The Jeep stops behind his car, and we walk over as the photographer gets out and starts unloading her gear. She's in her thirties, tall and blond, with an athletic build, as if she spends her days climbing around construction sites with her camera gear. Michael introduces us, and I give her my list of the shots I want.

"I'll probably have a few more, once we've finished the interview."

She nods and glances over at the house. "No problem. This ought to be fun. Lots of interesting angles on this house." She looks at Michael. "You built this place yourself?"

"Most of it. I got some help with the really hard stuff."

"You want a shot of you working on it?"

Michael hesitates. He's not dressed for construction work, but I can see he's tempted. He looks at me. "You think your publisher would want something like that?"

Why does every man want to imagine himself as a construction worker? When David patched the plaster on Chloe's bedroom ceiling last year, he spent the whole weekend walking around in a tool belt like he was auditioning to be one of the Village People. Still, it's not my job to keep Michael from looking like a fool. If we'd spent the weekend alone together, I might have gently steered him away from it, but today I'm here to get the interview and some photographs. That's it.

"That might be fun," I tell them. "I can't promise we'll be able to use it in the magazine, though. My publisher usually only allows one shot with the owners, and he likes them to look comfortable. That way, our readers can picture themselves living in the house."

Michael smiles. "Sounds like he's afraid they might get jealous."

"Something like that. If a house is empty, you can fill it with your imagination. That's true about people, too."

Michael looks at me for a moment, then nods. I hadn't meant it as any kind of deep message, but it looks like he's taking it that way.

The photographer grabs the rest of her gear, then slings a bag over her shoulder. "Okay, I'll get started with some exterior shots."

She heads down toward the house, and Michael and

I stand there awkwardly for a moment. Then I click on my tape recorder and ask him about the curtain-of-rain effect he'd designed for the solarium. Did he reprocess that water, or was it treated as runoff?

And that's how we spend the rest of the afternoon. We manage to finish the interview without any awkward moments, and then I spend some time working with the photographer. When we're done, Michael gets the cooler out of his car, opens a bottle of wine, and we all sit on the deck eating sandwiches and watching the light change as afternoon settles across the hills.

"So you're flying back to New York tomorrow?" Mari looks over at me. "It's a shame you can't spend a few more days out here and enjoy the sun."

"I wish I could. But my publisher wants to get this interview into the next edition, and there's quite a bit to do." I look over at Michael. "I'll send you a copy as soon as I get it transcribed. If you'd like to change anything, that's the best time, before we start getting into layout."

He nods. "Thanks. Will you give me a heads-up if you find I've said something completely stupid?"

"I don't think you need to worry about that. But if you don't like anything when you get the transcription, just let me know and we can fix it." I glance at my watch. "I should probably get back soon. My daughter's in Paris, and I want to give her a call before it gets too late."

Mari glances at her watch. "It must be almost midnight in Paris. Are you sure you don't want to wait until tomorrow? We were hoping to take you to dinner tonight."

The idea of spending an evening making polite conversation suddenly fills me with weariness. "That sounds really lovely," I begin, "but . . ."

Michael holds up a hand before I can even start my excuse. "Save your breath. We're taking you to dinner. No arguments." He turns to the photographer. "Can you join us, Haley?"

"I wish I could, but I have to be back in the city tonight."

Terrific. Just the happy couple and me. There's nothing to do but smile and be gracious—and stay away from the wine.

"Well, thank you," I say. "That's very nice of you. Would it be rude if I went back to my hotel to rest for a couple hours? I'm still on New York time."

So at least I get time to catch my breath. Back in my room, I stretch out on my bed. *You just have to get through a couple of hours.* Yet how can I complain? I brought this on myself.

At least I won't have to worry about gaining weight. I have no appetite, and just the idea of sitting down to dinner with Michael and his wife makes me feel sick to my stomach.

It seems I've discovered yet another new diet. How can you get fat when everything turns to ashes in your mouth?

# 124

Dear Eva,

I'm so sorry for putting you through all that this weekend. It must have been excruciating for you. I had no idea that Mari would want to come with me. Usually she couldn't care less about the house—or about anything I do, to be honest. We go through the motions for Emma's sake, but neither one of us is happy. That's probably my fault as much as anybody's, but it's unfair that you had to suffer for it.

Anyway, I just wanted to tell you how sorry I am. You handled yourself with real grace in a difficult situation. Mari said how much she liked you. I have to come to New York again in a few weeks. Any chance I could make it up to you?

And I never got to tell you how much I like your hair!

Michael

His email is waiting for me when I get home. He sent it Sunday morning, so he must have gone straight home from the inn, switched on his computer, and written to me. Where was Mari when he did this? Did they immediately vanish into different rooms when they got home?

They'd sure acted like a married couple at dinner. When I met them in the restaurant bar, I got the distinct sensation that they'd spent the afternoon making love. Michael seemed distant and abstracted, but Mari glowed like a bride on her honeymoon, a languid quality that I recognized from the way I'd acted just a week before.

Had he tried to distract her from any suspicions about me by rolling her around in the inn's king-size bed for a few hours? Or had he just lied to me about the state of his marriage?

Either way, it's not like I had any right to feel jealous. She was his wife, and I was just his . . .

What? His latest girlfriend? For all I knew, he'd done this lots of times before, picking up women on his many trips to Spain and Tokyo. The photographer seemed like a likely candidate. She'd been businesslike, snapping her photos, adjusting her lights and lenses, but it was clear they knew each other well.

I shouldn't care. He's not *my* husband. And even if he were, I'd have no right to complain, considering how I've behaved. I should just delete his email. And when he sends more, I should delete those without even reading them. I made a mistake in a moment of weakness, when I was starving for affirmation. But now I've come to my senses. It wasn't Michael I wanted: it was myself.

So why do I feel so lost? I'm only four pounds from my

goal, and since I've barely been able to eat for three days, I ought to reach it quickly. But nausea isn't what I imagined I'd feel when I got to this point, seeing the finish line just ahead. I pictured myself triumphant, fists pumping, the crowd cheering me on. Instead, I just feel ashamed.

I sat through our dinner with a smile pasted onto my face; answered Mari's polite questions about my work, my interest in architecture, and even my family. I barely looked at Michael the entire evening. It felt strangely like a job interview, as if Mari were checking my references. When she asked about Chloe, I found myself choking up. I had to excuse myself and go to the bathroom, where I fought back the tears that were trying to rise to the surface, then splashed cold water on my face before going back to the table.

"I'm sorry," I told them. "I think I'm feeling the time difference. I should probably call it an early night."

"But you haven't touched your dinner."

I looked down at the plate before me. The mushroom miso–glazed black cod with braised endive, totsoi, and local pomegranate looked and smelled wonderful, but I couldn't eat it. I couldn't eat the salad of organic baby greens with shaved young fennel, pixie tangerine, and red hawk cheese crouton, either. In fact, it felt like I'd never be able to eat again.

"It's a bit rich for me," I said. "I guess I'm not used to it."

"Can we get you something else?"

I shook my head. "Please, enjoy your meal. It all looks wonderful."

And so I sat there uncomfortably while they ate their

dinners, doing my best to hold up my end of the conversation. When it came time for dessert and coffee, Mari glanced at me and told the waitress, "I think we'll skip the dessert tonight. Just the check, please."

I was profoundly grateful. In the inn's lobby, I shook hands with Michael, then with Mari. "I'll send you the transcript of the interview sometime next week," I told Michael. "And we ought to be able to show you photographs shortly after that, if Haley can get them to us quickly."

"She's usually very fast," he said.

Mari just smiled.

"Well, it's been lovely meeting you both," I told them. "I'm sorry I wasn't better company tonight."

"Please," Mari said. "No apologies. I can only imagine how exhausting this must be for you."

*She can't know,* I thought as I drove back to my hotel. *It's just guilt that makes everything she says sound like an accusation.*

Back in my room, I took two Advil and crawled into bed. *Let it go,* I told myself. It was time to go home to David, go back to being myself and accept that the life I'd been struggling to escape wasn't a prison, but my home.

And with that thought, I began to cry.

⚬

Now, as I read Michael's email, I feel tears start to rise again. Even *Mari said how much she liked you.* God, what an awful person I've become. And he wants to see me when he comes to New York in a few weeks. He wants to *make it up to me*.

A week ago, the phrase would have excited me. Now it only makes me angry. What kind of person does he think I am?

*Exactly the kind of person you've chosen to be.*

It seems that my conscience, which went on vacation, is back now, tanned, rested, and ready for action. Clearly it's not going to cut me any slack—not that I deserve any. All those weeks in the gym, it's the one muscle I wasn't working. As my body got tighter, my morals lost all definition. And now my conscience has decided it's time for a workout.

I try to focus on simple tasks—unpacking, laundry, transcribing the interview—but the sound of Michael's voice on my tape recorder makes my throat close up, so I keep shutting the machine off. I check my email, scrub down the kitchen counters, strip the bed, and wash the sheets. Even an hour at the gym, sweating fiercely, doesn't lift this weight off my shoulders.

Tomorrow will be easier, I tell myself. I'll be back in the office, where there are simple tasks to accomplish, phone calls to answer, deadlines to meet. That's what I need right now—not time to think. David's trying to read manuscripts and I can tell I'm driving him crazy, chasing him from room to room as I search for more tasks to occupy me.

"You just got home," he says, plaintively. "Do you really have to get everything done tonight?"

What made me so greedy, wanting more than my fair

share of desire or love, so that I started stealing it from others? I've never thought of myself that way. That's the kind of thing movie stars do, or the filthy rich, those spoiled children of our culture of dreams. When had I become someone I wouldn't even want to know?

David dozes off over his manuscripts sometime after ten. At midnight he gets up to go to the bathroom, and finds me in there, down on my knees, scrubbing the shower.

"Eva?" He stands there, blinking in the fierce light. "Are you okay? Is something wrong?"

And suddenly I'm crying. He stares at me for a moment, amazed. Then he takes the sponge from my hand, and tosses it into the bathtub. He raises me to my feet and puts his arms around me. I stand there, stiffly, my head buried in his shoulder, weeping.

He doesn't ask me what's wrong. At some level, I'm convinced, he knows. I feel so terrible, standing there with his arms around me; I don't deserve this. He should be angry. He should push me away.

At last, my sobbing grows quieter. He draws back and looks at me carefully.

"You're tired," he says. "You miss Chloe. Come to bed."

And that's all we say. Sometimes silence is the only mercy we can hope to find.

He shuts off the bathroom light, and we get into bed. He holds me in his arms until I slip into a deep, dreamless sleep.

W e should throw a party," Ron says. Around the conference table, everyone looks up in surprise. He's practically bouncing with excitement, the photographs spread out before him. "We've got an exclusive, so why not make a big deal out of it? We could rent a nice restaurant, invite some of the architecture critics from the big media outlets. Maybe one of them will write about it and we'll get some publicity."

Haley sent me her best shots as an email attachment on Monday afternoon. By Tuesday, we had a disk by Federal Express with the entire set ready for layout. She was as good as Michael had said, worth every penny of her considerable fee. The photos made the house look even stranger and more interesting than it seemed when I first saw it: she'd shot neatly framed close-ups of the oddly angled walls and strangely textured light in the interior rooms. She'd even gotten Michael to waste some water by flicking the switch that allowed the cistern to drain down the solarium windows, getting a dramatic shot of the water curtains filtering the bright afternoon sunshine.

I'd given up on transcribing the interview and had gotten one of the magazine's interns to do it. But once the photographs came in, Ron got so excited by the visuals that he almost lost interest in what Michael actually had to say about the house. The interview, which cost me so much, has become just an excuse to run the pictures, and now it sounds like they'd both become just an opportunity for a party where Ron could schmooze the big names in our tiny, specialized field. From the way his eyes glitter, you'd think this was the moment he'd been waiting for, when he can finally outclass his competitors at *Architecture Today* and *House Fabulous!*

Ron looks over at me, and there's hunger in his eyes. "You said Foresman's going to be in New York next month, right?"

I nod. "He's working on a project out in Stony Brook."

"Can you pin him down on a date? Tell him we'd like to thank him by throwing a party in his honor." He looks down the table at our marketing director. "Cynthia, how quickly can you throw together a party?"

She looks surprised. "Me? I've never done a party."

"It's marketing, isn't it? Public relations, getting the magazine's name out there in the press?"

She hesitates. "I guess so."

"So? How quickly can you do it? We'd want to celebrate the publication of this issue, but the party should happen before it hits the newsstand, so we can get some press ahead of time."

Cynthia's rallying now, no doubt realizing that a marketing director for a small magazine can't afford to be seen hesitating about any suggestion for publicity. She starts scribbling notes on her yellow pad with a look on her face that seems to say, *Okay, you want a party? I'll make you a party. Shrimp on trays. Maybe an ice sculpture in the shape of the house.*

I desperately try to think of a way to derail this train before it gains speed, but Ron's got his hand firmly on the throttle and he's having fun, blowing off huge clouds of smoke as we race forward. How do I tell him that the bridge is out ahead? There's a woman tied to the tracks, with no brave cowboy to save her.

"I don't think he's really a party person," I say.

Ron looks impatient. "So, call it a dinner. Whatever it takes to get him here."

I haven't answered his last two emails, mainly because I don't have the guts to tell him I made a mistake. But I guess that will have to wait. Ron wants a party, and I couldn't send Michael an invitation right after I told him I didn't want to see him again.

David clearly senses that something's going on with me, but he's avoided asking me any direct questions. I don't know if it's politeness or fear about what I'll say, but the result is that we've spent the last several days tiptoeing around each other, both of us hoping I won't burst into tears again.

I won't sleep with Michael again, but I want to stay on good terms with him until after the party. All it would take is an encouraging answer to his emails. No promises, no flirtation; I just won't break it off yet. Would that be lying?

Why is it that the smaller my ass gets, the harder it is to cover?

I don't want to hurt anyone, and telling the truth would cause people pain. David's made it clear that he doesn't want to know, so now our apartment's got more sleeping dogs than a hillbilly's back porch. And given the tone of Michael's email, I'd obviously be hurting him if I broke it off now. This party will give me time to let him down easily. Anyway, when he sees the kind of magazine I work for up close, he'll probably lose interest. That would solve the whole problem.

> *Dear Michael,*
>
> *You don't need to apologize for this weekend. It's my fault, really. I'm the one who proposed an interview. Anyway, I'm a big girl—I can handle a little discomfort.*
>
> *Things have been crazy here since I got back. We're rushing to get the interview and the photographs ready for print, and I'm attaching both to this email. The text still needs editing, and we might play with the arrangement of the photos a little, but you should let me know quickly if you have any major concerns. My publisher would like to get these into final shape by the end of this week.*
>
> *So, when will you be back in New York? We'd love to host a dinner for you, to celebrate the publication of the interview.*

So there it is, on the table. Ron will have to live with it if Michael doesn't want to do it. We can find other ways to publicize the issue.

Not that Ron wouldn't still take it out on me if Michael declined. I hesitate, then type, *It would mean a lot to me*.

If he feels so bad about what happened in California, here's his chance to do something about it. I doubt that's what he had in mind when he offered to *make it up to me*, but life's full of little disappointments, isn't it?

⸻

Liz calls me just before noon to invite me out to lunch.

"I thought you signed up for that dating service 'Just Lunch.' Last week you said you'd be busy every day."

"I did. And that's what I got last week: just lunch." I hear her cover the phone and say something to her assistant, then come back. "Turns out it's boring to have lunch with men who want to tell you about how they're tired of being single and are looking for a committed relationship."

"Isn't that what you want?"

"Sure. Just not with these guys. I want to catch the fish myself, not have it served up to me. These guys have already been caught and filleted, and some woman has spit out the bones. I used to complain that the men I dated were emotionally unavailable. But these guys are so emotionally available that you want to tell them to put their hearts back in their chests and have a surgeon stitch them up."

"So, basically, you only like the guys who treat you like shit."

"That's old news, honey. I don't shop bargain racks."

We chat for a few more minutes, and then she says, "So, are you coming out for lunch with me? I'm standing up this poor guy from the lunch club, so you can tell me what a bitch I am."

"Seriously? You're standing the guy up?"

"I got a message on my voice mail this morning, and I'm supposed to call back if I want to meet him for lunch. It's not a big deal."

I look at the work piled up on my desk. "Can we make it quick?"

"You sound like one of my lunch dates."

❧

"So, how was California?"

"Exhausting. And now Ron wants me to arrange a party to publicize the interview when it goes to press. He seems to think this is the issue that's going to put us ahead of our competition."

We're at Dean and Deluca, getting salads and coffee. I get a table while Liz goes to get artificial sweetener for her coffee.

"Tell me this isn't the greatest invention ever," she says when she returns, holding up the tiny blue packets of sweetener. "All the sweetness of sugar with none of the calories. So you get cancer—I'd say that's a small price to pay for looking fabulous."

"You could start drinking your coffee black."

She shakes her head. "Pleasure without consequences. That's my motto."

I look up at her sharply. Is she hinting at something, or just doing her Dorothy Parker imitation? She catches my look, and her eyes move down to consider my coffee cup. Black, no sugar. I'm in the process of dipping a teaspoon into a tiny cup of low-fat dressing on my tray, scattering a few drops onto my salad.

"Not everyone can be as self-disciplined as you, Eva."

Her words take me completely by surprise. She can't be serious. Could she really feel defensive about her weight around *me*? I look at her, and for the first time, I realize that I've quietly slipped past her. Liz has put on a little weight over the last several months, but if I didn't know her so well, I would even have noticed. She took off her jacket when we sat down, and I can see that her blouse is pulling a little at the buttons. It's probably healthy that she's no longer a walking hanger. Anywhere but Manhattan, she'd still be the envy of her friends.

But the fact is that I'm now smaller than she is. And worse, she sees me noticing it. We both look away, tearing open the plastic knife and fork packets that came with our salads.

"When I was a little girl, I always used to think of these little plastic forks and knives as married couples," I say quickly. "Because they always come together. Now I know better. Married couples rarely come together."

Liz looks down at the utensils in her hand. "So what does that make me?"

*Crap.* There's no such thing as a safe subject anymore. There's nothing I can do but try to turn it into a joke.

"Well, the spoon comes separately," I suggest, "because it gets used more often."

She looks up at me, and I'm shocked to see tears welling up in her eyes. "Then I guess that's me."

How could I not have noticed that she's hurting? Have I really been that self-absorbed? I reach out, lay a hand on her arm. "Liz, I'm so sorry."

But she just shakes her head and walks quickly away to the ladies' room. I sit there, overwhelmed with shame. If I'd been a good friend, I would have seen . . . What? That Liz has put on some weight?

And suddenly I'm angry. Why is it my responsibility to worry about Liz's feelings? I haven't done anything to hurt her. So I've lost some weight—she should be happy for me. I can't help it if she's got her own body issues. She's done her best to sabotage me the whole time I've been on this diet. You read about this all the time: how your best friends are the ones who will try to tempt you with cookies or ice cream, demoralize you with comments that suggest you're only going to gain it all back again. They're envious, and they see your success as an accusation. If you can do it, why can't they? So it's comforting to them to imagine you failing. If Liz were a *real* friend, she'd support me in this difficult moment in my life.

But just as quickly, my anger fades. I haven't asked for Liz's support. I've kept my secrets, even enjoyed the feeling of not telling her what lies behind my success. So how can I blame her for not offering me her support?

Liz comes out of the ladies' room with an ironic smile fixed on her face. She sits down opposite me, picks up her plastic knife and fork, and starts to cut up her salad. "I must seem pretty ridiculous."

I shake my head. "Liz, I realize I've been pretty focused on myself lately. It's the diet, and everything that's going on with David. But I'm also very aware that you've stuck with me through everything—"

"Let's drop it, okay?"

We eat our salads in silence for a while, then she says, "So, tell me about your party."

# 119

Everyone asks me how I did it. As the waiters pass trays of shrimp impaled on toothpicks, the architectural critics gather around me, asking how I managed to get an interview with Michael Foresman for *House & Home*.

"It was the dress," Michael says, breaking away from Ron's monologue on the aesthetic challenge of restoring old houses. He winks at Ron and comes over to stand beside me. "How could I resist the dress?"

My red silk cheongsam. I'd been standing at my closet a few hours before the party bemoaning my lack of clothes, when David spotted the dress and pulled it out. "What's this?"

I hesitated. "It's the dress you brought Chloe during your trip to San Francisco. Remember? It was too big for her, but I found it in her closet a couple weeks ago, and I brought it in here to try it on."

"Does it fit you?"

"Yeah, it actually does."

He handed it to me. "Let's see."

Which is why I was late for the party. First, David made me put it on. Then he took it off me. And after that, I needed another shower.

"Where have you been?" Ron hissed when we finally arrived.

"Sorry. Wardrobe malfunction."

"The guest of honor got here ten minutes ago, and you weren't here to introduce him to everyone."

A task I'd been dreading—especially the moment when I would have to say, "And this is my husband." I remember the slightly pained look on Michael's face when he had to introduce me to Mari in California, but Mari and I had done our best to act polite and friendly. (Well, *I* acted. She *was* polite and friendly.) But men react differently at these moments. Even men as educated as Michael and David can get aggressive, puffing up their chests like roosters on the henhouse roof.

I have no idea how much David knows or suspects. Our affair is over, though Michael doesn't know that. But how could I let David know he's won without telling him how much he'd already lost? How do I let him know I've decided to give up my fantasy without admitting that fantasy didn't include him? And more to the point, how could I tell him I've decided to stay without making him want to leave?

Better to keep silent and let this mistake vanish into my past. All I have to do is get through tonight, and I can go back to my life with some painful wisdom.

In the end, the introductions were almost anticlimactic. Ron herded us over to where Michael stood by the bar, talking with our production manager about the photo layout.

"Well, here's Eva," Ron called out in his master-of-ceremonies voice. "And this is her husband, David. Have you found the food?"

Michael looked at David with curiosity, but Ron was already hustling him away to meet some media types he'd invited. And that's how it went for the next hour, with Ron steering the party like the captain of an ocean liner in search of an iceberg.

❧

And now we may have reached it: everybody's staring at my red cheongsam. David's over by the buffet, so I don't think he heard Michael's joke about the dress, but Ron's laughing a little too hard and several of my co-workers are exchanging glances.

"It's certainly quite a dress," Ron agrees with a bit too much enthusiasm. Catching a look at my face, he says more seriously, "Eva's been an inspiration to all of us this year. It's been quite a transformation."

Inevitably everybody looks at my body, and for the first time, I register my colleagues' responses: envy, even some disapproval. A successful diet brings out the worst in everyone; failed diets are more satisfying. Who really wants to see someone you know become that woman on the late-night commercial showing off her buffed body in middle age? That just makes everyone else feel bad.

Michael looks like the cat who ate the canary, feathers still sticking out of his mouth. Just a few weeks ago, that look would have sent a shiver of desire through me. Now it just makes me feel sad. It's not me he's seeing, but an image in his mind. And I've spent the last six months trying to shape myself to match that image. If he really wanted to see me, the Eva who's spent the last twenty years as a wife and mother, he should look at his own wife. *That's* the reality. This body everybody's staring at right now was created by shared memory and fantasy.

I'm proud of it, don't get me wrong. And the moment two days ago when I first saw the scale go under 120 was like seeing an angel smiling and waving me into the Promised Land. But now that I'm here, it's just another day to get through: breakfast, lunch, dinner, workouts. No victory parade, just the long walk to work and six flights of stairs to climb.

As with any fantasy, I'd expected more. But life rushes on, like a riptide pulling you out into the deep water. In a way, that was true about Michael, too. Somehow, I'd expected more. Not more sex—that could hardly have been possible—but a more powerful sense of the moment, as this thing we'd spent months imagining became real. I'd lingered over every moment in my fantasies—how we'd undress each other, the moment when he first touched my breast, or gently slid my panties down to leave me naked to his eyes—but especially that first moment when he'd enter me, slowly, both of us looking into each other's eyes, savoring this long-imagined fulfillment. But that's not how it happened. A bit of fumbling, an awkward pause, and then suddenly he was inside me, moving urgently, the moment already gone.

Is everything like that? Do we always miss the crucial moment when we expected to feel something? And, if so, why do the awful, embarrassing moments seem to take so long?

Like this one. A waiter passes with a tray of shrimp and I grab one, just to show people I'm not starving myself. I swipe it through the ginger sauce, grab a napkin, and turn back to my audience.

"Party food is one of my favorite things." I take a bite. "It's like sushi on the move."

Michael takes one also. "I've always thought of it as a test. Can you eat it without spilling it down the front of your shirt? When they serve those little puff pastries, you *know* your host has a hidden camera somewhere."

So now everybody has to take one. It's an orgy of shrimp with ginger sauce, and we all watch to see who spills. Funny how quickly parties can degenerate into something so primitive, like a gang of monkeys sitting around, and one of them picks up a stick. So now they all have to pick up sticks, just to show they can do it, and the next thing you know, it's Guy Lombardo and his Royal Canadians, playing music to dance the night away.

But the novelty eventually wears off, and Ron turns to Michael and asks, "So, how did you meet our Eva?"

*Our* Eva? His Eva. Everybody's Eva. Can you choke yourself on a shrimp?

Michael looks at me and smiles. "We met in Florida when I was doing an architectural internship down there and she was in college. She told me my buildings were ridiculous."

David's wandered over just in time to hear this, and he looks at me with raised eyebrows.

"He told me he wanted to build beach hotels with all their windows facing inland," I explain. "I thought he was just trying to be provocative, and I told him so."

Michael laughs. "I still carry the scars. So when she got in touch to ask about an interview, I saw my chance to get some payback."

David's moved into the circle of people around us, and I feel as if the room's suddenly gotten very small.

"And did you?" Ron asks.

Michael looks over at me. "Let's just say she's a worthy opponent."

"*And* I deserve a raise."

He looks over at Ron. "*And* she deserves a raise."

Nervous laughter all around. Ron raises both hands in surrender. "Alright. I can see I'm outnumbered."

"So I get the raise?"

"We'll talk about it."

"You must be a parent," Michael says, laughing. "That's the same line I always use with my daughter."

Suddenly David says, "Eva, you never mentioned that you two knew each other before."

Everybody looks at David, then at me, and I feel my face get hot, knowing I must be bright red. David sees it. Everyone sees it. Our bodies betray us.

"So," Ron says quickly, turning to Michael. "Tell us about this new project in Stony Brook."

❦

David was silent on the cab ride home. We sat on opposite sides of the taxi's backseat, looking out at the passing lights, tension crackling between us. When the cab pulled up at our building, David leaned forward to pay the driver while I got out and waited for him in the lobby. When he joined me, neither one of us spoke. We waited in silence for the elevator, then stood gazing at the numbers as it climbed to our floor. David dug in his pocket for the keys to our apartment while I waited a few steps behind him. Then he disappeared into his study, and closed the door. I went into the bedroom, hung up my dress, and climbed into bed, feeling sad and depressed.

I had the television on an hour later when David came in, although I couldn't tell you what I'd been watching. He sat on the end of the bed and said, "I think we need to talk."

I shut the TV off. "I agree."

"What's going on? You haven't been yourself for months. Is there something you should tell me?"

It was the question I'd been dreading for months. But now that David had finally asked it, I couldn't think of an answer. That I screwed up but it was over now? That I'd learned my lesson? Anything I told him would be only a half-truth at best.

"Are you angry about my history with Michael? Is that what this is about?"

"I find it interesting that you never mentioned it."

If I'd told him about it when the idea of the interview first came up, it might have defused the bomb now ticking between us and my emails never would have taken on that secretive, flirtatious excitement.

"Because it happened long before I became that person who let herself gain all that weight," I told him. "When I met Michael, I wasn't a wife or a mother or an editor at *House & Home*. I was just Eva, a girl who wanted to do things with her life. The interview was Ron's idea and I couldn't say no. But I felt like my history was nobody's business but mine."

David looked at me. "Did you sleep with him?"

"Yes. And we talked about architecture. And we went out to dinner, and we talked on the phone, and then we didn't cross paths for twenty years. That's how it works when you don't marry someone."

We sat in silence for a while. Maybe I'd talked my way out of this trap, like a wolf chewing its own leg off to get free. David wasn't satisfied, though; I could see he was still brooding on it.

"But nothing's happening now," he said.

And there it was, the moment of truth. Did I lie to save my marriage, making it up to David over the years to come? Or did I tell him what I'd done, and risk losing everything?

The way he'd phrased it, as a statement he wanted me to confirm, made it clear that he wasn't looking for any confessions. He wanted reassurance that he had nothing to worry about, that we could put this behind us and go on with our marriage.

Still, he knew *something* had been going on. You don't burst into tears for no reason, and the growing silence between us had to be explained.

"I've been exchanging emails with him."

"Tell me about it."

I looked down at my hands. "Ron was putting pressure on me to get the interview. He kept saying we needed something to take the magazine to the next level, and an exclusive with a major architect would do that." I raised my eyes to meet his. "And I admit, it was affirming to have somebody remind me who I used to be when I was young. It helped motivate me to stick with my diet."

"So I wasn't being supportive about your diet?"

"You've been very supportive. But the person you were supporting was always *me*. I was trying to imagine a different person: somebody who wouldn't just go back to being *me* when the diet was over. When you look at me you'll always see me as who I am, not who I *could* be."

I could tell by the way he looked at me that he was hurt, and I rested a hand on his arm. "I don't mean that in a bad way; it's just the nature of being married. We enforce each other's identities. It's hard to change when you've been living with someone for twenty years. Every time they look at you, you go right back to being who you've always been."

I realized that somewhere in there, I'd gone from try- ing to avoid telling him what happened between Michael and me, to explaining it. I desperately wanted him to understand what was going on in my mind. An affair is the opposite of a diet, where everything is written on your body for the world to see: your despair, your failures, your hunger for change. In an affair, what you do with your body is just an attempt to express the hidden longings of your heart. What drives you isn't the desire to be *with* someone else; it's the desire to *be* someone else. And you think you can see that new self reflected only in a stranger's eyes.

David wasn't looking at me, and I suddenly felt very scared. It was like we were balanced on a narrow beam; one wrong move could send us both tumbling into the pit gaping beneath us.

David looked up at me. I couldn't read the expression on his face. "You were crying the night you came back from California. What happened out there?"

"I met his wife. She was very nice. It made me feel ashamed."

"And you didn't feel ashamed before that? Meeting her made you feel ashamed, but not cheating on me?"

"I was too caught up in it to know what I felt," I told him. "I can't explain it, but the diet, the exercise, Michael, it all got confused in my mind. It's like I got lost in it. All I could think about was what I needed to do to lose the weight. Nothing else mattered."

"Well, you look great now," he said bitterly. "Everybody tells me so. They all want to know how you did it."

We sat in silence for a while. Then he looked over at me, and I could see the exhaustion in his eyes.

"We can't go on like this, Eva."

Tears filled my eyes. "Are you saying you want a divorce?"

"I don't know what I want. I just know we haven't been a couple for a long time." He got up, went into the bathroom, and bent over the sink to splash water on his face. He dried his face, then looked at me with an expression of determination. "I think we should try living separately for a while."

And that was it. I'd destroyed my marriage. No amount of talking would bring him back.

"Is that what you want?"

"It's not *about* what I want. Neither one of us is happy. I don't see any point in living that way."

"What about Chloe?"

"She's a big girl. She'll understand in time." He'd made his decision, and nothing was going to change his mind.

And suddenly, like a light coming on, I saw something else in the way he turned his back on me, the decisiveness with which he drew the line under twenty years of marriage.

"Is there someone else, David?"

He shot me an angry glance. "You'd like that, wouldn't you? Then this whole thing would be my fault."

But even as he said it, I could see I'd hit the truth. "There is, isn't there? That's why you haven't asked me what's been going on before now. You were too busy hiding something from me. And now you see a chance to get out and try to make the whole thing my fault!"

He walked out of the room. A moment later he came back carrying a suitcase from the hall closet. Neither of us said a word as he angrily emptied his drawers into the suitcase, then went back into the hall for a garment bag.

It's hard to maintain self-righteous anger while fighting with a tangle of hangers, but David kept at it until he'd stuffed the garment bag with four suits, an armful of shirts, and three pairs of shoes. Then he went into the bathroom, gathered up his toiletries, and threw them into the suitcase.

But when he went to close it, he found he'd packed too much. It wouldn't close, no matter how hard he shoved the clothes down to give the zipper room. Finally he grabbed a handful of clothes at random and threw them on the floor. Then he zipped up the suitcase, and turned to look at me.

"I'll call you with an address where you can send my things." He sounded like he was speaking lines from an old movie he'd seen, but there was a pleading look in his eyes.

"If that's what you want," I said. "I'll have them ready when you call."

The look vanished from his eyes. He picked up his suitcase, slung the garment bag over his shoulder, and walked out. A moment later, I heard the front door close.

Twenty years of marriage, gone. I closed my eyes, and now the tears came—too late to do any good.

at something, okay?" Liz nods toward my un-touched salad. "Take a piece of chicken. That looks good."

She talks to me as you would a child. What makes it particularly annoying is that I think I'm doing pretty well. I get up in the morning, go to work, go to the gym. The only thing I'm not doing so well with is food. I make meals and then can't eat them, so I wrap them up in plastic and shove them in the refrigerator. When Liz takes me out to eat, I end up bringing my meal home in a takeout box. After a few days, I go through the refrigerator and throw out the stuff that's start-ing to smell. I'm down a size since David left, which I guess is good. Liz looks at me and shakes her head like I've turned into some famine child, walking around on fragile stick legs. But the whole range of high fashion is now open to me. I could be a model, if any designer ever needed a fortysomething recently dumped depressive who fucked up her marriage. God knows, I'm not the only one. Liz invites me to join her group of bitter divorcées for drinks. I probably make the other ladies feel better about themselves, since they no longer burst into tears on a daily basis.

"Look at you! You're so skinny," they cry when they see me. "How'd you do it?"

"Adultery," I say. "Divorce. You stop eating. Works like a charm."

They stare at me, until one starts to laugh. "Oh, you're wicked. Really, how'd you do it?"

Diet and exercise. Healthy life choices.

⁓

"He's staying with her now," I tell Liz.

"Who?"

"Maribel Steinberg. She writes diet books."

Liz raises an eyebrow. "There's an irony. Out of the frying pan, huh? So let him find out what it's like living with a real diet queen. He'll realize how good he had it with you."

Wishful thinking, but I know he's not coming back. Husbands never come back once they've left you. *He'll be back* is just a story we tell ourselves to get through the first few months, until we can get used to the idea that we'll spend the rest of our lives alone. You can't go back; you can only go forward.

"Have you told Chloe?"

I shake my head. "She's been traveling in Eastern Europe. I thought I'd wait until she got back to Paris, so I wouldn't ruin her trip. I was thinking I might fly over and talk to her in person."

"Now, that's a good idea! Take a few days in Paris. Sleep with a Frenchman. There's nothing better to cure yourself of an American husband."

The idea has occurred to me. But as much as I'm trying to be realistic, I also know that I've put off talking to Chloe in the hope that it might blow over, that I'll come home from work one evening and find David there. Instead, I come home to find that more of his things have disappeared. He didn't call me with an address. Instead, he came on his lunch hour, let himself into the apartment, and carried away the things he hadn't thought to pack during the drama of his departure. I've taken to packing up boxes of his belongings and leaving them in the entryway by the front door. When I come home, they're gone.

And then there are the phone calls. I'm drowning in commiseration. It seems like everyone he tells that he's moved out calls me to share my pain. All I can think is that these were the people who knew he was seeing somebody else but couldn't bring themselves to tell me. They've been waiting for this moment to say how much they wanted to tell me. Edie, from his office, is the first, and she calls only two days after he moved out. He must have told his co-workers, in case they needed to reach him.

"Eva, I'm *so* sorry," Edie tells me. "I saw what was happening, and I felt terrible about it. Please let me know if there's anything I can do."

I thank her politely, tell her it's kind of her to call, then get off the phone as quickly as possible. What can anyone do for me? I've already done too much for myself.

"Anyway," Liz says of Maribel, "you're probably thinner than she is these days. And where's her book gone? It was in the window of all the bookstores for a week back in the fall, and now you can't even find it on the shelves."

"Well, she can't blame her publisher. David always said diet books need a hook. I guess nobody wants to buy a book that tells you to be true to yourself."

Liz laughs. "Ain't that the truth. Life's hard enough. If I buy a diet book, just tell me how easy it'll be and how often I can cheat."

"That's my diet plan. All cheating, no truth."

She looks at me, surprised. "Is there something you're not telling me?"

Confession is good for the soul, so I tell her.

When I'm finished, she stares at me in amazement. "Eva, I'm so disappointed in you! How could you have an affair and not *tell* me?"

"It's not the kind of thing you brag about."

"Are you kidding? Where have you been? The culture's fascinated by cheating wives. They're in all the movies, on TV, everywhere. Now men who have affairs are bastards, but women who do are just *hot.*" She leans forward. "Seriously, honey, you should write that diet book. 'Cheat your way to a new you.' Wives everywhere would read it."

"You think so?"

She gives a wicked smile. "And just imagine how Maribel Steinberg will feel."

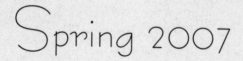

Spring 2007

Mom, you're on!"

I carry my coffee mug into the living room, where Chloe sprawls on the couch, her feet on the coffee table. She's got the television remote in her hand, bringing the volume up just in time for me to hear the morning anchor say, "And we're back. Our guest is the author of a new weight loss program that's causing quite a stir."

"It's so funny, the way they all say that," Chloe comments. "Like they're not the ones stirring up the controversy."

"And they all think they're so clever, using the food metaphors."

The anchor is wearing her "concerned citizen" face, the one she puts on whenever she reports a social trend that signals the end of Western civilization. "But is the suggestion that infidelity is the most effective weight loss plan for married women just too much to swallow? We have with us Eva Cassady, author of the *The Adultery Diet*. Welcome."

The camera draws back, showing me seated on the couch, wearing my latest red dress and a slightly ironic smile. "Always wear red when you do TV interviews," the publicist Edie had hired told me. "It's the color of adultery."

"Isn't that a little obvious?"

"Obvious is good, honey. You do the obvious stuff first, then you can get ironic."

And so far, she's been right. She'd managed to stir up a small scandal over the book by sending advance copies to right-wing pundits who were always looking for evidence of the culture's moral decline. Then she'd staged a series of events at book signings she'd scheduled at several large chain stores in Midtown. She'd called around to the city's Baptist churches, posing as a "concerned citizen," alerting their ministers to this celebration of immorality. After a few tries, she found a guy in Queens who'd once gotten some publicity by leading his congregants in nightly "pray-ins" outside a Broadway theater where a famous film actress who'd once played Mary in a film of Christ's final days was now disrobing nightly as Mrs. Robinson. He'd brought out his congregation to wave signs and shout slogans for the local news cameras, while I signed books in my red dress inside the store. Then she'd recruited a dozen of the publisher's female employees, dressed them in matching T-shirts with large scarlet As on the front, and sent them out to stage a counterdemonstration as happy, skinny adulteresses. The women found it funny, and a clip of them chanting, "Two, four, six, eight, ask us how we lost the weight!" at the Baptists made the news. By the time I started my twelve-city book tour, Edie had the campaign running like a well-oiled machine. She'd send copies of the video to the local TV newsrooms, then place more "concerned citizen" calls to the suburban mega-churches. In the bookstores, there'd be a life-size cardboard cutout of me in my red dress and ironic smile, leaning on a giant scarlet *A*. There'd be a stack of T-shirts for sale beside the stack of books, and as often as not, a crowd of laughing women already wearing them lined up to get my autograph.

"It's amazing," I told Edie on the phone. "They all put on their shirts and proudly declare themselves adulteresses. I've never seen anything like it."

"That's the power of a good publicity campaign, honey. Just stay thin and keep smiling, and they'll follow you anywhere."

I keep smiling. As long as we keep treating it as a sly joke, maybe women will get the book's central point: they don't actually have to *be* adulteresses, just think like them. Claim your own unruly desires, I tell them. Recognize how, by turning you into wives and mothers, the world creates hungers in you that only grow as you consume. Honor your inner adulteress by refusing to be consumed by your desires. Remember that you were once a girl with your own dreams and aspirations. Take back *your* life. Eat right, work out, and allow yourself the freedom to dream. Refuse to be adulterated.

And there are recipes, too. It's impossible for me not to smile while promoting it.

Staying thin on the road is the hard part. I haunt the hotels' workout rooms, where business travelers sweat before walls of mirrors while CNN plays on the

TV mounted near the ceiling. These rooms are as impersonal as airports, and just as transient. I go from city to city, and find the same five machines in every hotel.

"It's TV interviews next," the publicist warns me. "Just remember, the camera adds ten pounds."

That's nothing, compared to what the book would have added if I'd let it. How did anyone write before rice cakes? I sat at my desk every evening for nine months staring at the computer screen and crunching my way through a bag of low-sodium rice cakes. Nine months of fierce cravings: Fig Newtons, Oreos, pistachio ice cream, M&Ms. When I was carrying Chloe, at least I had an excuse to eat. But how could I let myself get fat while writing a *diet* book?

But writing the book helped me survive David's abrupt exit. Edie Boyarski kept me up to date on his romantic woes. It turned out that Maribel Steinberg wasn't thrilled to find him suddenly available. She'd enjoyed having a married lover, who didn't disrupt her life. But now her lover had moved in with her "until he could find his own place." In Manhattan, that can be a long process. She gave it three months, then threw him out.

"And to make it worse," Edie told me gleefully, "she's changing publishers. She told her agent we hadn't done enough to publicize her book."

For a few weeks, I half expected David to show up at my door. But apparently he found a place to live, and he was still too angry or too proud to go back to his wife.

So I kept typing. I didn't tell anyone except Liz that I was writing it, so it was like I'd traded one secret for another. And turning out a small stack of pages each week felt strangely like watching the numbers go down on my bathroom scale. In both cases, it was nine months of slow, tedious effort. Writing, dieting, giving birth: all the things that take time and patience, but that change your life.

When it was done I sent it to Liz, who called me the next day to say, "When did you become so *wicked*? You have to publish this!"

I felt encouraged enough to send it to Edie, and she called me a week later to say she wanted to take it before the editorial board.

"Will David be at the meeting?"

"Didn't you know? He left two weeks ago. I meant to call you, but I had so much extra work on my desk."

Maybe I shouldn't have been so surprised, but the information sent pain rushing through my heart. Why didn't he tell me? It must have been a huge decision, but apparently he considered it none of my business.

"Where'd he go?"

"He's 'exploring new opportunities.' That's what they say when they force you out. Apparently things haven't been running smoothly, and there have been problems on a number of projects. Then Maribel Steinberg walked, and her agent spread some nasty talk, so somebody upstairs let David know that it might be time for him to explore those new opportunities. And now I'm bringing your book before the editorial board. Isn't it just *delicious?*"

Not particularly. I felt sad when I got off the phone. So, I called Chloe at college. She'd come back from Paris last summer to find that her parents had separated. Yet in many ways, she'd returned with a new maturity and sophistication that made her seem like she hardly needed parents anymore. She'd stayed with me for a few weeks until she left to go back to college, but I'd hardly seen her during that time. She'd lined up an internship with a French media firm's New York office, using contacts she'd made through a boy she'd met in Paris who had wealthy, influential parents. All she wanted was to finish her senior year and get back to Paris, this time with a job. Our problems seemed just another reason for her to want to go. If your past is vanishing behind you, what can you do but grasp at the promising future ahead?

Anyway, I called Chloe at college and told her I was going to drive up for the weekend to see her. She seemed surprised, even a little annoyed. It was the spring semester of her senior year, and she was terribly busy. Wouldn't I be coming up for graduation in a few weeks, anyway?

"There's something I need to talk with you about," I told her.

"Is it about you and Daddy?"

"In a way. But it involves you, too."

We agreed that we'd have lunch on Saturday. So I packed up a copy of my manuscript and carried it with me as I drove up to see her. Over lunch we chatted about her work on her senior thesis, the job interviews she'd lined up the following week, and her plans immediately after graduation. Some of her friends were going to rent a cottage on Cape Cod for a week right after commencement, and she thought she'd join them. I told her it sounded lovely.

When we'd finished off all the obvious parent-child business, I said, "Listen, Chloe . . ."

"You're getting remarried, right? Or Dad is. So you're going to file the divorce papers."

I looked at her in surprise. "Chloe, I'm not even seeing anyone. Has your father told you he's getting married?"

She shook her head. "He doesn't talk about that stuff with me. The only woman he ever mentions is you."

"*Me?* What does he say?"

"He asks how you're doing, if everything's okay at the apartment, that kind of stuff." She smiles. "And I tell him you're doing fine. Busy, but okay."

For a moment, I was thrown by the idea of David asking if I was happy. But I pulled myself together and said, "Chloe, I know it must have been a terrible shock when Daddy and I split up."

She shrugged. "Not really. All my friends' parents are splitting up lately. I was kind of wondering when you two would get around to it."

All I could do was stare at her in surprise. This wasn't going at all the way I'd planned. "We'd been growing apart for some years. I guess it happens in lots of marriages."

"Which is a polite way of saying Daddy was having affairs."

"It wasn't only his fault."

She laughed. "You mean you were having affairs, too?"

There was a pause, and then I took a deep breath. "We both made mistakes, Chloe."

She stared at me. "Really? You had a boyfriend?"

My throat felt like I'd swallowed a rock and it had gotten stuck halfway down. Finally, I looked down at the table and nodded.

"That's so awesome, Mom! All this time I've been feeling sorry for you sitting at home waiting for Daddy to come home. And it turns out you were out having a good time."

What's happened to young people? Have they lost the capacity to be shocked by their parents? Is that what we get for refusing to be shocked by what they do?

"I wrote a book, Chloe. If it gets published, all this will become public. I don't mention any names, and I leave your father's affair out of it for the most part. But I thought I should tell you, because it could affect you."

"You wrote a *book*? About you and Daddy?"

"In a way. It's a diet book."

She sat back and laughed until tears came. "Oh, that's great. Poor Daddy! All the women in his life write diet books." She wiped her eyes with her napkin, looked at me, and burst out laughing again. "You're seriously worried that a *diet* book could embarrass me?"

I reached into my briefcase, took out the manuscript, and pushed it across the table to her. "Maybe you'd better read it."

She looked down at the title page and her eyes widened. "You're kidding."

"Just read it, then give me a call. If you think it's going to be a problem for you, then I'll shove it in a drawer and that'll be it." I got up from the table. "C'mon, I'll give you a lift back to your dorm."

That evening, I let Liz take me out for a stiff drink. In

the bar, two men started giving us the eye, but I was too nervous about Chloe to do anything about it.

"Don't worry," Liz told me. "She's a big girl. She can handle it."

But that wasn't really what worried me. It was the idea that Chloe's whole image of me would change when she read my manuscript. I'd expected her to be shocked when she first saw me after I lost all the weight, and in truth, she'd barely recognized me when I met her at the airport. But it only took a few moments to get past the "You look *fabulous*" and "How'd you *do* it?" to when she looked around and asked, "Where's Dad?" Now she'd get her answer, and it was hard for me to imagine that our relationship could ever be the same.

When I got home that evening, there was a message on my answering machine, the light flashing like a warning. I pressed the button.

"Mom, it's Chloe. I love the book! Can I show it to my roommates? When did you get so *funny*? Call me when you get home, okay?"

❦

Now Chloe sits on the couch, wearing her own T-shirt with its ornate scarlet *A,* as we watch my interview with the local morning show anchor, taped the previous afternoon on an empty set. The anchor's doing her best to suggest both amusement and stern moral disapproval. I just keep smiling. None of the questions are new to me.

"So, are you really suggesting that women should lose weight by cheating on their husbands?"

"Not at all. In fact, it's not even about sex. It's about reclaiming your body by reclaiming your dreams. In our dreams, we're individuals, but in our lives, we're wives and mothers. Losing weight is a selfish process in the sense that you have to spend time thinking about yourself: what you eat, how to get enough exercise, setting daily goals that help move you toward your larger aspirations. We've been conditioned to think about others' needs before our own, and that's one reason why we see this close association between successful weight loss and extramarital affairs. Women lose weight when the desire they feel is greater than the daily pain of dieting and exercise. What I'm saying in the book is that we have to learn how focus that same desire on ourselves, rather than looking for somebody else to fulfill our dreams."

"So you're not advocating adultery?"

Chloe rolls her eyes. "God, where do they *find* these women? Didn't she hear what you just said?"

"They're not really interested in what you say," I tell her. "They sit there looking thoughtful while you talk, so that the camera can get a reaction shot, but they keep sneaking looks at the script. All they're worried about is what they have to say next. That woman's on camera for two hours every morning. She doesn't have time to listen to what her guests say. After me, she had a segment with a dog groomer on getting your pet ready for winter. So I come on, give my soundbites, and afterward they shake my hand and tell me how much they're looking forward to reading the book."

Chloe looks at the anchor in her Chanel suit. "She doesn't look like she's ever had to worry about her weight."

"You're kidding, right? She worries about her weight every day. The camera adds ten pounds, so she's always on a diet."

"Well, if she keeps flirting with the weather guy, she won't have a problem."

The anchor suddenly leans toward me, one hand raised as if to keep me in my chair a moment longer, playing the hard-hitting journalist with a tough follow-up question. "But you admit in the book that infidelity destroyed your marriage."

"Yes, and that's why I wrote the book. It's easy to confuse the desire to change your life with desire for another person. All any of us wants is hope, Joan. When it's not there, we'll go to incredible lengths to get it. We want to be defined by our futures, not just by our pasts. What I'm telling women is that they can choose those dreams for themselves."

The anchor gives me a benign smile. "An interesting and provocative argument, and I'm sure we'll be hearing more about it in the weeks to come. Thanks for joining us."

"Thank you."

The camera cuts away to her male co-anchor, who throws it to the weather guy. They both shake their heads and make some clucking noises, then the weatherman warns us about a cold front that could bring rain at rush hour tomorrow.

Chloe picks up the remote and shuts off the television. "I don't know how you do it," she says. "Just smiling away, no matter what kind of stupid question they ask."

"I imagine that Maribel Steinberg is watching."

"Dad's girlfriend?"

"*Ex*-girlfriend. Who would have killed for this kind of publicity."

"You should have thanked her in the acknowledgments." Chloe glances at her watch. "Speaking of Dad, I'm having lunch with him today."

I sip my coffee. "Have you told him you're moving back to Paris, yet?"

"I haven't seen him since I got the job. I'll tell him today."

She goes off to take a shower, and I try not to think about what it'll be like when she's gone. I spent most of last year living alone in this apartment, writing my book in the evenings after work, and while it had its pleasant moments, I'm not sure I'm really cut out for that much solitude.

*You should have thought of that before you lost your husband.*

I still miss him. That feels like a weakness on my part, especially now that I'm playing the strong, independent woman in television interviews. And, really, it's not Maribel Steinberg I think about when I do those interviews. It's David.

Has he read the book? I sent him a copy of the proofs with a note that said, *I thought you had a right to see this before it came out.*

He never replied.

"I wouldn't have bothered," Edie told me. "It's not

like you mention him by name. Nobody but your close friends will even know he's the husband in the book."

But I know. And I can't help wondering what he thought when the proofs arrived and he saw my name on the cover. When I'm doing these TV interviews, is he watching? Does he understand what I'm trying to say, or is it only my fantasy?

I get hate mail from those who see me as the devil's handmaiden, but I also get plenty of erotic fantasies. I've even received a few marriage proposals, sent—I have to assume—by men who enjoy the idea of their wives with other men. It's all there at the zoo.

And I can't help thinking that David would admire the marketing campaign. With all the interviews and protests, all the hate and titillation, the stores can't keep the book on the shelves. It's tempting to be cynical, watching the publicists stir up controversy just to sell books, until you do a morning news show and see people working just as hard to sell all the *other* stories the anchors are reporting. War, scandal, the latest corporate merger: there's somebody promoting all of them. At least in my case, their audience might lose a few pounds.

Chloe comes out drying her hair with a towel. "Dad's picking me up at noon, okay?"

I look around at the apartment in panic. "God, I should straighten up."

She looks at me with interest. "I don't think he's planning to come up. He'll probably call me from the lobby."

"Right. Of course." I sit back, relieved—but also a little disappointed. I haven't seen him since Chloe's graduation, and then we barely spoke to each other except to agree that she looked happy. How strange that people who've been so intimate can suddenly have nothing to say to each other. Do they really see each other differently, or is it just that they no longer feel confident that what they say will be taken in the sense in which it was meant? Is that all that makes a marriage possible? A sense of trust?

"If you want, I could invite him up." Chloe's smiling now. "Or you could join us for lunch."

"No, you two go ahead. I've got work to do."

I'm still writing my column for the magazine, although Ron has granted me a leave of absence to promote the book. When I first told him about it, he seemed to find the idea unsettling. But as my notoriety began to grow, he quickly started imagining ways to use it to get publicity for the magazine. When I started my TV interviews, he called me to ask, "Can you mention the magazine?"

"Ron, it's a little hard to see how I could work it in. The book's about sex and dieting."

"It's all renovation, right?"

This from a man who worries about alienating his advertisers with an article about replacement windows. But I made sure to note my work as a columnist for a magazine on architectural renovation in the materials the publicist sent out to interviewers, and sure enough, several of them asked about it.

"Do you find there's a connection between renovating your home and renovating your body?"

"Absolutely, Meg." Always call them by name, the publicist emphasized. It makes the interview sound like two friends chatting. "They're both about finding the beauty that used to be visible. A good architect should be able to help you find what lies hidden under the pressures of daily life."

I said this with a small private smile, during an interview on a Los Angeles TV station. When I got back to my hotel room, there was a message on my phone from Michael.

"Eva, you're a celebrity! I'm going to run right out and buy your book this morning. How long are you in town? Any chance I could see you?"

We met for coffee that afternoon. He hadn't bought the book yet, but I had a copy with me, so I gave it to him, inscribed:

> For Michael,
>   A good architect should be able to help you find what lies hidden under the pressures of daily life.
>   Eva

He looked at the cover, which shows a tiny bride parachuting off a wedding cake. "So am I in it?"

"You're all over it," I told him. "You're the inspiration. But if you're asking whether I mention your name, then, no, you're not in it."

He nodded, then looked up at me and smiled. "You look great. Fame agrees with you."

"I wouldn't call this fame. I'm just on a book tour."

"Are you kidding? You were on *Mornings with Meg*! That's like currency in this town. I'll bet the studios are bidding on the movie rights as we speak."

I laughed. "It's a diet book, Michael."

"So they'll give it to Kirstie Alley."

It really was nice to see him. But I couldn't help thinking about Mari. After a while, he reached across the table, took my hand, and said, "Can I see you tonight? I'd love to get some time alone with you."

I shook my head. "It's really tempting, Michael, but I've made enough of a mess already. You've got a lovely wife. Why don't you spend some time alone with her?"

It felt good to say that, but I have to admit that I regretted it later, as I lay in my vast hotel bed imagining what I'd given up. *It's a little late to be playing Miss Morality.* But maybe being lonely wasn't such a bad thing. And luckily the hotel had a nice, strong shower.

Anyway, when David arrives to pick up Chloe for lunch, I'm sitting at my computer in my bathrobe, trying to finish a column on the connection between renovation and dieting. I had lots of ideas on this subject this time last year, but now they all seem too obvious. Our lives are too complex. We can't restore our past; we can only create a *new* self using the past as a model. And even that idea seems false to me. There's no such thing as a new self, just new pages in a single book.

So maybe dieting isn't like renovation; maybe renovation is like dieting. We think of our houses as versions of ourselves, always dreaming that we can go back and fix our mistakes.

The buzzer rings. Chloe calls out, "That's Dad!" Then I hear the hall door close, and the apartment is suddenly empty and silent.

I sit there feeling strangely hollow and depressed.

What did I expect? That David would come upstairs and I would make us all a nice salad for lunch, then we'd sit around the kitchen table telling jokes, the way we used to when Chloe was in high school? That life is gone, and what I've got in its place is time. I should concentrate on my column, and not allow myself to get distracted by dreaming about the past.

But isn't the past what my column's readers are trying to restore? Old houses are a fantasy of a simpler life, when families still sat around the kitchen table telling jokes. My diet is about restoring not that past but an earlier one—before I even had a kitchen table, much less a husband and daughter to sit at it. That's the problem with restoring the past: you have to destroy one version of it to find another. We're never satisfied with what we have, so we try to reach back for something hidden beyond it. We try to escape the present by grasping at the past. It seems a basic human impulse, wired into us by the way we constantly compare the world we see around us with our memory of what we once knew.

So what does that say about my life? There's a lot to enjoy about this moment: I'm thin; the book's threatening to make me rich; I'm even a minor celebrity. I get invited to parties that I don't attend. No time, I say apologetically—the book tour and all these interviews. But the truth is simpler: no date. I don't even have the gay friend every socialite needs for those moments when you don't have a man handy.

I'm out of practice at being single, and despite Liz's best efforts, I can't seem to get the hang of it.

"Why are you still living in that awful apartment?"

She shakes her head sadly. "You've got the money to move, so put the past behind you! Just think of the fun we could have decorating."

I look around at the apartment. She's right: it's depressing to be reminded every day of my failed marriage. But the last thing I want is to become one of Liz's clients, filling her empty life with stylish home decor.

There are some nice things about my current life— but would I go back if I could? Damn right. Or maybe not back, exactly, but forward, without giving up the best parts of the past. After all, nobody restores a Victorian house to its original condition. You put in modern appliances, central heat and air, a home entertainment center, and a wireless network. We all like the pleasures of the past with the conveniences of the present.

David and I had our problems, but now that he's gone, I find myself noticing what's missing from my life: Laughter, mostly. And talk. Not deep conversation, but the simple stuff: *How was your day? Okay, and yours? You won't believe what happened.* Someone to curl up against when you're tired. Someone who laughs at the same movies, who gets angry at the same stuff on the news. Someone who can share my pleasure at the smart, strong woman our daughter has become.

And suddenly, without warning, I'm crying. That's how it happens lately, and this one's a real monsoon. I'm looking for tissues when the phone rings.

"Hi, Mom. It's me."

I'm crying so hard, it takes me a moment to speak. "Hi, honey. What's up?"

"Are you okay? You sound like you've been crying."

"I'm fine." I finally find a tissue and blow my nose. "I think my allergies are acting up."

"Right. Listen, Dad wants to talk with you about some stuff. I think he's got a problem with the whole France thing. Talk to him for me, okay? I can't seem to make him understand. He can meet you for coffee at two."

I'm so surprised, the tears stop. I wipe my nose, wondering what this could be about. Is he angry at me for not consulting him about Chloe's plans? It's not up to me to decide what she does with her life. Or is it something else? We've never filed divorce papers. Maybe he's met someone and he wants to get remarried. The tears return to my eyes, but I fight them back.

"Sure, honey. I can meet him."

She covers the phone, and I hear her talking to him. Why hadn't he just called me himself? Then she gets back on the phone and says, "Okay, he says two at Cupola."

I get dressed, do my best to fix the mess that is my face, and head downstairs a few minutes before two. David's sitting at a table in the window, gazing out at Broadway with tired eyes. When I come in, he stands up and we shake hands awkwardly.

"Nice to see you," he says. "You look great. Even better than on television."

"Thanks. You look good, too."

He's been spending time at the gym, it's clear. Probably goes there to meet women, or to stay competitive in the single world.

He gestures toward the counter. "You want something?"

"I'll get it."

I order a nonfat latte, mainly to give myself time to take a deep breath and get my balance while the kid behind the counter goes through the elaborate ritual of brewing, steaming, and pouring. David watches me carry the latte back to the table. He's got a plain cup of coffee in front of him, his hands on the cup like it might get away from him.

"So," he says when I sit down. "What's up?"

"Chloe said you wanted to see me."

He looks surprised. "She told me you wanted to see *me*."

"You're not worried about her moving to France?"

"No, not at all. Good for her. How about you?"

"I want to go with her."

We look at each other, perplexed. At that moment, both of our cell phones go off with the signal that Chloe set as our text message alerts years ago. We look at each other, simultaneously say, "Excuse me," and reach for our phones.

*Sorry,* says the message, *but U R both 2 :( Figure it out. C.*

Across the table, David laughs.

Summer 2007

Dear Liz,

You can't imagine how long it takes to get an internet account in Paris. It took ten days just to get a phone, and now the internet company won't have somebody out until next week. Fortunately, it gives me a nice excuse to sit in a café. The apartment's lovely, and Chloe's only a ten-minute walk away. I love walking here; I walk everywhere. Much better than a StairMaster. And the waiter just brought me a brioche. I really am in heaven.

David arrives on Thursday. No cynical remarks, okay? We're just giving this a try. If it doesn't work, he can stay with Chloe, but I don't really think that'll be necessary.

Did I tell you the titles Edie's marketing people suggested for the new book? She sent me a list the other day: Break Up, Make Up; The Round-Trip Marriage; Ex Marks the Spot; and my personal favorite, Cheat to Win: How Infidelity Saved My Mar-

*riage. They want David and me to write alternating chapters. I told her we'd think about it. The money would certainly be nice, but it's still early, and I'm not sure we could survive writing a book together. Besides, I think I'd rather enjoy being back together than writing about it.*

*"Reader, I married him." Again.*

*Uh-oh—look at the time! Got to go or I'll be late for my appointment with Jean-Marc. Have I mentioned him? He's my personal trainer, three times a week, to work off all the brioche. He's exactly what you'd imagine—or at least, exactly what I imagined. And thanks to him, I'm* very thin!

*But don't mention him to David, okay?*

*Love,*

*Eva*